Protocol

Jeff Zwagerman

Black Rose Writing | Texas

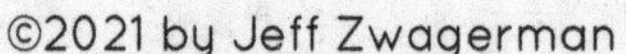

©2021 by Jeff Zwagerman
All rights reserved. No part of this book may be reproduced, stored in a retrieval system or transmitted in any form or by any means without the prior written permission of the publishers, except by a reviewer who may quote brief passages in a review to be printed in a newspaper, magazine or journal.

The author grants the final approval for this literary material.

First printing

This is a work of fiction. Names, characters, businesses, places, events, and incidents are either the products of the author's imagination or used in a fictitious manner. Any resemblance to actual persons, living or dead, or actual events is purely coincidental.

ISBN: 978-1-68433-799-6
PUBLISHED BY BLACK ROSE WRITING
www.blackrosewriting.com

Printed in the United States of America
Suggested Retail Price (SRP) $20.95

Protocol is printed in Book Antiqua

*As a planet-friendly publisher, Black Rose Writing does its best to eliminate unnecessary waste to reduce paper usage and energy costs, while never compromising the reading experience. As a result, the final word count vs. page count may not meet common expectations.

Protocol

Prologue

Niemand Weet Waar Een Ander De Schoen Wringt
No One Knows Where The Shoe Pinches, But He Who Wears It.
–Dutch Proverb

Kevin Grienne was an enigma. People around him said he had many faces. There was the serious and business-like Kevin Grienne. There was the fun-loving Kevin Grienne. There was the smart-ass Kevin Grienne. There was the compassionate Kevin Grienne. There was the practical joker Kevin Grienne. There was the performing Kevin Grienne. Maybe there were countless other faces of Kevin Grienne that he let people see.

There was, however, a darker side to Kevin Grienne that he let no one see. Layers and layers separated the visual from the hidden. He had perfected his subterfuge, and those around him had no idea of his hidden darkness.

Kevin was a master manipulator. He could turn on the charm and people would melt. That was the best part of his darkness. Everything else in his arsenal became much more murky.

No one seemed to know where he came from. He mentioned the Midwest a few times to some of his co-workers, but that's as much as he would divulge. How he ended up in Florida seemed to be a puzzle to everyone but Kevin.

If anyone had bothered to check, they would have found that Kevin's education had been spread out over much of the Midwest. He attended secondary school in a small rural community outside of Council Bluffs, Iowa. He attended and was graduated from Iowa State University with an agri-business degree. From there, he went to graduate school and received his master's degree from the University of Nebraska at Lincoln. There he would change from agriculture to counseling. He thought he could be a counselor for the farming community. It was not to be.

The need for farmer-counselors was almost non-existent, so he went to work for the federal government. He bounced around the country in various positions until he landed in a facility that dealt with government employees who needed intense therapy. It was located somewhere in Miami. It was a secret facility that could be accessed only by the elite few.

Kevin had built a reputation and was highly sought after. If there was a file somewhere on Kevin, no one could find it. Educational transcripts were his only history. Kevin had his own protocol that he kept in a lock box hidden somewhere in either the floorboards or walls of various apartments where he had resided. Some might call it a journal or diary. A protocol in Kevin's mind was a memorandum or record of a diplomatic negotiation. It was a road map explaining his methods, and it should have never been written down.

Kevin could not stop himself. For some reason he felt the need to record methods used to humiliate women. It continued to be a work in progress, and the protocol was always mutating which kept him busy with the many revisions. He knew it to be a dangerous game. Kevin reassured himself that this one flaw would be less dangerous than taking trophies from his conquests.

There had been many women. Kevin was careful not to mix his employment with his pleasure. He met women in public places. Public transportation had yielded some very satisfying adventures. He was a fan of the theatre and met a few older, lonely women who were thrilled with his company. None of these relationships lasted more than a few clandestine meetings.

Kevin was a master at recognizing the loneliest of the women he met. Those were the poor souls that he targeted. He was smooth and won over many confidences, before he had sex with them. After one or two of these encounters, he would disappear, leaving each woman wondering what happened. Kevin prided himself on only taking a life when it was absolutely necessary. He highlighted it in his protocol many times. There were times, however, when it could not be avoided. He was careful to explain the "whys" in all of the records.

It was a life that Kevin relished without any disgusting commitments. He told himself that he avoided committing any crimes and prided himself on loving the women before he left them. He always left them with more than he received. It was a lie but one he could justify in his mind. Even the women who had to be eliminated were much better off than they had been in their miserable existences. Kevin had never experienced the encumbrance of a conscience.

Kevin tried to stay out of the dives and honky-tonks. The women in those places seemed to be able to see through Kevin's façade. It was his fantasy, anyway. Those places scared him because he felt his personality was too sensitive to relate to the scum drawn to that seamier side of life. Besides, he was never much of a fighter, and there was a deep-seated fear of hitting on some cretin's woman and losing his good looks to some fists.

He possessed no opposition to spending time in the bars of supper clubs and hotel restaurants. The government paid him well, and he could afford the best of the places Miami had to offer. It was in one of those bars that he met Margaret Powers.

Margaret was a few years older than Kevin, and he made the assumption that she was just another one of his lonely conquests. It would be another one of his mistakes.

Kevin called her Maggie after they had introduced themselves. She never corrected him, but she had never been called anything but Margaret. She had shoulder- length blonde hair. Kevin called her style the "wet" look. She made it look like she had just come from the shower and hadn't straightened all the kinks in her hair. The style appealed to Kevin, and found he was quite attracted to her. As Kevin began playing his new mark, he never realized that she was actually playing him.

Kevin bought Maggie a number of drinks, and she let him. He tried not to show his surprise at how well she held her alcohol. Liquor had always been the favorite tool in his arsenal. Women lowered their guards when drinks passed the usual two or three limit.

The conversation was light, and neither pried into either of their backgrounds. There was no "tell me about yourself" or "where are you from originally?" Kevin was surprised, because he usually needed to push the conversation away from those topics. He thought about turning the tables and asking Maggie about her background, but something in his head said it might not be a good idea.

Kevin ended the night by asking Maggie out to dinner. She accepted and suggested they meet at one of the trendier nightspots on South Beach on Friday evening at 7:00. She would make the reservations. It was a red flag. Kevin was the one who usually was in control. If this were some kind of power grab, he would need to be vigilant. It would give him, however, a few days to do a background check on Margaret Powers. He needed to know what he was getting himself into.

He was attracted to this woman, but there was something that made him uneasy. He had always been careful around his targeted women. She didn't share any personal information, and Kevin wondered if she was just cautious. He needed to find out more.

***

The name of the restaurant was called OLA. Kevin arrived at 6:45 and waited outside for Maggie to arrive. He saw the menu near the entrance in a glass case and went over to look at it. When he saw the prices, he was instantly angry. This place was crazy expensive. He could afford it, but there was reluctance about spending money on someone he just met unless it was going to pay off. The feeling was compounded by the fact he could find nothing on any Margaret Powers that matched. There were three women who shared her name, but they didn't live anywhere near Florida and all were much older.

Kevin checked his watch a few times. A few minutes after 7:00 he began to wonder if he had been stood up. A moment later the receptionist asked him if was waiting for a woman by the name of Margaret, and he affirmed. She was waiting for him at the table she had reserved. He became pissed once again and huffed into the restaurant. He considered telling her to go to hell but changed his mind when he saw her stand and smile. She motioned for him to join her, and Kevin immediately calmed himself down. He noticed that she was wearing a bright yellow dress with a plunging neckline, leaving little for the imagination. Yellow was his favorite color, and a plunging neckline was his favorite type of dress. She had a small waist, and it was cinched with a black belt. He glanced down at her feet and saw she was wearing black heels. Margaret had everything in all the right places.

"I'm sorry if you had to wait. I told the receptionist about you. I guess she wasn't paying attention," Margaret said.

"It doesn't matter. We're here now," Kevin said, trying to mask his real feelings.

"What do you think of the place?"

"Looks like they are pretty proud of their prices."

"They match what they charge. Everything is superb."

"I'm more of an informal type of diner. Sports bars are more my style and much more reasonably priced." Kevin was in the process of using his subtle manipulation.

"Well, you don't have to worry about anything. This night is on my tab." Margaret smiled.

Kevin wanted to strangle her right there at the table. He disliked women who failed to play along with his game.

"I couldn't let you do that."

"Nonsense, I was the one who chose this place, and I should be the one who pays. I won't hear another word about it."

Before Kevin could make an objection, the waiter approached the table and asked for their drink order. Kevin looked over the wine list and was about to order when Margaret preempted him.

"Let's do a bottle of your finest Cab. You pick it out," Margaret said to the waiter.

Kevin had never been with a woman like Margaret. He was puzzled and had no idea of what to make of her. She was strong willed, and he usually avoided uncontrolled personalities. There was something different about her, however. This would be a conquest that would change his entire protocol if he were successful in breaking her. The rest of the evening would be spent following her lead. It would be a reverse manipulation, and Kevin was excited to venture into this new territory.

Margaret ordered from the menu for them both. Kevin nodded in agreement at her every suggestion. She was right with her observation. The food was indeed superb.

The table was cleared, and the waiter asked if they wanted dessert. Margaret declined but ordered two old fashioned instead. Kevin was irritated. He preferred Manhattans. There was too much sugar in the old fashioned. He kept his mouth shut. It was a difficult task. Playing along was so much different from taking the lead with woman. He realized that he was enjoying the role reversal, and that surprised him.

While they finished their drinks, Kevin tried to keep the conversation moving along. It was difficult because of the lack of sharing anything personal.

"I think we should go for a walk. It might help to settle dinner," Margaret said.

Kevin nodded in agreement thinking that she had just used his line.

"I was thinking the same thing. South Beach has its share of weirdos and I think it will be entertaining."

"I can't argue with you. I have no idea where all this strange humanity comes from."

Margaret called for the check, and Kevin used the moment to go to the restroom. He needed some place to think about how he was going to proceed. His inner voice was telling him to get away as soon as possible. Somehow, he knew the woman was trouble. His curiosity would not let him run, however.

When he exited the restroom, he saw Margaret waiting for him at the door. If he had considered leaving, that door had closed. He walked over and Margaret put his arm through hers, and together they left the restaurant.

It was a pleasant evening, and the humidity had dropped. There was a slight breeze and Kevin was thankful for his suit coat. He noticed Margaret shivering when a breeze gusted. He took off his coat and draped it over her shoulders. She looked over and smiled and nodded.

Kevin could still see most of her ample breasts with the coat only covering her shoulders. He liked what he saw, and they walked together without saying much. Kevin was content to look over at her. He tried hard not to ogle. If Margaret noticed him looking at her she appeared to be oblivious. They walked for a time until they came to a park bench overlooking the Atlantic.

"Let's sit here," Kevin said, trying to make it sound like a suggestion rather than a command.

"I have a better idea. My hotel is just down the street. There's a beautiful view of the ocean from the veranda of my room," Margaret said taking his hands in hers.

Kevin's first inclination was to be angry. He had made one suggestion about the park bench, and she had vetoed it immediately. The fact that she had just invited him to her room in the hotel tempered his mood. He still needed to have some control. He was searching for something tangible, when he realized exactly how to proceed.

"Do you have anything to drink?"

"Well, there's a mini bar. I suppose there would be something in there we could drink."

"Oh please, not that swill. Why don't I go find something we both would like to drink? There are a host of liquor stores down the block. What do you prefer?"

"I like almost anything. What do you prefer?"

"Bourbon and water."

"Get that then. I'll go up and make sure the room is presentable. The room number is 315. Here's an extra key, so you can let yourself in."

They walked together until they reached the hotel entrance. Margaret took off Kevin's coat and returned it.

"Don't be too long, or I might be asleep."

Margaret entered the hotel, and Kevin walked quickly down the block looking for some bourbon. He realized that this would have been the opportune time to make a quick retreat. He knew it was the rational thing to do; however, he was engaged in the situation and was beyond being rational.

Margaret failed to realize that Kevin had taken back some control. He decided not to be seen walking into the hotel with her if things degenerated, and he would have to make an immediate exit.

Kevin found a bottle of Maker's Mark and walked around the block searching for a rear entrance to the hotel. He was in luck and found a rear entrance into the hotel bar. He walked through holding the brown paper bag that held the bourbon. There were a few people sitting at the bar. No one paid to attention him as he walked through toward the hotel stairs. He always used the stairs rather than the elevators because of the possibility of cameras. There was no need to have a record of his visits to any hotel.

Kevin climbed the stairs and found the room. He fished the key card from his front pocket and put it into the door's slot. Somehow the protocol that he had been following was no longer relevant. So far, there had been no diplomatic negotiation on his part. This woman had generated everything.

It should have made him wary.

1

Kevin used the key card to let himself into the room. He glanced around and saw that Margaret was seated outside on the veranda.

"I found the bourbon. How do you like it?"

"There's ice in the bucket," Margaret said.

It was not the response Kevin wanted. He was irritated once again.

"That doesn't answer my question."

"Bourbon on the rocks with a splash of water."

Kevin was surprised that she liked her bourbon the way he did. It was an interesting coincidence.

"Coming right up."

"When you have the drinks, come join me. It's a beautiful evening, and there are a host of weirdos out tonight."

Kevin was pleased to see that the little bar had glasses. He hated drinking any type of alcohol out of plastic. For him, presentation was everything.

When he joined Margaret, he almost dropped the drinks. She was in a terrycloth robe that was supplied by the hotel. Margaret's legs were crossed and Kevin could see her right leg halfway up. He tried not to stare as he delivered her drink. He wondered what she was wearing underneath or if she was wearing anything at all.

Kevin sat across from Margaret and forced his eyes to look out streetside to avoid staring at her legs. He had an odd feeling that he knew her from somewhere in the past. It was nothing he could put his finger on, but it was unnerving.

"I've got this nagging feeling that we've met before," Kevin said turning toward Margaret.

"Really?" Margaret looked at Kevin. "I don't think so. It would be something I would have remembered. Maybe you have me confused with someone else from your past. You have a past I presume?"

Kevin sat up straight.

"What kind of question is that? Everyone has a past."

Margaret sat back, smiled, and finished her drink in one gulp.

"Would you be so kind as to refresh my drink? This time please fill the glass, because as you see, I can handle more than the two fingers you just poured."

Kevin took her glass and left the balcony to pour two more drinks. If she wanted him to load her up, he would accommodate. He would be using more water in his drink, however. He could handle his alcohol, but he needed to be in control. So far, it had been Margaret controlling the evening. Given enough alcohol, Kevin knew the tide would be turning.

Kevin finished making the drinks and was picking up the glasses, when he felt Margaret's body press up against his back. He froze for a moment amazed at the degree of stealth she possessed. He decided to take the next cue from her and remained motionless.

"Do you have the drinks ready?" Margaret asked.

"I do."

"Could you please hand me mine?"

Kevin picked up a drink, making sure it was the stronger one, and turned around. Margaret's robe was open, and the terrycloth belt was in her hand. Kevin looked with his mouth open.

"Is this something you might appreciate?"

"It's provocative, to be sure," Kevin said, not caring if he was ogling.

Before she took the drink, she dropped the robe to the floor.

"How about this? Would you say this is also provocative?"

"We are way beyond provocative, I'm afraid."

"Try not to be afraid. Just do what comes naturally."

Margaret took the drinks from Kevin and placed them back on the bar.

Kevin didn't like that particular action, but he was too far into his own arousal to dwell on it. He started to remove his coat and was reaching for his belt, when Margaret put her hand on his to stop him.

"Slow down there, slugger. I never have sex on the first date."

Kevin was pissed, again.

"What's the game here? You are standing in front of me completely naked, and you want me to slow down? What kind of freak are you?"

"Time will tell, I'd imagine."

Kevin realized that he had been so shocked to see her naked, that he failed to take in the full available view. He stood wondering about his next move, and then he rectified that error. Margaret was put together in all the right places. He started with her chest and worked his way down. It was almost too much to fathom. He had never been with a naked woman without taking full advantage. This was just showing how much control she possessed. Kevin wondered how long he would let this go on.

"What is it you want?" Kevin asked.

"I would take my drink if you don't mind."

Kevin took the bourbons from the bar and handed Margaret hers. He was hopeful she would down the entire glass in one swallow. Margaret took a drink, but Kevin was disappointed in the amount she consumed.

"Are you uncomfortable?"

"What do you think?"

"Why don't you join me then. It probably would be less stressful if we were both naked."

"I tried that, but you stopped me."

"I stopped you from trying to have sex with me. Now that you know the rules, you may continue to take off your clothes."

Kevin took a slug from his drink. He had no idea about how to proceed. He was in uncharted territory. This was completely foreign. He decided to try and antagonize the situation.

"I think I'll pass. Why don't we go back and sit on the balcony."

"I'll do whatever you want."

Margaret turned and went back to her seat on the veranda. If Kevin thought she would put her robe back on, he was mistaken. He followed but didn't sit. Instead, he leaned against the railing and looked out toward the ocean. He made sure he didn't look at Margaret.

"What's your game here?"

"There's no game. Just two people enjoying each other's company."

Kevin thought she sounded entirely too smug.

"You've got something on your mind, and you're trying to play me."

"Am I doing a good job?"

"I should just walk out the door and be done with this shit."

"But you won't will you? You are engaged, and you want to see where all this ends." Margaret drained her glass and pushed it into Kevin's back. "I'll have another."

Kevin was forced to turn around. He had to admit it was easier to think straight when he wasn't looking at her. He took her glass and went back into the room without saying anything.

Margaret followed him into the room, and Kevin started mixing the drinks. He would make Margaret's straight bourbon without the water this time around.

"You're pretty good at pouring strong drinks. Tell me, would that be so you can take advantage of me sexually?" Margaret asked while moving next to him.

"Of course. What's your point?"

"It might be working."

Kevin turned and faced Margaret. She took the cue to begin undressing him, and he let her. It was a slower process than Kevin wanted. He started to help her, and she slapped his hands. This seemed to be her show, and Kevin knew he just needed to be patient and play along. When he was down to his briefs, Margaret stopped and pushed him over to the bed. She pulled down the covers.

"You may take off your underwear. Do it slowly."

Kevin was in full arousal. He didn't want Margaret to see she was in control. He knew he was beyond the point of no return. He did an uncomfortable striptease. When his underwear fell to his feet he stepped out of them. With his right foot he flipped them over to Margaret trying to hit her. His aim was poor and they went wide missing her by two feet.

"Let's hope you have better aim with what's between your legs."

Margaret pushed Kevin onto the bed and fell on top of him. Kevin wrapped his arms around her and they rolled over on their side.

"How do you like it?"

"What?"

"Do you like to be on top or does the missionary position have more appeal? Maybe you have a more perverted approach. I'm here to please. Just tell me how to proceed." Kevin liked the power he was taking back.

"I'm not particular. You just need use whatever technique you have to give me the most pleasure."

Kevin knew he was thinking with his penis, but he was powerless to stop. At any other time, her last statement would have been his option to leave. He decided to stop talking and do what gave him the most pleasure. It was the least he could do to regain his manhood.

Before he could make a move, Margaret rolled over to the edge of the bed. She reached into the drawer of the nightstand. Kevin assumed she was reaching for some protection. He was wrong. When she turned and faced him again, it wasn't a condom she was holding

He felt something cold slide between his penis and scrotum. He looked down and saw that Margaret was holding a knife to his favorite parts. He looked back up at her face. She was smiling.

"So, what do you think of my style of protection? I'll wager you were thinking I had something way different in that drawer."

Kevin's eyes were wide open. He knew she could slice off what he held dear in one fluid motion if she wanted.

"Tell me what you want," he said trying to mask the fear in his voice.

"What do I want? I want you to suffer, you bastard." Margaret put more pressure on the knife.

Kevin realized he needed to do something before he lost everything dear to him.

"I don't understand. What's this about?"

"It's about your lifestyle. It's about your perversions and who you hurt. It's about how I'm going to stop you from ever hurting anyone else. It's about a woman named Demi."

Kevin looked up at her without any understanding.

"You don't recognize the name? I suppose I shouldn't be surprised."

Kevin continued to look puzzled.

"She was my sister."

"Was?" Kevin asked.

"Yes. After you took advantage of her, you just left her. She was too fragile for that. Demi never had much luck with the men in her life. She always chose badly which led to her spiraling depressions. She was in love with you, however. After your little tryst, she lost her will to live."

Kevin was mesmerized.

"How did she do it?"

"Do what?"

"How did she kill herself?"

Margaret put pressure on the knife while staring at him in total disbelief.

"Only a psychopath would get pleasure from the details of someone's death." She put more pressure on the knife.

Kevin squealed.

" Keep your mouth closed, or I'll cut it off." Margaret's spoke with a low voice.

Kevin realized he was seconds away from losing his favorite body part. He tried to deflect.

"I don't enjoy anyone's death, but I work with people who need help in their personal lives. This story might help others."

"I know what you do. I've been following you for the past three months. You have an inflated sense of self-worth. You use your position to prey on the women who are most vulnerable while using your government position to remain untouchable. For you, all good things have come to an end."

Kevin was frantically trying to think of anything to stop Margaret from making the final cut. He looked around for something to use as a weapon. A phone on the end table could have been used to give a shot to Margaret's head but it was attached. The lamp was out of reach in his current predicament. The only other possibility was his drink glass. He needed only a slight diversion.

"You'll never get away with this. What do suppose law enforcement will do to you?"

For the first time, Margaret laughed.

"Do you think you're getting out of this alive? This is only the first step. I'm here to make you suffer for what you've done, and suffer you most certainly will. I have a list of the women you have harmed and made disappear. I will leave it with your body after I'm finished with you. It's in my bag. Here, let me read it to you. I think you'll agree it's quite damning."

Margaret reached for her bag to find the paper and Kevin felt the pressure of the knife ease. He took the opportunity to grab for the glass and before Margaret knew what happened, he came around with the glass in his right hand in some type of windmill fashion. The glass caught Margaret on the left side of her face. She went down immediately, but in doing so, drug the knife from Kevin's exposed genitals. Unconsciously, she was able to draw blood, and Kevin howled in pain. Looking down, he realized that he was still intact. Incensed, he grabbed the knife and slit Margaret's throat and sat on the bed next to her to watch her die. He had comfort in that.

Blood was everywhere. Some of it was Kevin's, but Margaret had bled out on the bed. Kevin was dazed but realized he needed to stop his bleeding and get out of the hotel. He looked down at the body that used to be a woman named Margaret. He was sad that he had over reacted and cut her throat. He would have liked to have sex with her first. Unconscious women hadn't been off limits in the past. Margaret was dead, however. He didn't know how he felt about that. He told himself that some things were out-of-bounds even for him. Looking at what could have been one of his most interesting conquests surprised Kevin.

Kevin chased the thought away and found some tape in Margaret's purse. He went into the bathroom and pulled out a handful of tissues and blotted the blood from around his genitals. He saw a small cut almost an inch long between his penis and scrotum. It appeared to be clotting, so Kevin wrapped the tissues around the best he could and made a few passes with the tape to keep them in place. It was the best he could do with what he had at his disposal.

He cleaned the blood from his body with towel and washcloth. When he finished, he got dressed and made sure to eliminate any sign of his being in the room. He considered all the places he touched and wiped away any prints including the murder weapon. He was ready to leave the room, when he remembered the towel and washcloth with his blood on it. Both needed to leave with him as well as the tissues he had used. He would take the knife with him. It would be a great trophy and much better than a bloody towel.

Margaret's bag was on the end table. Kevin emptied the contents on the bed next to her and stuffed the items into it. It was big enough, and after Kevin slung it over his shoulder, he felt that little attention would be drawn to him. They were in Miami and men carrying bags was not uncommon. He left the hotel the same way he had entered.

He would be watching the news for the next few days to keep tabs on the investigation to Margaret's death. He would also be enjoying and reliving his handiwork. It was a beautiful evening. Kevin enjoyed a leisurely walk down the South Beach strip, before he found his way back to his condo.

2

Sander Van Zee left the Perry city limits in a vehicle that Millie DePont had loaned him. He wasn't sure how it would be returned to her, but he had more important issues to deal with at present. No one knew him as Sander, of course. His nickname had always been Zander. Most people didn't know he had another name. He was like Cher or Sting, at least in his own mind. The only things that listed his given name were legal documents. Most of his mail came to his home in Frisco, Colorado, with the Zander moniker.

Leaving his newborn had been tough duty. Leaving her mother, not so much. His old nemesis and lover had become a bane to his existence. Sara Jane's influence had followed Zander from pre-pubescence until his final awakening in Key West. Sara Jane, or Jayne, or whatever she was calling herself at the moment, had finally pushed Zander to a point of no return. Then he found out she had a child. It was his child, and it would change his life forever.

He was leaving Perry, and his daughter, to try and salvage his relationship with Aubrey Moreno. He was in love with her. It was the first time in his life that he loved someone unequivocally. His other relationships had been more about lust and that included the mother of his daughter. He knew he needed to find a separate peace with Jayne if he were to have any chance of ever having influence in his daughter's life. He thought that maybe he was on his way to making that happen. There was no blueprint, so he needed to be careful.

He was on his way to his friends, Herbie and Gail, at their home in Cedar Key. There he would meet Max who would have Aubrey with him. Max helped free Aubrey from a Cuban prison, and Zander owed him a great deal.

Herbie and Gail had always welcomed Zander with open arms and would do whatever he needed. It was hard for Zander to comprehend the magnitude of their friendship. It was something he never had growing up in the small town of Hospers, Iowa.

Zander tried not to think about what had happened to Aubrey while she spent months in the Cuban prison. Max had told him that she was broken but would have the best of care from people in a secret government facility. The state department had used Aubrey as a spy in country because of her ethnic background. In order to have her survive any future involvement with the agency, Max had to see to it that she was listed as deceased and consequently procure a new identity. How deep Max's influence ran was unfathomable, but Zander was thankful they had a history together. He could only hope that whatever facility Max had found for her, it would be enough to bring her back to him.

The drive to Cedar Key was short, and Zander would have three days before Max could deliver her to him on Friday. He hated disrupting his friends' lives and decided to spend time away from their home as much as possible. He questioned why his life had to be so complicated.

He knew his friend Fats would be wondering what was happening and decided to give him a call. Zander found that talking to Fats on the phone, while he was driving, eased the irritation his hippie friend caused. Most of the time Fats pissed him off with his roundabout lingo. But he had a good heart and tried hard to have Zander's best interests at the forefront. He failed at that.

Zander called the Branchwater's phone in Frisco. It was the bar he and Fats had owned together until Zander sold out his share. Fats answered on the third ring.

"It's always summertime at the Branchwater no matter what month you choose to visit. How may I be of service?"

"Fats," was all Zander said.

"Hail-fellow, my palsy-walsy, what's shaking?"

"On my way to Cedar Key. Max is bringing Aubrey on Friday," Zander said.

"An outstanding and remarkable pronouncement from my main man. What is your stratagem henceforth?"

"It was something you said to me earlier."

"I verbalize and articulate many pearls of discerning and insightful sagaciousness. I beg of you to be more explicit."

"You are a smartass. How's that?"

"Cuts to my soul but hardly relevant."

"Fats, you told me to come home. If Aubrey will let me, I'm planning to bring her back with me to Frisco."

Fats was overjoyed at the news and lost his hippie-speak without realizing it.

"It's about time you came to your senses. Do you want your share of the bar back?"

"No, the bar is yours. My main concern will be Aubrey, but I wouldn't be adverse to helping you out down the road."

"That's great news because I wasn't going to sell you back your share anyway. I would like to be your boss, however."

Zander had to smile. It was one of the reasons he wanted to go back to Frisco. Fats always made him feel better, no matter how convoluted his method.

"When will you be gracing us with your persona?" Fats asked.

"I have no idea. I'll have to see how Aubrey is doing and what she wants before I make any more plans. I'm all keyed up just thinking about her return, but it isn't without a great deal of fear."

"To Hades with your consternation. Seize the day, and when you do, call me." Fats left the conversation.

Zander tried to reply, until he realized the phone was dead. Fats needed to be contacted and kept in the loop when it concerned Zander, but he always left on his own terms. It was just one of the many quirks that made their relationship work. It was odd, but Zander knew it was a shared friendship of idiosyncrasies. He knew every one of Fats' odd and peculiar habits, but he had a difficult time seeing his own. He knew he had many, however. Fats was not averse to pointing them out from time-to-time.

Zander crossed the third bridge that led into Cedar Key, as he was putting down his phone. He decided not to go directly to his friends' home. A parking spot opened up adjacent to the boardwalk, and Zander pulled in. He was across from the fishing pier and felt it would be a good place for him to sit and think. He needed some time to sort out the twists and turns his life had taken over the past few weeks.

Zander noticed an open bench near the water, and he claimed it. A man and his daughter were fishing a few feet from where he sat. Zander didn't notice any fish being caught, and soon the little girl lost interest. After a few minutes, she walked over and sat down next to Zander. Zander had no clue how to talk to kids. He had never been around children long enough to gain that skill. She made him nervous, and he wanted her to go away.

"Hi mister. What's your name?"

"My name is Zander. What's yours?" Zander tried to sound interested.

"My name is Sandy."

Zander didn't believe in coincidences, and the fact that this little girl shared his daughter's name, made the hairs on the back of his neck stand up. He wasn't very good with ages but thought that she was around four or five.

"That's a pretty name. I have a daughter with that name."

"Oh, maybe we could play together."

"I'm afraid that wouldn't work very well. You see, she was just born a few weeks ago, so she wouldn't be very much fun yet."

"Maybe I could babysit her. Where is she?" Sandy looked around.

"She lives in another town not very far from here."

Sandy looked puzzled.

"If she is there, why are you here?"

It was a very good question, and one that Zander had thought about at length. He decided not to share it with the pretty young thing, however.

"She's with her mother and grandmother right now. I have some business I need to take care of around here."

The explanation seemed to pacify Sandy, and she started rattling off a number of other things on her mind. Zander let her talk and answered questions when she had them. She was cute, and he found he was enjoying himself. There were all types of surprises in Zander's life lately. This was one of the few positives.

When the father came over with his fishing gear, Zander was disappointed.

"It's time to go, Sandy. I hope she didn't talk your ear off. She's a real little spitfire," her father said to Zander.

"Nonsense. It was real pleasure spending time with her. You should be very proud."

He smiled.

"Do you have children?"

"A newborn. A baby girl."

"Well, hold on tight. They grow up so very fast."

Zander watched the two leave hand-in-hand. It made him think about his own Sandy. He didn't want to think about all that right now. He needed to concentrate on Aubrey.

As he watched them leave, he noticed Herbie and Gail's home in the distance. They were expecting him sometime Thursday evening or Friday morning. It had been his plan until Millie DePont told him to leave. She had been right to push him on his way, and he realized it was for the best. His friends wouldn't find him very good company, however. He made a decision not to show up to their home until early on Friday. It would mean a change of plans, but it gave him time to process his future.

Zander stood and walked directly to the car he was using. He made a mental note to call Millie so someone could pick up the car at Herbie's. He drove back the way he came, making sure not to get to close to his friends' house.

He crossed the second bridge and came to a stop in front of a little boutique hotel called "Low-Key Hideaway." Zander had stayed there before when Herbie and Gail were looking for their new home. The hotel only had five rooms, so Zander hoped they had something available. Since it was mid-week, they had a few openings. He booked a room and decided to go to the market down the road and pick up a few items that he could cook for himself. He made a list of what he would need for each meal through Thursday evening. The units all had a small kitchen, and it would give Zander the privacy he needed.

When he got back from the market and had put all his groceries away, he noticed it was after 4:00. The hotel had a funky little bar on the premises that was constructed completely with glass bottles. They called it their tiki bar, but it was far more unique than anything Zander had ever seen.

Pat and Cindy Bonish owned the property, and Pat was opening the door as Zander followed him into the bar. He recognized Zander from his past stay.

"You must be thirsty. Welcome back." He stuck out his hand for Zander to shake.

Zander realized he didn't remember his name, so he eliminated any embarrassment and said his name as he took his hand.

"Zander. I am thirsty. So much trail dust."

They both laughed at the dusty old joke.

"What can I fix you this fine afternoon?"

Zander thought for a moment.

"Bourbon on the rocks."

"What's your preference?"

"Surprise me," Zander said looking around.

Pat poured the drink and went about his business getting ready for his guests to arrive for the happy hour. Zander sipped his drink and wondered what kind of bourbon he was drinking. He decided it didn't matter. It was just the thing he needed to adjust his attitude.

Zander drank with a number of guests far into the evening. He wouldn't be cooking anything for dinner that day.

3

Kevin Grienne went back to work after his weekend misadventure, but all in all, it had been another successful conquest. It was unfortunate that the woman had to be eliminated, but some things could not be helped. It had been his biggest screw-up and almost ended with him lying dead in the hotel bed instead of her. He tried not to think about it. He promised himself that he would be more careful in the future.

Kevin's work had begun to bore him. It was the same old set of problems with the same old clients. He wanted to work with more women clients, but it was not a part of his employer's protocol. Female counselors worked with female clients, and male clients were seldom assigned any opposite sex duty. Kevin wondered if there was a problem with male predators taking advantage of females in their fragile state. It was interesting that he did not include himself in that predator category.

When he first saw the woman being led down the long corridor, Kevin was thunderstruck. She reminded him of someone, but he couldn't place her. Underneath the swollen eyes and bruising, he knew she was beautiful. He asked around about her, but no one seemed to have any information. She was a ghost.

That same evening Kevin returned and pretended to do some work in the records department. His tenure was such that no one questioned his access. Kevin was able to locate the recently admitted female without a problem. The name on the file said, "Female Moreno." Her background was interesting, and Kevin was lost in the twists and turns of her life's story. Her Cuban decent was a little troubling, but her beauty outweighed Kevin's prejudice against Hispanics. He wasn't thrilled when he read about a boyfriend waiting for her somewhere in Florida.

He put away Aubrey's file and sat back to think about how he would proceed. He needed to make some kind of move before discharge. He went back to her case file and found her counselor's name. Kevin frowned and threw the file on the desk with disgust. He knew the counselor, Connie McGill and hated her.

She was a big and forceful woman who was not intimidated by anyone. Kevin knew it to be true, because he had tried. She was not unattractive, and originally Kevin thought she would be a fine specimen for his list of conquests. When she didn't respond to his manipulations, he tried some sarcasm. She put him up against the wall and would have pounded him senseless, but some of Kevin's coworkers intervened. It was the last time he made any notice or contact with Connie McGill. He knew he would never get any information from her. He had to find another approach.

The intake secretary was a mousy little thing and had no interest for Kevin. He caught her staring at him different times but ignored her. He decided to make an effort to stroke her in some way, so he could gain the information he needed concerning this Aubrey Moreno. He knew he had to work fast, because there was no telling how long

Aubrey would remain a patient. He would begin the process the next day.

Kevin kept his office door open the following day in hopes he would catch McGill and Aubrey coming down the hallway. He cancelled most of his appointments for the day under the guise of catching up on paperwork. He decided to take lunch in his office making sure not to take a chance at missing them.

Just before 1:30 Kevin's patience paid off. Connie McGill was walking down the hall with Aubrey. He noticed they were side-by-side in conversation. Aubrey no longer had to be led. Her face showed no bruising. That had not been the case the last time Kevin had seen her. Kevin was shocked seeing that she was even more beautiful than he had imagined.

Timing would be crucial, and at the precise moment Kevin burst into the hallway with a handful of files. He effectively cut off the pair's forward progression.

"Well, good afternoon, Connie. Who do we have here?"

Connie had been quite happy at having no contact with Kevin after their incident. She prided herself at having a good sense at reading people. She knew Kevin's motives were no good. It puzzled her how he could keep his position when her creep radar was pinging off the charts every time she came near him. He had seniority over her, so she had to be somewhat deferential.

"Kevin, this is one of my clients."

There was a distinct note of distain in her voice, but Kevin pretended not to notice.

"Hello. I'm Kevin. Pleased to meet you."

Before Aubrey could answer, Connie broke in.

"Her name is not important. It is classified." Connie took Aubrey's hand and stepped around Kevin.

Kevin watched them walk down the hall. He knew her name, and he knew there was secrecy surrounding Aubrey and her background. It only served to make him more interested.

He walked over to the secretarial area and waited for the secretary on duty to finish speaking on the phone. He looked for her nameplate on the desk and found her name was Elaine Taggart. He noticed she was looking at him while on the phone, so he smiled broadly. Elaine immediately flushed at the unusual attention.

Kevin was trying not to show his impatience at her phone conversation. He knew he had to play the game to get the information he needed. Finally, Elaine hung up the phone and looked at Kevin.

"Can I help you?" Elaine asked.

Kevin could tell she was interested. Her question was businesslike, but her tone was much softer. She wasn't his type, but she could be of some value.

"How are you today, Elaine?"

Elaine immediately flushed again.

"It's a beautiful day, so I'm quite fine, thank you."

"It's always a beautiful day in Florida, isn't it?"

"Yes it is, and it makes me very happy to be here."

"Where are you from originally?"

"North Dakota."

"Really? North Dakota, wow, you're a long way from home."

Elaine eyes lit up.

"Are you familiar with North Dakota?"

"Just a little. I'm from the Midwest also." Kevin was careful not to reveal where he was actually from.

"Where 'bouts in North Dakota do you hail from?" Kevin asked trying to interject at bit of midwestern dialect into the conversation.

"I'm from Minot."

"Why not Minot?" It was an expression Kevin had heard somewhere in his past.

Elaine smiled broadly.

"You got it."

"That's pretty far up there, isn't it?"

"Maybe sixty or so miles from Canada is all."

Kevin whistled.

"Boy, what brings you all the way down here?"

"Well, living in Minot might be the reason, don't you think? It seems like it's mostly winter all the time up there."

"I hear you. How did you end up here?" Kevin was playing her, and he could see she was enjoying the attention.

"I was a pretty good distance runner in high school, but it's hard to train in the winters when it's so darn cold. Minot State University tried to get me to commit, but who ever heard of a runner from there?"

"So, you came to Florida to run?"

"Not really. I was recruited by a number of colleges and universities. I guess my times were impressive."

Kevin thought it was lucky she was good at something, since she had nothing in the way of physical attributes. He was starting to become bored with the conversation and wanted to get to the real reason he was speaking to her.

"Looks like you were built for running." Kevin wondered if the comment would put her off.

Elaine flushed again, and Kevin realized she took what he had said as a compliment. There was no explaining how a comment could offend one person and be a compliment to another. If he could figure that one out and write a paper about it, he would be famous in the psychological world.

"Where did you end up going to college?"

"I got a full ride at the University of Colorado at Boulder."

"Well, that's not very far from North Dakota."

"It seemed like light years to me. At least the weather was better. I majored in business and graduated with honors. Pulled a hamstring my senior year and missed most of the season."

"How sad. Terrible way to end a running career."

"It wasn't so bad. I was burned out and tired of the training it took to be competitive. It was kind of like it was meant to be."

Kevin was beginning to get impatient but did a good job of still trying to sound interested.

"The question still would be how you ended up here in southern Florida?"

"I met a guy on the track team. He had all these grand ideas about moving to Florida and opening a business and getting rich. So, we moved to Florida. He talked me into getting a job to support us; while he researched what business we could get into to become rich. I should have figured it out, but I thought I was in love. He was the first guy that ever paid much attention to me."

Kevin thought he knew why.

"What happened?"

"After a few months, he took a job on a fishing charter boat in the keys. When he wasn't busy he would come back to tell me that he was learning the trade. He dreamed of getting his own fishing boat. We would be in business. I would take care of the bookkeeping end of it, and he would do the charters. We would be rich."

"A pipe dream?"

"Worse. His trips back to Miami became fewer and fewer, until they stopped altogether. I even made a trip down to where he said he was working. I checked with all the charter boats, but no one had ever heard of him. He played me."

Kevin almost choked at her last sentence. He smiled to himself because that was exactly what he was doing. People like Elaine tended to lend themselves to being used.

"Did you ever find out what happened to him?"

"No, he just vanished. That's when I found this position. Been here ever since."

"What a sad story, but you're doing just fine now."

"Yes I am."

Kevin would have liked to meet Elaine's flim-flam man. He was someone after his own heart. He thought they could be good friends.

"It always nice to hear good things come out of bad experiences, especially in my business."

"I'm sure you could tell amazing stories."

"Yes, but unfortunately my code of ethics doesn't allow me to tell these tales of woe." Kevin smiled.

"You know, even I have to be careful about talking about my job outside of the office. There is just too much that goes on around here that can't be shared."

"You are a good employee, and we're lucky to have you."

Elaine smiled but suddenly sat up straight in her chair.

"I'm so sorry. Here I am talking about myself, and you are obviously here on business."

"Think nothing of it. My job is listening to others and trying to help them. It's nice to listen to someone who is not a client and not on the clock."

"You made me feel better by just talking. Thank you. Now let me help you with what you need."

Kevin thought about how to proceed and decided to just get to the point. It could be that he had established enough trust with Elaine to keep her talking.

"Did you see the woman who was with Connie just now?"

"Isn't she beautiful? She reminds me of Natalie Wood."

The comment made Kevin smile. That's exactly who he thought she resembled. It took Elaine to jolt his memory.

"She is beautiful. What's her story?"

"I don't know very much. Everything about her is pretty secretive."

Kevin realized that all the effort he had invested in Elaine might have been a big waste of time. He was ready to excuse himself, when Elaine let the information slip that he had wanted all along.

"The only thing I know is that she's going to be discharged this Friday."

Kevin's mind went into hyperdrive. He turned and walked back to his office.

Elaine sat in her chair wondering what had just happened.

4

Kevin had too much to do before Friday. He didn't know if he could tie all the loose ends together. He knew he would have to make it work, because this was bound to be the greatest opportunity of his lifetime.

He decided to take two weeks of his vacation starting on Friday. It was easy to juggle his schedule and assign a few of his clients to other caseworkers. By the end of the day everything was arranged. He would finish out on Thursday and be free on Friday to follow Aubrey.

Kevin was up and packed by 7:30 on Friday morning. Most of the patients were discharged between 9:00 and 11:00. He was waiting in his plain and unobtrusive rental car at 8:30 in the parking lot with a full view of the exit. The rental was some foreign model. Kevin wasn't sure what it was. He never paid much attention to automobiles. He did like the fact that the color was white just like thousands of others. He would be invisible and melt into the traffic making it difficult for his prey to realize they were being followed.

Kevin sat drinking his coffee out of his 20-ounce mug. The coffee and his own adrenalin jacked him up. The minutes ticked slowly. He was afraid he would have to find a bathroom to get rid of the coffee he was processing.

At 10:00 he began to panic and wondered if someone had changed Aubrey's discharge time. Just as he opened the car door, a large black SUV pulled up to the exit door and a tall slender man jumped out and rang the bell. Kevin eased back into his rental to watch.

Forty-five minutes later the door opened back up, and the man walked out and looked around. Kevin slumped down into his seat. The driver seemed satisfied and motioned for someone inside the doorway to come out.

Kevin could see it was a woman by the way she walked, even though she had a hoodie pulled around her head. He knew it was Aubrey, and he forgot about having to go to the bathroom.

The car began to head for the parking lot exit before Kevin started his car. He would have to be careful. The man in the vehicle looked to be a professional. It would be in his best interest to go undetected. It would have been better to put a tracking device on the SUV, but there hadn't been time. Kevin wondered if he had made a mistake. There was no time for that kind of thought now. It would serve no purpose. He would just need to be vigilant.

Then the unexpected happened. The black SUV pulled up alongside of Kevin's rental and the man got out. He tapped on the passenger window, and Kevin pressed the button to roll the window down. The man was friendly enough and asked for the best route to Fort Meyers. Kevin gave him his opinion, and the man got back into his vehicle. It was a brief encounter but it shook Kevin. He knew he had to be careful. He tried not to look directly at the man to avoid having him see his face. Surprise would still be his best tactic, and being unidentifiable was always preferable.

The SUV headed west out of Miami. Kevin kept his distance and was happy when he saw the vehicle find the entrance to I-75. Kevin didn't mind traveling on I-75 but he hated I-95. It was always too busy to suit him. There were too many East coasters for his taste, and it seemed like there were countless accidents every day. Those idiots didn't know how to use their turn signals. The Floridians joked that they must have all run out of blinker fluid.

Alligator Alley always amazed Kevin. The sheer number of alligators sunning themselves on the side of the interstate was amazing. It was good that there was chain link fencing between the shoulder and the banks of the waterway. Otherwise, Kevin knew there would be a number of accidents and many more dead 'gators.

At a turn-off between Naples and Bonita Springs, Kevin saw the black SUV make an exit. He signaled and did the same. Aubrey's driver pulled into a Shell station, and Kevin made a quick decision to do the same. He thought he'd take a chance and pulled next to the SUV. It was a huge risk but one Kevin decided was worth the chance that he might be recognized. He got out and began to pump gas into his tank. He was careful not to let Aubrey see him and kept to the rear of the car.

He waited for the opportunity to engage the driver in conversation. Finally, the driver emerged from the vehicle and began to pump gas into his vehicle. Kevin took his chance.

"Nice day isn't it."

The man looked at him. Kevin felt he was sizing him up.

"It seems to be."

Kevin smiled. The man didn't seem to have recognized him from the parking lot.

"Never know in Florida, I guess. Where you headed?"

The man looked at him again.

"North."

"Me too. Maybe I'll see you again down the road."

"Never know."

The man went back to the driver's door and leaned in and handed something to Aubrey. Kevin wondered if he had been using her credit card for gas. It would make sense.

He hung up his nozzle. He got back into his car and made a quick decision to get back on the interstate. There were three northbound lanes, and Kevin exited to the right lane and reduced his speed. It was a gamble, but he felt he could spot the SUV when it passed him in the far lane. If the guy hadn't told him the truth, it would be a gamble gone badly.

After twenty minutes, Kevin began to panic. He dropped down to forty and cars were passing him and honking. He didn't dare to go slower and risk getting picked up for going too slow. Finally, when he was convinced he had made a bad decision, the SUV whipped by him in the far left lane.

Kevin put the hammer down but stayed in the right lane. He didn't want to follow Aubrey's vehicle directly. It would be better if he stayed out of the range of the SUV's rear view mirror.

The traffic flow was good. Kevin passed a few vehicles in the center lane, making sure not to drift to the left lane. When they passed Sarasota, Kevin began to wonder how far up the coast they would be traveling. He was getting tired of driving.

There was a sign north of Bradenton that displayed the exit for I-275. The spur would take them over the Sunshine Bridge. Kevin had never been over the bridge. If he had business in Tampa he took I-4. The Sunshine Bridge was out of the way unless one was traveling to St. Petersburg. He hoped that this was going to be the destination. His ass hurt, and his back ached.

Kevin's disappointment was pronounced when he watched Aubrey's vehicle turn on highway 19 and head north. The interchange was busy so he kept closer to the SUV than he had previously. He didn't want to lose them in the traffic. Highway 19 was a toll road, but Kevin blew right through the tollbooth without paying. The SUV had done the same. He figured the vehicle might have had some type of prepaid pass attached to the windshield, but since he was driving a rental, there would be a surcharge tacked on when he turned the car back to the rental agency.

When they passed New Port Richey, the traffic began to flow along faster with less traffic. It was still a four-lane road, so Kevin could relax a bit and change positions from time to time to ease his aching butt.

He had never been this far north of Tampa and found the difference between southern Florida and northern Florida quite impressive. Huge pines lined the road, and there were no longer palm trees visible. When they passed Crystal River, there was a sign that pointed toward the power plant on the coast where there was a viewing area for manatees.

Kevin made a mental note to return to take in that tourist attraction. Manatees always fascinated him. They were the gentle giants of the ocean that were totally susceptible to mankind. That thought puzzled him somehow. How could a mammal be completely defenseless and not be completely wiped out by its many predators? Had he let his thoughts drift even more toward his own life, he might have seen the extreme contrast between himself and the manatees. Who protected the defenseless women from his predatory conquests?

He didn't have the wherewithal or the time to make any comparisons. He needed to focus on what was happening in the here and now.

Thirty-five miles north the SUV's turn signal indicated a left turn. Kevin slowed down and watched as the vehicle turned on to highway 24. There was a sign ahead indicating it was twenty-one miles onto Cedar Key. It also said it was the only road to "old cracker" Florida. Kevin would be sure to ask what that meant if he had time.

Cedar Key was a small place, and Kevin realized he would have to be careful not to follow too closely to avoid being detected. When the SUV reached 1st Street, it turned right and parked in front of a house a half-block down. Kevin turned left, and then took a right on Dock Street, following the loop back to 1st Street. There was a city park two blocks toward where the SUV had turned. Kevin could see the vehicle and the house from that vantage point. He would wait and see what happened from here. He was getting hungry and wanted to return to Dock Street where he had seen a number of restaurants. It would have to wait until later, however. This was much too important. He was happy not to be discovered on the long trip from Miami. Now all he had to do was wait.

Kevin had packed binoculars, and he took the opportunity to retrieve them from his bag in the trunk. It felt good stretching his legs and getting the kinks out of his back. He decided to take a seat on a vacant picnic table. Here he played the typical tourist and took in the sights around him through the glasses. He would rest his panoramic view onto the black vehicle for a few moments during each of his viewings. It was empty, so he knew everyone was inside the house. He wondered if he was going to have to spend the night in the car, keeping an eye on the house and vehicle. He would not be looking forward to that at all. He used the opportunity to empty his exploding bladder in the park's public restroom.

After he finished, Kevin sat on the table for almost an hour before the tall man emerged followed by Aubrey and an even a taller man. It looked like the SUV driver was planning to leave. Aubrey gave the man a hug and stepped away. The taller man shook the SUV driver's hand. Kevin wondered if this was the boyfriend. He also considered that this might be his house, and they would be staying here. That would be a good thing. If it were so, he could begin planning his next move.

As he moved the binoculars around he was suddenly disappointed. There was a couple on the second floor deck watching the scene unfolding. They were arm-in-arm, and Kevin figured that they were the homeowners.

The goodbyes were short, and when the black SUV pulled away, the couple returned into the house. They would be staying there for a while. Just how long, Kevin had no idea. He knew he needed to find someplace to stay, and he had to get something to eat.

Hodges Resort On The Water was located diagonally across the street from the house where Aubrey was staying. Best of all, it was well hidden from the view of the house. That was both good and bad news. No one could see his car parked next to his cabin, but he also could not see what was happening across the street. His surveillance would take more effort than he wanted. He had no choice, so he booked the room and soon found himself under the shower. It felt good to wash the day's stress away. When he finished, he asked the desk clerk where he could find something to eat within walking distance. The clerk gave him a few suggestions, and as he suspected, they were all on Dock Street.

Steamer's Bar and Grill looked promising. It was a second-floor establishment with an outside staircase that boasted more drinks than selection of food. Most of their offerings were fried. Kevin wanted to sample the local cuisine, and he chose a sample platter that was long on clams and oysters. It had fried green tomatoes and some fish the locals liked. Kevin didn't share their taste in fish, but everything else was passable. After a few beers to wash away the taste of the fish, Kevin returned to his room.

He needed sleep and was out before the sun had even begun to set. Had he been able to stay awake, he would have seen the same tall man walking around the resort until he stopped at Kevin's rental. He paused for a moment and then turned around and went back the way he came.

5

Max entered the parking lot and pulled up to a side door to pick up Aubrey for transport to Cedar Key. The door that most people used was around the front. The side door was used for those who didn't want to draw attention to comings and goings.

Max looked around as he exited the SUV. It was instinctive and something he always did. Getting the layout of the surroundings was important. If anything looked questionable, it probably was going to be a problem.

He noticed a white sedan with someone sitting in the driver's seat. Not unusual in itself, but at this facility it was strange. People were here for the long term, and no one waited for anyone outside in the cars. He made a mental note to check if the car was still there when he and Aubrey left.

It took Max a few moments to adjust his eyes to the dimly lit corridor when he entered. Most of these places didn't believe in bright lighting. He figured it probably was used to subdue behavior. Many of these patients suffered from some sort of PTSD and exhibited violent behaviors. Max respected the people who gave their lives to helping these poor souls. He knew he could never do it.

He checked in with a receptionist behind a wall of glass. She asked for his credentials, and he slid his driver's license, passport, and something in a small envelope. The receptionist routinely looked at the first two items without much fanfare. When she looked at the item in the envelope, her facial expression changed. She looked up at Max without changing her facial expression, but Max noticed something in her eyes that hadn't been there before. He was always amazed at how people responded to the memo from the National Director of Intelligence. It opened many doors that would have been closed to most others.

The receptionist buzzed Max into another corridor where she met him. She was a big woman, and Max thought that she didn't get out of her chair for just anyone. The thought made him smile. She must have thought that he was some big deal, but he knew nothing could be further from the truth. He liked the subterfuge, however.

The pair moved quietly down the first corridor and through a set of doors that needed another receptionist to allow passage. The big woman spoke through a small opening in the glass window. Max couldn't hear what she was saying but soon heard a click and the doors opened. The woman turned and headed back to her post without engaging Max. He hoped he had made her day. At least he helped her get a bit of exercise.

Max entered the hallway and could see doors all the way down the long corridor. The place looked like a hospital and he supposed, it many respects, it was. The second receptionist turned and spoke to Max. Unlike her co-worker, she didn't get up. Max thought she could have used some exercise as well.

"Please have a seat against the wall. I will ring for an orderly to show you to the room." The woman's badge showed her name to be Mary.

Max looked at her for a moment.

"Thanks, Mary. It seems kind of sterile around here."

Mary stared at him and then turned around to continue to deal with some paperwork on her desk. Max was an unknown, and the employees were cautious around people of importance. Max liked having people think he was a person of importance, so he did little to dissuade it. People were more pliable when they were uncomfortable.

Max didn't have to wait long before a male orderly approached him.

"If you would follow me please, I'll take you to the subject's room."

Max noticed that no one used names in places like this. He liked it. Anonymity was preferable when dealing with anyone from the outside. It insured that the same people who had used and almost killed her wouldn't bother Aubrey.

Max was amazed at how large the facility seemed. The hallways went on forever, and it would be easy to get turned around snaking through the windowless labyrinth.

The orderly stopped, and Max almost ran into him.

"This is the woman's room. I will announce you, and you will enter. I will stay outside the door, and when you are ready I will accompany you both to the exit."

"Thank you. I don't think I could manage to find my way out of this maze on my own." Max stuck out his hand.

The orderly looked at him for a moment and turned and knocked on the door without shaking Max's hand. Max didn't care. He was bullshitting the guy anyway. He knew exactly where he was and could easily find his way back without any help. It was the kind of thing he had always done, but he was trying to be pleasant with the staff. It was hard work for Max, and he was relieved he didn't have to pretend any longer.

"Excuse me. You have a visitor. I am going to unlock your door, and he will be entering your room." The orderly was nothing but professional. Max thought he might be an okay guy.

After the door was unlocked, Max entered and closed the door quickly behind him. The room was windowless but pleasant enough with plenty of light. There was a large television on the wall opposite the bed. It was turned off, and Aubrey was sitting on the bed. Max kept an appropriate distance.

"Hello Aubrey. My name is Max Kuhn. I'm a friend of Zander. I'm here to take you to him." Max tried to keep everything simple.

"What's his real name?" Aubrey asked.

"His name is Sander Van Zee."

"I don't know you. You could be anyone."

"Do you believe I could get into this facility if I didn't have the right credentials?"

Aubrey rolled her eyes.

"Those people who put me into Cuba had all the right credentials."

Max liked her. She was cautious.

"Look, let's start over. Do you mind if I sit?"

Aubrey motioned to a desk chair nearby.

Max took the chair and sat next to the bed. He kept a reasonable distance to keep from invading Aubrey's space.

"You don't know me, and you have every right to be cautious. I am impressed with your pluck." Max thought he saw a hint of a smile pass over her lips. "Tell me what you want to know."

"What is your relationship to Zander?"

"As I told you, we are friends. It was because of him I found the love of my life." Max could see confusion in Aubrey's eyes. "It's a long story and one that should probably told by Zander."

"Why isn't Zander here?"

"You are in a secret facility. He would not be permitted to enter under any circumstances."

"Just who the hell are you?"

Max smiled.

"I'm the guy who rescued you from your Cuban fiasco. Well, Zander played an important role as well. If it weren't for him you'd still be there, or worse, buried in some shallow grave on the prison grounds. You weren't in very good shape when we found you."

"I have no recollection of anything but lying in my cell."

"You've had a trying recovery both physically and emotionally. It wouldn't have happened without access to this place, such as it is." Max motioned with a broad sweep of his arm.

"And I have you to thank for that?"

Max shrugged.

"I did what I could for you and Zander."

"Why?"

"I feel like I owe him and quite frankly, it feels good to get back into the game." Max paused. "He loves you, you know."

Aubrey looked down and blushed. It was the first Max saw of her emotional side. He liked what he saw.

"What's going to happen now?" Aubrey asked when she recovered.

"I'm going to return you to Zander. He's been waiting, and I can't say it was with any patience. It will be good not receiving his daily phone calls."

"Where are we going?"

"To his friends, Herbie and Gail. I believe you know them?"

"Where do they live?" Aubrey was quick and still testing.

"Cedar Key, Florida. Do you want to continue this banter, or do you want to get out of this place?"

Aubrey jumped up and opened her closet door. Everything she owned was in a large bag. She threw it on the bed.

"I'm ready, but I've got questions."

"I've got the answers, and we'll have time for both on our five-hour drive to Cedar Key." Max stood and grabbed her bag.

Max grabbed the door handle to open it and was surprised to find it locked. He pounded on it twice.

"Hey, open this door."

He heard a key enter the lock, and the door opened.

"Why would you lock the door when you knew we were leaving?"

"Sorry, it is procedure." The orderly turned and began walking back the way Max had entered.

"Friendly folk," Max said to Aubrey, as they followed behind.

"If you only knew," Aubrey said, and she rolled her eyes.

Max retraced his steps following the orderly. When they got to the second checkpoint, the three walked through without stopping. Mary, the receptionist, didn't bother to look up.

"I wonder who schools these employees on public relations?" Max asked.

Aubrey laughed out loud.

"I don't think Mary has much time for men. Especially men with credentials."

"So, that's what I am. A man with credentials?" Max paused. "I like it."

When they passed the first checkpoint, the first receptionist looked up.

"Have a nice day," she said and looked back down at her paperwork.

Max thought the words sounded hollow and knew Aubrey thought so as well, when she rolled her eyes again.

The orderly almost pushed them out the double doors, and they found themselves in the hallway that led to the side door and freedom. Max couldn't wait to get out of the facility, and he wondered how Aubrey felt.

When Max opened the door, the day's heat rushed them both. Max thought it felt wonderful and saw Aubrey smile, as she shed herself of her sterile environment. Max guided her to his vehicle. He unlocked the passenger door and opened it. Aubrey stood away from the car, letting the pent-up heat partially escape the car's interior. Max went around to the back and unlocked the trunk. As he placed Aubrey's bag inside, he glanced to his left. The car with the driver sitting inside was in the same place. The car was running, and Max figured it was to keep the interior cool so he could remain in place.

Max closed the trunk lid and moved toward the driver's door. He was in no hurry. Aubrey was waiting beside her door and, Max told her to wait until he started the car and got the air conditioner pumping.

He started the SUV and then got back out. It was too hot to sit in the car. He kept his door open and talked to Aubrey through the open doors.

"I want you to look at me and casually answer me. When I ask you a question, just look at me and don't look around. Can you do that?"

"Sure. What's up?" Aubrey asked as she concentrated on looking directly at Max across the top of the car.

"There's a white sedan across from me and to your left."

Aubrey fought off the urge to glance over to the spot Max had just mentioned.

"Okay."

"There's a person sitting in the car, and he was here when I got here. I think it's unusual."

"I agree."

"I would like you to take a look when you get into the vehicle and see if you can recognize this person."

"Okay."

"I think it is cool enough to get into the SUV, why don't you get in and take a look. I'll wait a few moments before I get in. It should give you enough time to take a good look. Whoever it is would still be concentrating on me."

"Got it." Aubrey went into the vehicle headfirst looking straight at the white sedan. She pretended to be moving something around in the back seat but never took her eyes off the car.

Max waited a few more moments and then got in.

"What do you think? Do you recognize this driver?"

"Well, it's definitely a man. I think I may have seen him someplace, but I can't be sure. He's a little too far away to be sure."

"Let's fix that. I'm going to drive by him on the way out. I'm going to stop and ask him for directions. You need to study his face before we stop, but after I roll down my window, you need to pretend you're reading something in your lap. Glance at him only from your peripheral vision."

"Let's go." Aubrey was already doing an appraisal.

Max swung the car around and moved toward the exit. He stopped when the black SUV came next to the white sedan. Since the vehicles were both facing the same direction, Max got out and tapped on the white car's passenger window. The driver hit the button, and the window rolled down.

"Hot one today," Max said.

"How can I help you?" the driver asked.

"We're headed to Fort Myers. I was wondering if there is a better way to go than I-75?"

"Well, you could certainly take 41 but I-75 will be much faster."

"Hey, thanks. You have a nice day." Max smiled as he used the receptionist's line.

Max got back into the car and moved to the parking lot exit. He didn't say anything until they turned onto highway 27. Just before they found the entrance to I-75, Max turned to Aubrey.

"What do you think? Did you recognize the guy?"

"I can't be completely sure, but I think he was a counselor at that place. I remember someone creepy staring at me a few times. I think it might have been him. My counselor told me to be careful and avoid him at all costs. I guess I didn't pay close enough attention. He didn't bother me, other than the stares."

Max looked straight ahead. After a few moments he glanced at the review mirror.

"Well, it appears he is tailing us. He must have seen something he liked, and I don't think it was me."

6

Aubrey's instinct told her to turn around and look at the vehicle following them, but she caught herself partway.

"Sorry. I'm a little jumpy when it comes to people following me."

"It's understandable. He's far enough behind, so he won't be able to make out much happening inside our vehicle."

"This is making me nervous."

"As it should. I want to do some checking. What was your counselor's name?"

"Connie McGill. She was really good. You don't think she's involved in anything do you?"

"I doubt it, but it could be she could provide some information about our new-found friend."

Max took out his SAT phone from under his seat. He punched in one number and waited as he drove.

"You shouldn't be on electronics when you're driving," Aubrey said.

"Distracted driving. I know. Maybe just this once." Max smiled, and Aubrey smiled back, which surprised them both.

Max recited a few numbers into the phone followed by one word, "Jackson." He put the phone back down on the seat.

Aubrey was intrigued.

"What's going on?"

"We wait. Someone will call back. In the meantime, why don't you grab the satchel under your seat." Max continued driving, glancing in the mirror from time-to-time.

"Is he still behind us?" Aubrey asked.

"Yes. I'm doing my best not to lose him. I don't think he's a professional, if that's any consolation."

"It helps somewhat, but it also leaves us with more questions." Aubrey reached into the bag and pulled out three plain envelopes. "What's this?"

"Open them," Max said.

The first envelope had a driver's license with her picture on it. The second was a passport. The third held a birth certificate. They were all hers.

"Where did you get these?"

"Best money can buy."

"I don't understand."

"Look closer."

Aubrey looked again at each document until she noticed her name. It wasn't Aubrey Moreno. The name on all three documents listed her as Audrey Wood. The new name wasn't lost on her.

"Very funny. Who picked this out?"

"I think you might have a good idea." Max smiled as he glanced over at the new Audrey. "He wanted to call you Natalie, but that was just a bit too obvious."

"Do we really need all this cloak-and-dagger stuff?"

"You are listed as dead. What would happen if someone did a random search and your name popped up again? We want you to have a life without interruption from the Feds. From now on everyone will call you by your new name. Get used to hearing Audrey."

Aubrey glanced back at the documents.

"I guess it's an easy name to remember. Aubrey is close to Audrey, and I never could escape the Wood comparison."

"Not that you're complaining, right, Audrey?" Max winked.

"I suppose I'll have to get used to people calling me that."

"Sure, but what's nice is that if someone screws up, the names are so close most people wouldn't notice."

"I assume the screw-up you are speaking about is Zander."

"Of course. Everything should be great unless he starts calling you Natalie."

The former Aubrey, now Audrey, began to answer when the SAT phone rang.

Max picked it up and listened while someone spoke on the other end. He repeated the numbers from before, followed by the word "Jackson."

"I need some information from someone in our facility in Miami. The name of the contact is Connie McGill. She worked with a patient named Aubrey Moreno. We need info from this Connie. She mentioned someone that Aubrey Moreno should avoid. He might be another counselor or some other employee at the facility. Whatever you can give us would be helpful. Thanks." Max put the phone back under his seat.

"Now what?" Audrey asked.

"We wait. The information will get to us before we reach Cedar Key."

"Who are you?"

"I'm nobody any longer. I used to be somebody but not anymore. It's the way I like it."

"You still have resources that no one else can access."

Max smiled.

"It's the price you pay for formerly being somebody. It can be a very big burden at times."

"Other times it comes in handy when helping friends."

"It's true."

"Am I your friend?" Audrey asked.

Max looked at her.

"I think so. I think I really like you. You have a sense of humor even after all the shit you went through. I can see why Zander is so taken." Max avoided the word love, because he didn't think it was his place to say.

"But which one does he expect, Aubrey Moreno or Audrey Wood?"

Max didn't answer but smiled at her question.

Audrey sat back and decided to watch the road. She saw a sign that listed Marco Island with arrow pointing left.

"Where are we, anyway?"

"Just making the turn north."

"Did I miss the Everglade City exit?"

"That was about 15 miles back."

"I wanted to stop and see some of the people from the Rod and Gun Club."

"Sorry, Audrey. That can't happen. You can never go back there. You are dead, remember?"

"How can I forget, with you reminding me constantly?"

"It's something that's going to take a great deal of discipline on your part. You can never go back to any part of your old life."

The reality hit Audrey hard.

"I didn't realize how difficult this was going to be."

"It's going to be much harder than you can imagine. Everything that you were is gone. There is nothing left of your past life. It has to be a complete restart. I can't stress this enough."

"I'll do my best."

"I know you will, but that won't be good enough. It will be difficult not to slip into old habits and make mistakes. You can never contact former friends for any reason."

Audrey nodded, still trying to process what had just happened.

The SAT phone rang, making Audrey jump.

Max fished it out from under his seat. This time all he said was "Jackson." There was no conversation on his end. Max listened intently without speaking. Finally, he thanked the caller and put away the phone.

"The man following us is indeed a counselor at the facility. His name is Kevin Grienne. Connie McGill doesn't seem to hold him in very high regard. She knows that he abuses women outside of work, but there is no proof. He has a history of being a womanizer and chooses those that he considers most vulnerable."

"How do we know it is him following us?" Audrey asked.

"He put in for vacation at the time of your discharge. He rented a car from the airport. The license number matches the car following us."

"How in the world were they able to get all this information?"

"We've got some very good resources," Max said and smiled.

"You amaze me," Audrey said, never taking her eyes off Max.

"I know. I amaze myself sometimes."

Audrey knew that it wasn't arrogance fueling Max's comments but his attempt at keeping things light. She appreciated anything that would keep her panic in check.

"I think we'll pull off up ahead and get some gas. It will be interesting to see what our new friend does."

"What do you want me to do?"

"Do you need to use the restroom?"

"I'm good."

"Do you have a knife or a scissors in that bag of yours?"

"Nope."

Max reached into his pocket and pulled out a knife and unfolded it.

"Cut up your old identification into small pieces and give it to me."

"I don't have my birth certificate."

"No problem. The other two are the important pieces."

Audrey began to rip up her license and passport with the knife as Max got out to fill the tank.

Max had just finished cleaning the windshield when Audrey noticed the white sedan pull into the next set of pumps. She kept looking down and paid attention to what she was doing while trying to keep the scene in her peripheral vision.

Max continued to fill the tank and she could see him responding to the creep who was also filling his tank. The conversation didn't last long, and soon Max handed the receipt from the gas pump to Audrey. She took it from him but had a puzzled look on her face. Max said nothing. He turned and watched the white sedan turn back toward I-75 and finally, when he was gone, got back into the SUV.

"Why did you give me this?" Audrey asked.

"I wanted to make sure you saw this guy."

"I was watching him the entire time."

"He must either be stupid or arrogant to think that we wouldn't recognize him from the parking lot."

"Maybe he's both."

"That presents a real problem. Stupidity and arrogance don't mix well together, and they make for a great deal of unpredictability."

"Now what?"

"We follow the plan. The next stop will be Cedar Key and Zander."

That comment made Aubrey both excited and apprehensive. She didn't know how Zander would respond when he saw her. She wasn't the same woman physically or emotionally. She had lost some weight, but she also knew she had lost some of her spark. Maybe Zander could help her get them both back.

Things were quiet after that. Audrey was considering how her meeting with Zander would go, and Max was considering various options with this person in the white sedan.

The Sunshine Bridge at St. Petersburg was fun. The view was amazing and they both commented on it. When they reached the turnoff to Highway 19, Audrey was beginning to feel excited. She had missed Zander, and the anticipation of seeing him again was almost too much to handle.

"It won't be long now. Are you ready to begin your new life?" Max asked.

Audrey hadn't thought of it that way, but it was true. Everything was about to be brand new. There was nothing from her past that could be carried over. The more she thought about the idea, the better she liked it. Her life before Zander hadn't been very good at all. She had been miserable for most of her adult years. Now she could forget all that because she was told she had to. It turned out to be a huge perk in her mind.

"This is the new me."

"Be sure you keep Zander appraised of the new you as well. It will take him some time to get used to the idea. It would be best for both of you to remain in Cedar Key until the transition is fully realized."

"That shouldn't be a problem since we both like Herbie and Gail. They are great hosts. I don't think they will kick us out until we're ready."

"I like what I'm hearing."

"Good. But what will we do about this guy on our tail?"

"That will be a decision that needs to be made by all of us. There are many options, and I'll help with the one that you and Zander decide is the best."

Audrey wondered what he meant by that. It sounded ominous to her and she wasn't ready to make more decisions just yet. She hoped this could be put off for some time. That would depend on Kevin Grienne, however.

As those thoughts were swimming in Audrey's mind, Max made the turn into Cedar Key. Audrey had no idea where she was until Max pulled into Herbie and Gail's home. She recognized the house the moment her mind came into focus.

"We're here," Max said.

"I'm not ready."

"What? Do you have to put on your face or what?"

"I'm just not ready to see anyone just yet."

"You'd better get ready because they are coming out the door."

Audrey turned to see Zander rushing out the door toward the car with Herbie and Gail right behind. She opened the door and Zander pulled her out of the SUV in one fluid motion. He put his arms around her and looked her in the eyes.

"I don't know what to say."

Audrey put her finger on his lips and kissed him gently on the cheek and then removed her finger and kissed him on the lips. Zander finally broke away and was about to speak.

"Don't talk unless you know what to say." Audrey smiled.

At that moment everyone knew things were going to be better.

7

The reunion moved inside when everyone had enough of the moment. Gail went to work making some appetizers, while Herbie took the drink orders. Max went back out to the SUV to have a look around and retrieve Audrey's bag. He placed it inside the door and then walked around the house pretending to look at the grounds while searching for the white sedan. He walked down the street toward Hodges' Resort. Max knew that their tail would want to be as close as possible without drawing attention. As he suspected, the white sedan was parked next to cabin number 3. Max walked around the area making sure it was the right sedan, and when he was satisfied, he walked back to Herbie and Gail's home.

When he let himself back into the house, he could hear Audrey explain her new identity to the others. He wondered how Zander would react to his little joke. His reaction was immediate.

"What idiot came up with that?"

"That would be me," Max said as he entered the room.

"Very funny," Zander said.

"I thought it might be just a little bit," Max said.

Everyone in the room smiled with him except Zander. He was trying to show his annoyance.

"Audrey is entirely too close to Aubrey don't you think?" Zander asked.

"That's by design. If you screw up and call her Aubrey, it's close enough that people will overlook it. Besides, it's all about the last name anyway. She's in the system as Audrey Wood. When people look her up, they will see an interesting background that is total fiction. Even better for you, you can live out your Natalie Wood fantasy with Aubrey's new last name."

There was a good deal of smirking going on after Max's comments. The new Audrey Wood did most of the smirking. Zander knew he was defeated. In truth, he wasn't all that upset about her new name.

"Herbie made reservations for dinner at the hotel for 7:00," Gail said, as she passed around the appetizers.

"What do you want to drink, Max?" Herbie asked.

"I'm afraid I'll have to pass. I need to get back on the road. I promised Mona I would return when I completed this last task. It's never wise to break a promise to a woman who waits for you." Max looked at Zander.

"Truer words have never been spoken," Zander said and put his arm around Audrey. "We both thank you. I know that we can never repay you for all you've done, but if you ever need anything, don't be afraid to ask."

"That's good. I always like people owing me," Max said.

"I don't have a clue how I can be of service, but I am forever in your debt."

"We both are," Audrey added.

"You need not mention it. Zander, I wonder if you would walk with me. I've got a few questions for you."

Zander dropped his arm from around Audrey and followed Max out the door. He was concerned that Max wanted to speak to him and not Audrey. Max stopped at the end of the sidewalk and leaned against his car.

"There is something you need to know."

Max told Zander about Kevin Grienne following them from Miami. Zander needed to sit down, so they walked to the park down the street and found a bench. Zander had questions, and Max answered them not holding much back.

"Is this more interference by those government men?"

"No. There is no evidence pointed at any interference. My sources tell me he has a questionable past. One of the counselors at the center believes he's into some very bad things. She put Audrey on high alert. Apparently, he's not one to be messed with."

"What do we do now?" Zander asked.

"That's for you to decide. Audrey knows all about this. I didn't want to involve your friends in case you wanted me to take care of this."

Zander sat without speaking. Max could see he was weighing what Max told him. He also knew Zander always factored in consequences.

They both sat in silence looking out into the bay. Max wanted to get moving, but he knew Zander needed to sort things out before he could move on. The minutes ticked away, and Zander turned to Max when he had made a decision.

"I think we need to take care of this ourselves. You've done more than enough for us."

"Are you sure? This problem could be eliminated without much effort. It wouldn't need to involve you or Audrey."

Zander looked directly at Max.

"There's been entirely too much of that in my life. I need to figure out a way to handle this without killing the guy."

Max liked what he heard.

"That may not be possible. Your motives are certainly admirable, but don't leave the option out. This man may be dangerous and leave you no choice."

"I realize that. I've got to try not just for me but for both of us."

"If that's your decision, you'll need to have all the information. Walk with me."

Max led Zander to the resort entrance.

"His name is Kevin Grienne. That's information I'm sure he doesn't know you have. It could be of use, depending on how you proceed. He's here and staying in cabin number 3." Max pointed toward the cabin. "There is a white sedan parked next to the cabin. He may think he's clever, so you'll need to stay one step ahead of him."

"Thanks. I'll try."

"Do you have an idea about how to handle this?"

"It will be a work in progress. I'll need to involve Aubrey, I mean Audrey.

"You'll get it." Max smiled. "But you'll need to act quickly. The longer this guy has to size you up, the more serious the situation will become."

"I'm aware of that. I think I'll try something tomorrow morning, early."

"Do you want to share?" Max asked.

"No. This has to be Audrey and me."

Max looked at Zander. Zander understood what he was thinking.

"I can't keep secrets from Audrey or our relationship will be short-lived."

Max put his arms around Zander and hugged him. It surprised them both.

"You take care. If you need anything at all, I'm a phone call away."

Zander nodded and watched as Max walked over to the SUV. He got in and made a U-turn, and as he passed Zander, he hit the horn once. Zander waved and watched until the black SUV disappeared.

Zander went back into the house. Gail was picking up the dishes and glasses.

"We've got a few minutes before our dinner reservation. Herbie, you need to help me pick up."

Gail's command gave Zander and Audrey a few moments to talk.

"Did Max explain things to you?" Audrey asked.

"Yes. We'll talk about it after dinner."

"Is he going to take care of the problem?"

"He offered, but we need to figure this out on our own."

"I see."

Zander thought he could detect disappointment in Audrey's voice. He took her hand.

"There's been too much killing. We'll need to handle this another way, and I'll need you to help with that."

Audrey looked at Zander, and he could see the disappointment was gone. Zander thought it might have been the best thing he had done in quite some time.

****

Dinner at the hotel was filled with light-hearted conversation and attempted wit. Some of it hit the mark. On the way back to the house the two couples decided to stop at one of the bars on the boardwalk for a nightcap. It was there, with Audrey's help, that Zander explained their latest problem.

Both Herbie and Gail listened without interrupting. When Zander had shared as much as he knew, Audrey filled in the rest.

Herbie was the first to speak.

"You are telling us he's basically across the street from our house right now?"

"Max showed me the exact cabin he rented," Zander said.

"What are we waiting for? Let's go get him." Herbie put his hand on the bar table ready to push himself up.

Gail reached over and put her hand on Herbie's to stop him.

"Zander has not asked for your help."

"He doesn't have to ask. He knows I'm always here for him."

"You are not listening, Herbie. Listen to your friend. He's got some idea about how he wants to see this thing play out. If he needs your assistance, he will tell you."

Herbie grunted his displeasure.

"She's right, Herbie. This is something Audrey and I need to do. I'm telling you all this so you don't go off half-cocked. We are keeping you two in the loop, so if we need your help you'll understand the stakes."

Herbie calmed down and nodded.

"Thanks for all this sharing, but I would rather help you take care of things right now."

"I know. I just feel our first step should be to try and defuse this before it gets to the point of no return. All this bad shit just seems to lead to more bad shit."

"We just want it to stop," Audrey said and took Zander's hand.

"So, what are you thinking?" Herbie asked.

"Tomorrow morning at sun-up, I'm going over to this Kevin Grienne's cabin. Surprise will be the key element in this visit. He has no knowledge of what we know. It should come as quite a shock."

"Do you think it will be enough to deter him?" Herbie asked.

"I have no idea, but it's worth a shot. If he's not some psychopath, it may scare him enough to leave Audrey alone." Zander looked at Audrey. "I'm sorry, but this Audrey thing is very difficult for me. Aubrey is such a beautiful name, and I have a hard time letting it go."

"Maybe it will only be for a while, and we can get back to who we are when we know I'm safely out of the Fed's fingers," Audrey said.

Zander motioned to the waitress to bring the check. After he and Herbie argued who was going to pay, Audrey paid the bill. Gail laughed, while the boys looked sheepish.

When they got back to the house, Herbie poured some kind of flavored whiskey as a nightcap. It was too strong for the girls, so he put theirs on the rocks while he and Zander drank theirs neat.

When they were settled, Herbie asked the first question.

"How long are you planning to stay?"

"Have we worn out our welcome already?" Zander asked.

"Of course not. I just need to adjust my work schedule. I want to be here for you if you need me."

"I'll be here. So you are free to go to work. I would be much better help anyway," Gail said, winking at both Audrey and Zander.

Herbie looked perturbed and stared crossly at Gail.

"Don't give me any of your stink eye. You know it's the truth," Gail said.

"Why don't we all catch our breath and drink some drinks," Audrey said.

Everyone seemed to relax after that and little was said about what was going to happen. Zander was relieved. He didn't really have a plan and thought he would just go over and see where the conversation would take him. He didn't know much about the guy in question. Max had said he needed to be careful, so he couldn't go in totally impromptu.

After the drinks were finished, Gail suggested they call it a night and everyone seemed to be relieved and happy to follow her wishes.

As Audrey and Zander climbed the stairs, Zander felt anxious. He didn't know how to handle going to bed with Audrey. He thought it might be too early to be intimate.

They undressed with their backs to each other and slipped into the bed. Zander was on his back starring at the ceiling wondering how to proceed.

"I know what you're thinking," Audrey said.

"What's that?"

"You're thinking with all that's happened to me, I might not be ready for sex."

"Would I be right?"

There was a long pause, and Audrey rolled on her back and looked at the ceiling as well.

"I think it could be the case."

The comment didn't surprise Zander. He could feel her nervousness.

"How about I just hold you like this."

Zander rolled over and put his arm across her stomach. Audrey responded by rolling onto her side and Zander draped his arm around her and pulled her close. Audrey sighed and seemed to melt into Zander.

Together they stayed that way all night. Zander didn't think he had ever felt closer to anyone before that moment.

8

Zander woke up the next morning at 5:30 and couldn't feel his right arm. During the night he had slipped his arm under Audrey's body and held her as close as possible with his left. His right arm went to sleep, and he couldn't feel a thing. His main waking goal at the moment was to try and remove his arm without waking her.

His careful efforts seemed to pay off. When he removed his arm, Audrey simply rolled over. Zander grabbed his clothes and went to the bathroom to get dressed. He would shower later. Right now, he had something to do, and he wanted to make sure it involved the element of surprise.

He padded down the stairs to the kitchen holding his shoes. He was hoping not to wake anyone. When he entered the kitchen he saw

Gail sitting at the table looking at him. Being quiet and not bothering anyone never seemed to work for Zander.

"I'm sorry, I didn't mean to wake anyone."

"You didn't. I was awake. You want some coffee?" Gail asked.

"I do, but I have a favor to ask."

"It must be a big one for you to be up so early."

"Not such a big deal. I need two cups and a carafe of coffee to go."

"Can I ask why?"

"Sure."

"But you're not going to tell me, right?"

"You are correct. At least not right now. I don't want to get you involved unless it's necessary. I'll tell you everything before Audrey and I leave."

"I suppose that will have to do."

"You're the best, Gail."

"I know. You keep on telling Herbie that," Gail said, as she got up to get Zander's coffee mugs.

"Hey, I can do that. Just tell me where everything is located."

Gail looked at him and rolled her eyes. Zander laughed, as he realized how good she was at that particular maneuver. It was easy to understand, after he thought about living with Herbie. She definitely had all kinds of opportunities for practice. He would have to remember to share that thought with Herbie.

Gail placed the carafe and mugs in front of Zander.

"Now, I'll need to make more coffee."

"Why don't you let me do it?"

Gail laughed and turned around to go make more coffee. Zander took the opportunity to grab his stuff and make an exit before he could give Gail occasion to ridicule him even more.

Zander walked across the street and headed into the parking lot of Hodges Resort. He found cabin number 3 and sat down on the little deck that was big enough to hold two chairs and a small table.

He placed the mugs and coffee pot on the table and took the chair opposite the door. It was a typical warm Florida morning. It was 6:00 a.m., and Zander poured himself some coffee and sat back to wait. He waited for over forty minutes and was almost ready to make some noise when the door opened.

The occupant had on some sweats and looked like he was going out for a jog. He startled when he saw Zander.

"I'm sorry, I think you have the wrong cabin."

"Oh, this is the right cabin. Why don't you sit down and join me for some coffee this fine morning." Zander filled the second mug.

"What do you want?" Kevin asked.

"I want many things, but I have questions that need answering." Zander took a drink of his coffee.

"I don't know who you are."

"I'm sure you have some idea, since you have been following my friends from Miami." Zander saw Kevin tense.

"I don't know what you're talking about."

"We can dance around and play games, or we can settle this."

"What's there to settle?"

"Once again, you are dancing. I don't want this to end badly for you. I think there is a way to end this game-playing before it's too late for you."

Kevin snorted. He knew this guy was trying to intimidate him, and he was not going to buy into it.

The snort pissed Zander off. He reached into his boot and pulled out "Old Sparky" and placed it on the table. He pressed the "On" button, which sent an impressive shower of sparks cascading between the two poles.

"We can do this anyway you want. My preference would be to come to some kind of amiable compromise. The choice is entirely yours."

"What do you want from me?" Kevin asked, glancing at the stun gun.

"Before we get to that point, I think we need to figure out why you are following my friends."

"What I do is my business. It has nothing to do with you."

"I believe it does, Kevin. Let's see, your full name is Kevin Grienne, I believe."

Kevin's mouth dropped open.

"How do you know my name?" Kevin asked, spitting in anger.

"I know a lot about you, Kevin. I know where you work. I know the people you work with and what they really think about you. I know you took a vacation to follow my friends, and I know where and when you rented this white sedan. What I don't know, for sure, are the whys and wherefores. Maybe you could enlighten me."

Kevin stared at Zander. He wondered what his relationship was to this Aubrey woman. He hated being put on the defensive and wanted to have this little meeting over. He needed more information, however.

"What's your name?" Kevin knew he had to take control of the dialogue.

"My name is Sander Van Zee, but people call me Zander." He reached into his wallet and fished out one of his cards. He handed it to Kevin.

"Check me out. I think you will be unpleasantly surprised."

Kevin slipped the card into his pocket.

"Since you know where I work, you must realize we do follow-ups on our patients to see if they are thriving or slipping back into their old routines." Kevin sat back and took a drink of his coffee.

Zander made "Old Sparky" talk again. Kevin almost did a spit take.

"That's your first lie. I told you, I know all about you. I talked to Connie McGill. I think you know her." It was a lie, but Max's information helped to make Kevin think it was the truth.

Kevin tried to mask his concern by drinking more coffee. He weighed his options and decided to tell some of his truths in an effort to ward off this man who knew too much.

"I have been enamored with the resemblance of Aubrey Moreno to the actress Natalie Wood. I think maybe I let it get away from me."

"Do you think?" Zander asked.

Kevin didn't overlook the mocking tone in his voice.

"Now that I've had some time to consider everything, I can see that I may have let my emotions take over."

"Just what exactly were you planning to do?"

"I don't know that I thought it out that far. I was hoping to make some contact down the line. I just wanted to know more about her and perhaps form some sort of relationship."

"I would agree that she has a remarkable resemblance to Natalie Wood." Zander decided that Kevin knew nothing about Audrey's new identity. "I've found it quite fascinating as well. The difference is that she is with me, and you will never have the opportunity to even get close to her."

Kevin did an excellent job of masking his anger. He didn't appreciate anyone trying to tell him his business. He knew, however, that this man was not someone he could manipulate.

"I can see the folly of my ways. I hope you can accept my apology for this stupid behavior." He put out his hand.

Zander looked at his hand but decided not to shake it. He returned the stun gun back to his boot. It would be his only gesture of acceptance to this half-baked apology. He didn't trust him. His mannerisms seemed slimy somehow.

"How do you plan to proceed from here?"

"Well, I think I need to go back to Miami and leave you all alone."

"That would be an excellent idea. I wouldn't wait if I were you. I would pack up and leave within the hour," Zander said and stood up grabbing the coffee mugs and carafe in one motion. He was walking across the parking lot before Kevin could even stand.

Kevin watched Zander walk across the parking. He didn't know how to proceed, but he knew he would have to move out of his current situation. He needed more information about this man. He reached into his pocket and pulled out the card. He decided to make use of the receptionist back at work, Elaine Taggart, for information. He knew she could find out almost anything about anybody. If this Zander thought for one moment he could push him around, he was badly mistaken. Kevin knew he needed as much information on this guy as he could get. He was certain he would have to eliminate him in the near future. No one told him what to do. It only served to strengthen his resolve.

He went back into the cabin and made the phone call to Elaine Taggart. He was smooth, and she was more than happy to go out of her way to do him whatever favors he requested. Kevin smiled after he hung up the phone. He wouldn't have been averse to "doing" Elaine, but you never shit where you eat. The thought made him smile. He threw his stuff together and was heading out of the parking lot in twenty minutes. It was less time than this Zander gave him, and he knew he would be watching. He decided to drive past the house, making sure everyone saw him leave.

Two men were sitting on the second-floor deck. He bumped his horn once and waved with his arm out of the driver's window. He didn't know if his performance would further anger these people, but he didn't care. In his mind Zander's challenge had been accepted. He would never stop until he got what he wanted. Right now, that was the woman Zander was claiming. The interesting part for Kevin was that he knew if he couldn't have what he wanted, this Zander character would not have her either. Elimination of his subjects was not his first choice, but sometimes it was necessary. It would be too bad if that were the case in this instance.

Kevin turned onto the road that led from Cedar Key, and soon he was heading back to Miami. This was merely a small setback. It would actually be good to take another perspective and a second run at this problem. Elaine would give him the needed information about Sander Van Zee, and he would find them both when they least expected it.

Kevin Grienne's trip back to Miami found him as happy as he had been in a long time. The trap had been baited, and now all he had to do was make the necessary plans. Kevin whistled some non-existent song as he drove back on I-75.

9

Zander and Herbie watched as Kevin Grienne drove past at a turtle's pace. His honk and wave made them both stare at the white sedan as it turned the corner.

"What an arrogant bastard," Herbie said.

"He's way worse than that. He's got sleaze written all over him."

"You've dealt with slimeballs before. He shouldn't be a problem," Herbie said.

"It is different when you factor Audrey Wood into the mix."

"You're right, of course. What was I thinking? How are you going forward with this?"

"I gave him an out. We'll see if he's smart enough to take it. I'm thinking that it won't happen. This guy is stuck on himself. I've seen it before. I going to have to stay vigilant, because I don't believe this will be the last we see of him."

"He is of no consequence," Audrey said, as she slid through the sliding glass door.

"How much of that did you hear?" Zander asked.

"I heard everything. He is an arrogant bastard," Audrey said and smiled as she sat down next to Zander.

Zander took her hand and held it close to his face.

"I won't let you out of my sight. We aren't going to have a repeat of what happened at that rest stop on I-80."

"It's going to be a little bit crowded in those women's stalls, when I have to go to the bathroom." Audrey winked at Herbie.

"You know what I mean."

"Of course I do, and I won't have you hovering over me like some baby who needs a diaper change."

Zander decided not to blurt out that he'd like to have the opportunity to change anything she might have. Herbie could see that Zander was about to say something stupid, and he gave him thumbs down.

"From what you guys have told me, this slimeball is some kind of narcissist. Is that about it?"

"That's what we've been told. Rather, that's what Max was told. Audrey could probably add more to the conversation," Zander said.

"All I know is what I was told by Connie McGill, my therapist. I didn't have much interaction with him otherwise. I did get a strong signal on my creep-meter, however. I don't know how relevant that information really is."

"Sometimes those instincts are our best precautions. I know that's how I felt about Herbie when I first met him," Zander said, trying to lighten up the conversation.

"Me too," Gail said as she entered the conversation. "You three need to come inside. Dinner is served."

"Are we eating crow?" Herbie asked. "Seems like I'm always the butt of everyone's joke."

"That's why I keep you around. It's all about the comic relief." Gail went back into the house.

"Let's not keep the boss waiting," Audrey said jumping up and following Gail into the house.

"Well, I've got something to say about all this," Herbie said trying to show he still had some say-so.

"What are you talking about? You've never had anything to say. Accept it, and just go along for the ride."

Herbie shrugged and got out of his chair.

"You are right, but it would be a nice to think I had some say-so." He smiled, as he followed the women into the house.

Zander sat for a moment. He knew he needed to make some decisions concerning the future, but he knew he would never be permitted to arbitrarily do it on his own. If he wanted Audrey to truly be his partner, he would have to start by involving her in all decisions. That was true, even if he thought she should be protected from some of them. Zander got up and went into the house.

Audrey was helping Gail dish out what looked to be some kind of pasta. Zander walked over to her and put his arms around her waist.

"Now that this Kevin Grienne knows where we are, how do you want to proceed?"

Gail turned around.

"Are you shitting me? You are asking this question just before dinner? Use your head, Zander. This is something you need to discuss in private at some later time. Now sit down, and shut it."

Zander was stunned. Herbie could hardly stifle his smile of complete delight. He leaned over and whispered in Zander's ear, after he sat down.

"So, how much do you have to say? Accept it, and go along for the ride."

"This household is tough."

"You should stay a while and find out what I go through."

"I don't think so. The quicker we leave the better for all concerned."

"I can hear you boys. If you want dinner, you'd both better button it."

"Yes, dear," Herbie said pretending to look down.

"Yes, dear," Zander mimicked.

"Be very careful. This pasta might just slip off the tray right into your laps," Gail said, but this time with a smile on her lips.

"This looks good," Herbie said looking into his bowl.

"Cannelloni with vodka sauce. It's my own recipe. I hope you like it."

Herbie grabbed his fork and was about to dig in, when Gail slapped it out of his hand.

"Ouch. What did I do?"

"Mind your manners. We've got other items for the table, and you need to wait for everyone to sit down before you begin."

"I knew that. It just smells so good I couldn't help myself," Herbie countered.

"Good answer," Gail said and returned with a basket of garlic bread and a tray of antipasti.

"Everything looks delicious," Audrey said.

"Thank you, Audrey. I'm having a little tough time with your new name."

"I know. But thank you for using it. We all need to be vigilant," Zander said. "There's just too much going on, and we don't need to take any unnecessary chances."

"I'll try to keep Herbie from screwing up. You know how he is."

Before Herbie could make a rebuttal, Gail interrupted.

"Zander, could you please say grace this evening?"

The comment shook Zander. He hadn't uttered a prayer out loud since…he couldn't remember when.

"I'm not comfortable with that," Zander said to Gail.

"We aren't going to eat until you do, so I would suggest you begin soon."

Zander knew he would never be given a pass from this group. He looked over at Herbie and noticed he was enjoying the moment just a little too much. Zander gave him a dirty look, but it only served to tickle Herbie even more. Zander gave up.

"Let's join hands."

When everyone found a vacant hand, Zander bowed his head and began.

"Please bless this food that Gail has prepared for us today. Thank you for all the good friends we share, and that includes Herbie." Zander received a few hand squeezes but ignored them and went on. *"Herbie, and now*

Gail, have always been there to help me through the tough times. They both need to know how much I value their friendship and support. Thank you for putting Aubrey Moreno, and now Audrey Wood, into my life. I was a lost soul before I met her and was almost lost again, when she was taken from me. Thank you for giving her back. She has made my life complete, and I'll never need nor ask, for anything more. Amen."

When Zander looked up, the three of them were staring at him.

"What?"

"That was an interesting prayer. I don't think I've ever heard anything quite like it," Gail said.

"You never lived in my house. It was the only way I ever knew if my father was proud of me."

"Is that the same way you found out if he was disappointed in you?"

"No, that was always freely shared. The Dutch aren't very giving with their compliments, but they'll let you know immediately when you screw up."

"That doesn't do much for a child's ego. How did you survive?" Audrey asked, still holding his hand.

"I guess I never thought much about it. That was pretty much the way it was, so I didn't know any better."

"I think the prayer was perfect," Herbie interjected. "Let's eat."

He grabbed his fork and began tearing into the pasta. The remaining three diners followed Herbie's lead but at a much slower pace.

The plates were refilled, and the wine spilled out of three bottles before they were finished. They sat around the table and enjoyed each other's conversations until after 10:00. Finally, Herbie stood.

"Can I interest anyone in some port wine? I've got a great bottle that's just itching to be opened."

"I think we've all had enough for the evening. Thanks for the offer," Zander said.

"Just being a good host," Herbie said.

"Why don't you be a good husband, and help me with the dishes," Gail said.

"I'll help you," Audrey said and stood.

"Nonsense. You are our guests. Go out on the deck and enjoy the remainder of the evening. The no-see-ums should be gone." Gail knew Zander was getting restless and needed to make some plans with Audrey.

Zander and Audrey excused themselves and walked over to the deck railing. They both had been sitting long enough, and it felt good just to stand. Zander slipped his arm around Audrey's waist.

"I think it's time for us to leave."

Audrey was looking out over the bay.

"I suppose you've been thinking about this for some time."

"Not really. I was mostly just thinking about getting you back. Herbie and Gail have been great, but they need to get their lives back to normal. We are a huge distraction."

"I know. I've been thinking about that. I think we need to leave Florida."

"I agree. What would you think about going to Colorado, since our last trip was so rudely interrupted."

"I think I will let you make that decision. For the time being, I just need to be told where to go and what to do."

"That's great. Let's make some arrangements. I think there's a redeye that flies out of Tallahassee. Maybe I can book a flight for tomorrow. Herbie could give us a ride."

"Sounds fine."

"Of course, I'll have to let Fats know, so he can pick us up from the airport. Maybe Fran could check on the cabin to make sure everything is ready for us. I'll make some calls right now." Zander reached into his pocket for the phone.

Audrey caught his arm and stopped him.

"Don't forget that I said you can make the decisions for the time being. Don't think this is going to be a permanent thing."

Zander smiled. He realized he had pushed a little hard. He hadn't meant to utter those things out loud. That was something that happened to people who lived by themselves for too long. They started talking to themselves out loud. Now that he wasn't alone, he needed to talk to Audrey and not spew out every one of his own thoughts.

"Should we tell Herbie and Gail what we've decided?"

"What you decided?"

"You're okay with this decision, right?" Zander looked worried.

"I'm just messing with you. Of course this is okay. I would let you know if it wasn't."

Zander decided not to push. He felt Audrey was in a good place, and that was enough for right now. He took her hand, and together they went in to tell Herbie and Gail about their plans.

Soon, Herbie was calling the airport for the tickets to Colorado. Zander went back outside and made his call to Fats.

Fats picked up the phone, and Zander was disappointed. He hoped Fran would have answered.

"Greetings from the Branchwater, an establishment where you can select your poison, and we will be elated to be your sommelier and steward. How may I channel your communication?"

It was good to hear Fats' bullshit once again. It was so much easier to take when Zander wasn't experiencing a personal crisis.

"Close your mouth and listen," Zander said, trying to cut him off.

"My fiendish amigo has once again reared his repugnant cranium. I am here at your command awaiting your requisition."

"My first command was for you to close your mouth and listen. Apparently, you can't follow your own directive."

Zander didn't give Fats another opportunity to speak. He explained what was going to transpire. He asked him to have Fran check the cabin and to let the rest of their friends know he was returning. Just as he was about to allow Fats to speak, Herbie shared the flight schedule for the next day. Zander looked at it and continued to give Fats direction.

"Looks like we'll be arriving at the Denver airport at 9:15 pm tomorrow evening. You need to pick us up."

"Might I peruse the Thunderbird for this task?"

"Only if you decide you are going to find another ride home."

"No comprehendo."

"It's a two-seater. Since there will be three of us, that would leave no room for you."

"There was no mention of a triple threat. I can only surmise that one Aubrey Moreno will be in tow?"

"Her name is Audrey Wood. Aubrey Moreno has expired. We no longer will use that name."

"So sorry for your loss. I prefer the new moniker by comparison. It is past the expiration date of your sharing this woman of the world with the rest of us."

Zander had enough.

"See you tomorrow. Don't you be late." Zander didn't give him time to respond.

He was putting his phone back in his pocket, when the three dinner partners came back out. They were holding wine glasses. Audrey gave one to Zander.

"What's this? I thought we decided we were finished for the evening."

"I think that's what you decided. I told you that your decision-making would not be a permanent thing. This was my decision. Try the port; I don't think you will be disappointed."

Zander wasn't disappointed. He decided to try not to be disappointed ever again.

10

Kevin Grienne drove out of Cedar Key driving at pace that was pissing off all the drivers behind him. He pulled off into a parking lot just before he crossed bridge number 4. There was a boat ramp and some public fishing. It also looked like there was a museum. Kevin saw it had to do with the marine life of the area.

He turned off the engine and sat back to think. He needed to figure out how to proceed. His initial thought was to find a new hiding place to watch and follow this Aubrey woman. He knew she would be with the asshole he just met. What was his name? Kevin fished out the card from his front pocket. The name on the card said Sander, 'Zander,' Van Zee. There was a number and some other wording that he thought made no sense.

After a few moments, Kevin got out of his rental and walked toward the bridge. He needed some air to think things through. There were some people fishing from the bridge. When he got closer, he saw that they were throwing some contraption into the water.

"What are you doing?" Kevin asked a woman who had just pulled up what looked like some type of wire basket.

"Not from around here, are you?"

"No, I'm just taking in the sights."

"We are blue crab fishing."

"Are you having any luck?"

"The guy over there has a few."

Kevin walked over to the man. There was a five-gallon bucket with three crabs inside.

"Mind if I take a look?" Kevin asked the bucket man.

"Never seen a blue crab before?" the bucket man asked.

"Only in a restaurant and cooked on my plate. They are delicious, by the way."

"They are expensive. That's why we're here."

Kevin examined the blue crabs without putting his hands into the bucket.

"Interesting creatures. Thanks for letting me look."

"You ought to give it a try. If you don't eat the things yourself, the restaurants around here pay top dollar."

"Thanks for the tip. Maybe I will." Kevin walked away knowing full well he would never follow up.

He hated fishing. In his mind it was a huge waste of time. He hated the smell it left on his hands when he touched any type of sea life. That's why he never tried anything that wasn't fully cooked.

The weather was nice for this early in the morning, and he decided to stop at a bench and look out over the bay. It would give him time to roll over his options before he made another move.

Kevin took out the card again and looked at it. The card made the decision for him. His phone was in its holster on his belt. He took it and called the only number he had programmed. It went to his place of employment. He needed to talk to Elaine Taggart, the receptionist.

After two rings, someone picked up. The number he had just called was repeated on the other end, and the phone went silent.

"Please connect me to Elaine Taggart," Kevin responded.

"Eight digit code."

Kevin repeated his code into the phone, which allowed employees access. The phone went dead, and after thirty seconds, it was picked up.

"Elaine Taggart."

"Elaine, hello, this is Kevin Grienne."

"Oh, hello Kevin. I thought you went on vacation."

Kevin thought he could hear Elaine's voice warm up, when she found out who was calling. He knew he could ask her to do something that would normally be frowned upon.

"I thought I would take some time, but now I have something else that needs to be addressed. I'll be coming back today. I should be back in the office by mid-afternoon if all goes well."

"How can I help?" Elaine asked.

"I need you to do a background check on someone who has hooked up with one of our clients." He gave her the necessary information from the card.

"Is this something I should be doing?" Elaine said with concern in her voice.

"Probably not. I would be doing it myself, but it's time-sensitive. I'll need the info, when I arrive this afternoon," Kevin lied.

"I'd hate to get caught. I could lose my job."

"I'll have your back. If it comes to that, I'll take heat and tell them I made you do it," Kevin lied again.

"Well…"

Kevin could hear the concern in her voice.

"Elaine, how about you do this one thing for me, and we go out for drinks and dinner after work?"

Elaine's anxiety melted away.

"I'll get right on it."

"Thanks Elaine. You're a peach. I won't forget this."

Elaine actually giggled, as she hung up the phone. Kevin smiled to himself. She sounded like a pubescent teenage girl. It was somewhat of a turn-on for Kevin. He might have to reconsider his mantra, "you don't shit where you eat."

He would get the information on this Zander asshole and follow up when things cooled down a bit. That might give him some time to pursue something with Elaine Taggart. It had been some time since he had been with a woman, and he was feeling that same old urge once again. With any luck, he could get things going this evening. He could take it slow, but he would take his lead from Elaine. If she were ready, he would be accommodating.

Kevin walked back to his car and got in. He drove out of the parking lot and was about to turn right, when he had another idea. He turned left instead and proceeded back into Cedar Key. He drove directly to where he had last waved at the asshole and drove past the house as slowly as possible. When he was directly in front of the house, Kevin laid on the horn and stopped.

After a few moments, he saw a few faces looking out of the second story slider. Kevin stopped pushing the horn and leaned out the driver's window. He gave the one-figure salute. When he was sure they saw what he was doing, he mouthed the words "fuck you." People could hear his maniacal laughter up and down the street as Kevin drove off.

He settled back into his seat for the six-hour drive back to Miami, Kevin decided he was quite proud of himself. Things were going to work out just fine for him, but maybe not so fine for Zander asshole and his girlfriend. He knew he would need to take Zander out of the picture before he could have his way with Aubrey. It would make sense that she already was going by a new name. If things didn't work out the way he wanted, he was sure there was some government agency out there that would be happy to know she still existed. It would be a last resort, but one that he could use if he didn't get his way. It was unlikely, however. Kevin always got his way.

The gas tank of the rental showed a quarter tank when he decided to stop. The map showed he was between North Port and Punta Gorda. He filled the tank and went inside the convenience store to pee. There had already been too much coffee, and he didn't want to stop again. There wasn't much that spoke to him, as he looked over the items for sale. He needed something to sip on. He had also felt a few hunger pangs when he got on I-75 at Tampa, but nothing in the store appealed to him.

As he walked toward the door, he saw a Wendy's next door. It was still too early for them to serve lunch. Kevin knew he could talk them into making him a chocolate shake if he bought a few of their breakfast items.

His scheme worked, and he was back on the road with his shake and two sausage and egg breakfast sandwiches. He got the speedometer up to seventy-five. He always traveled at just five miles over the speed limit to avoid getting speeding tickets. Speeding tickets left a trail, and that was something he was careful to avoid. Those were the things that law enforcement would use to hang you. Kevin knew the things he did were federal crimes, and they would indeed hang him. Of course, these days they used lethal injections, but Kevin didn't want any part of either.

Kevin took a pull from his shake. Ice cream was one of his few food pleasures. He watched what he ate, so he could indulge whenever possible. There were few days when he failed to have some type of ice cream product.

The two sausage sandwiches were on the passenger's seat. He grabbed one and unwrapped it with one hand. As he was ready to take a bite, the egg slipped out and fell on his pants leaving a grease mark. Enraged, he opened the window and threw everything out. Things like that always pissed him off. Kevin knew he needed control. Sometimes things were beyond control, but this was something his carelessness had caused. Throwing the sandwich out the window was the only thing he could do to take back control. It showed once again who was boss.

Later, he was sorry he hadn't kept the sausage patty and had thrown everything else out. He was hungry, and his frustration was dulled by the fact he had another sandwich waiting for him on the passenger's seat.

This time he unwrapped it on his lap. There already was a grease spot on his pants. He clamped his fingers and thumb tightly around the sandwich, and this time he found success. He settled back down with his temper in check.

The hunger pangs stopped, and he enjoyed the rest of his shake as he made the turn on Alligator Alley. When he finished, he threw his garbage on the floor. In the past, he had tossed things out of the window because he had always hated clutter. The possibility of receiving a citation for littering had made him stop that practice. He pretended the trash wasn't there until his next stop. He would find the nearest trashcan.

It was 3:15, when he made the Miami city limits. His plan had been to go back to his apartment and change clothes. He didn't want to miss Elaine, however, so he drove right to his office building. He would need to get rid of his rental and make arrangements to meet Elaine that evening. First, he needed to get the information he had needed so desperately.

True to form, Kevin took all his trash from the vehicle and placed it in the receptacle next to the side door. He swiped his card and entered the dark hallway. The first person he saw was Connie McGill. He could have gone a lifetime and been happy never to cross her path. It looked like she was about to say something to him, when she must have thought better and walked away. Kevin noticed that she glanced at him, before she turned to go down another hallway. Her behavior puzzled him, and if he had more time, he would have pursued her to find out what was going on.

Instead, he went right to the receptionist area to find Elaine. There were two other people in the office besides Elaine, which bothered Kevin. It would be difficult to speak freely. Elaine saw him and got up from her chair immediately. She went to the counter and engaged Kevin as he walked up.

"Can I help you?" Elaine asked in her most businesslike voice.

"Ah, yes. I was wondering if I had any messages?"

Elaine went back to her desk and returned with a note. Kevin read it.

"I have what you asked for in a file folder, but I can't give it to you here. Can we meet later?"

Kevin couldn't believe his good fortune. This was just the opening he needed to get Elaine to meet him. He took the note and turned it over and found a pen. On the back he wrote: *"I'll go to my office and call you to make plans."*

He handed the note back to Elaine.

"Please call them back and set up an appointment."

Elaine looked at the note and nodded. Kevin smiled and walked down the hallway toward his office. Things were falling into place. First, he would work his magic with Elaine, and then after a cooling-off period, he would take care of Zander and Aubrey. The idea made him smile.

He settled into his office and decided what to say to Elaine.

Meanwhile, Connie McGill was in her own office holding a card and making a phone call to Max Kuhn.

11

The flight from Tallahassee was uneventful, and Audrey and Zander both slept most of the way. The tailwinds were good, and they landed just a few minutes after 9:00, Mountain Time. The time difference made it 11:00 in Florida, so falling asleep on the plane was welcomed. At least they wouldn't be dog-tired when Fats picked them up.

Arm-in-arm, Zander and the newborn Audrey made their way to the baggage claim area. Zander was still too uneasy to let go of Audrey in public places. He knew how easy it had been to snatch her when his back was turned. He vowed not to ever let that happen again. It was a risky business, however. There was always a chance at smothering the person you most wanted to protect. He had seen it before. He wanted to avoid being overprotective.

Audrey didn't seem to mind being close right now, but he would have to stay vigilant and back off if he noticed any change in her behavior.

When they walked through the door leading to the turnstiles, the first thing Zander saw was a huge sign. It was so large that everyone else noticed it as well. It read: *The Wandering Wayfarer Has Returned. Only The Rocks Live Forever. His Friends Are Jubilant At The Restoration Of His Countenance, And The Most Exquisite and Magnificent Audrey Wood.*

Zander looked at Audrey and saw she was smiling. That was a relief anyway. Zander was relieved that Fats had used the new name of Audrey Wood. It would have been just like him to slip up. He guided Audrey over to the sign.

"Come out from behind there." The sign was printed on butcher paper and so large that Fats had to hold it up in front of him with both arms well over his head.

"With tremendous pleasure my brother and newly-acquired sister. I never realized how heavy the ink on this banner really would be."

Fats dropped the sign and went over to where Audrey stood smiling. He dropped to one knee and bowed his head.

"Roland Sinning is the moniker. My amigos utilize Fats as my designation. I am optimistic that it would pleasure you to do the same."

Audrey was giggling by the time Zander had a chance to respond.

"I have some really fine friends. He isn't one of them. I just keep him around, because he's so weird," Zander said to Audrey while ignoring Fats.

"I think he's a hoot. We could all use a little humor in our lives. Stop trying so hard to be a stick-in-the-mud," Audrey said to Zander while taking Fats' hand and pulling him up. " I've never had a better welcome. I'm this Audrey Wood listed on your sign."

Fats kissed her hand.

"I surmised as much. Your beauty outweighs your description, however. My eyes have never beheld anything finer."

Audrey laughed.

"I think we're going to be fine friends, Fats."

The two new friends walked out of the terminal arm-in-arm leaving Zander to scramble for their bags. After he removed them from the turnstile, he had to run to catch up with Audrey and Fats.

"Thanks so much for your assistance with the bags," Zander said out of breath.

"We were busy introducing ourselves," Audrey said.

Fats said nothing and seemed to be lost in Audrey's beautiful face. Zander had to smile. Audrey had that effect on most of the men she met. It made Zander see how lucky he was to have her in his life. He knew she could have any man she wanted. The thought made Zander comfortable and nervous at the same time.

When the threesome reached the parking area, Zander could see that Fats was trying to put his best foot forward.

"You drove the Cameo. What's the special occasion?" Zander asked.

"Certainly it would not be you. I wouldn't pull this thing out for just anybody."

Zander liked the fact that Fats was easing up on his hippie lingo. Soon they were on I-70 heading for Frisco, and the three were swapping stories that seemed to put Zander in the middle of everything. He wasn't quite sure he appreciated all the attention. He knew he was the catalyst between his life before Audrey and after Audrey. Fats just wanted to be part of both.

After they passed through the Eisenhower Tunnel, Audrey stopped talking. She noticed a sign for the Silverthorne Outlet Mall.

"Hey there's an outlet mall. Could we stop please? I have a number of things I need to get, since most of my things got left in Florida."

"I don't know. Do we have time for this, Fats?"

"Anything for the lady."

"Such a good answer," Audrey said and gave Fats a kiss on the cheek.

Fats pretended to lose control of the vehicle.

"Try to keep it in your pants," Zander said. "I hate to disappoint you Audrey, but the place closes at nine and it's after ten already."

"Tomorrow would be just fine."

"Sure. I'll take you and we'll use my cargo van. I'm thinking you'll have more things than the T-Bird's trunk can hold."

"I'll take you in this Cameo," Fats offered.

"You need to work at the Branchwater. We've kept you away long enough."

"I thought maybe you wanted to work for me, and I could get to know Audrey better."

"You thought wrong, my friend."

"Boys, boys, boys. Let's not get into a pissing match on my account. How far before we get to Frisco?"

"It's just up the road. In ten minutes we'll be in front of the Branchwater."

"Good. I want to see the bar before we get to Zander's place. Maybe we can have a few drinks to celebrate his homecoming."

"It's already in the works," Fats said, without looking at Zander.

"What did you do?" Zander asked, not in his happy voice.

"People want to see you, and they want to meet your beautiful woman. I am just a mediator in this scheme. If you want to place blame, I would think you should talk to Fran."

Zander thought about what he said.

"Never mind."

"I am impressed. You seem to know your place among women."

"Mostly through years of failure. I think I might be on the right track now." He gave Audrey a peck on the cheek.

They pulled into a parking spot in front of the Branchwater.

"Why aren't you parking in the back?' Zander asked.

"We need to make a grand entrance. People want to see you and Audrey. They certainly don't need you sneaking in the back door."

Zander noticed cars lined up and down the street. It was unusual for this time of night, and he thought he should warn Audrey.

"When we go inside you'll be swept away by all my friends. They want to see you and get to know you. It will be harmless fun, but you probably won't see me until all of this is over."

"Well, I'm just fine with that." Audrey smirked.

"That's what I thought you'd say." Zander pretended to pout.

When they entered the bar, it was just like he had said. Audrey was whisked away and placed in the center of the tables where people could get personal access. No one seemed to notice Zander. He was thankful for that small favor.

Zander helped both Fran and Fats behind the bar making sure everyone's glass stayed filled. Zander was content to sip on a straight club soda with a wedge of lime for show. Audrey had ordered a beer, and Zander watched her glass closely but the level never got past half. He decided to check in and make sure she didn't need rescuing.

"Do you want me to freshen that up?" Zander asked.

"No, I'm fine. What are you drinking?"

"Not much."

"That makes two of us. Maybe we're not ready to celebrate just yet."

"Do you want me to get you out of here?"

"Absolutely not. I'm enjoying hearing all the stories about you. You can't buy that kind of information, and I may never have another opportunity to get all the dirt."

"I'll be behind the bar keeping an eye on you."

"I would expect nothing less."

Zander found his place back behind the bar pretending to be concerned for Audrey. He knew they were in the safest place that could be found anywhere. That thought made him relax and start to enjoy the evening.

"She's lovely," Fran said, grabbing his hand.

"Every time I look at her I'm blown away and wonder how I could be so lucky."

"That is the consensus among the general populace," Fats said, and Fran gave him a shove.

"Pay no attention to the man behind the curtain. He has his own set of difficulties, which he seems to be willing to add to this evening."

"That may be my cue to go out and get the drink orders," Fats said.

"A wise decision from someone who generally shoots himself in the foot."

Fats made a hasty retreat.

"Why don't you go out and visit with your friends. Some of them dropped plans on short notice to be with you this evening."

Zander looked at Fran.

"I think they're here more to see who I brought back with me."

"Don't confuse curiosity with whether they are here as your friends. They all want the best for you, and that's the reason they came."

"I think there might be some judgment involved. They want to see if I made a good choice with Audrey."

"Look at them. They love her."

"I can't argue with you. I just wonder what they would say to me if they didn't like who I brought with me."

"Zander. Why do you always worry about what might have happened? You need to get into the moment and enjoy what you have. In that regard, you could take a lesson from your friend, Fats."

Zander thought about what Fran had said. He decided she was right. He needed to be with his friends and not worry about things that never happened.

"Fran, would you care if I went ahead and joined the party? I don't want to leave you in the lurch." Zander indicated the packed bar.

"You already dropped the ball on that one when you hooked me up with Fats."

They both laughed.

"You go and be with your friends. Fats and I can handle this measly crowd."

Zander wiped his hand on a bar towel and walked from behind the bar. He looked around and noticed Bert and Jo. They were at a table with Roger and Lilly who now lived in Aspen. Zander decided to join them, and when he reached their table, the front door opened. His old friend, Danny Bloemendaal, and his wife Ingrid, entered the bar.

Zander rushed over and gave them both a hug.

"What in God's green earth are you doing here?"

"Fats called and said you were coming back, so we got in the car and here we are," Danny said.

"Shit, that's over a twelve-hour drive."

"And yet, here we are," Ingrid said. "It wasn't that bad. We actually took a flight from Sioux Falls."

Zander held her tightly and found she felt good in his arms like always.

"Hey, go easy, mister. That's my wife you've got in that bear hug," Danny said.

Zander released Ingrid, reluctantly.

"Sorry, Danny. It's just so good to see you guys."

"You didn't hug me like that."

"Well, you're a guy. So there's that."

Zander looked around and realized he had been involved sexually with a number of his female friends in the bar. The list included both Ingrid and Lilly. It was amazing to him that they still remained his friends. He knew that wasn't always the case with past lovers.

"Come over and sit down. I think you know most of the people here. Many of Zander's friends had made the trip to Hospers, Iowa, for his parents' funerals and Danny and Ingrid had met them there.

Soon, everyone was talking about old times. Audrey came over, and Zander re-introduced her to his Hospers friends. Zander made Fats get him a double Jack Daniels on ice. It was time to catch up to the rest of the crowd and throw abandon to the wind.

Zander's phone rang, as he was ready to take a drink. He looked at the screen and saw it was Max Kuhn. That wasn't a phone call he wanted right now. Try as he might, Zander could not let the phone go to voicemail. He believed in confronting things immediately. Some might think it was a character flaw, but it was what made Zander who he was.

He stood and went out the front door to take the call.

12

"Hello, Max. I was hoping not to hear from you. No offense."

"None taken. I got a call from Connie McGill. Kevin Grienne is back at his employment."

"That's good news, isn't it?"

"Possibly. She's not so sure. She's going to keep an eye on things, and if anything changes, she'll call me. I'll let you know the minute I hear anything."

"Thanks, Max. I do appreciate what you continue to do for us."

"You know I have no choice. You've met my Mona, right?"

Zander laughed.

"Yes I have. We're lucky guys, aren't we?"

"Without a doubt. Now go back and enjoy your party. Sorry to have bothered you, but this was semi-good news. I wanted to share it while you were having a good time."

"Wait. How did you know about the party?"

"Fats called. Mona wanted to drop everything and fly out there. I just couldn't do it right now. I have a few things going on. Sorry to miss your homecoming."

Zander knew enough not to ask Max what he had going on. He would never tell him anyway.

"Thanks for thinking of us. We owe you more than we could ever repay."

"That's the way I like it," Max said, and the phone went dead.

Zander entered the Branchwater, and Audrey caught his eye. Her demeanor told Zander that she was concerned with his absence. He gave her a thumbs-up and a smile. He could see relief in her face, and she went back to talking with their guests.

Zander could see that the party was beginning to wind down. He went over to the bar and spoke to Fran.

"How about I clear tables? You can start washing the glasses, and I'll dry. Maybe everyone will get the hint and leave."

"Fats can help me. You need to be with the people who came to see you and Audrey."

"I suppose you're right."

"Always. Tell Fats to get his ass over here."

Zander could see Fats in the middle of everything. He was working the crowd as only he could do.

"It might be a tussle getting him away from his audience."

"Just tell him I said so."

Zander went over to where Fats was entertaining and whispered in his ear. Fats turned and went over to the bar. Zander watched Fran's animation while Fats stood and nodded his head.

Zander smiled and found Audrey. He wrapped his arm around her waist, and she put both hands on his arm. Zander thought he never had a more provocative gesture. Audrey must have felt his reaction.

"Down boy," she said loud enough for him to hear.

"It's hard."

"Bad choice of words. You might have said 'difficult' instead."

"Both would be true."

"Incorrigible."

"It's getting late, don't you think? Maybe we should wrap this thing up so Fats and Fran can clean up."

"We can help them."

"We can try, but I don't think Fran will be in agreement."

"What about Fats?"

"He has no say in the matter."

"As it should be." Audrey had enough of the banter and turned to thank some of the people who had begun to leave.

Zander sat at the table with Lilly and Roger, Bert and Jo, and Danny and Ingrid.

"Ingrid and I think she's gorgeous," Lilly said.

"Thank you. I don't know how I got so lucky."

"We don't either. Don't screw it up," Jo said.

"I could use some help around here," Zander said to the men at the table.

"You're on your own," Danny said.

Roger stood.

"It's getting late, and we've got to head back to Aspen."

Zander got up and shook his hand.

"Thank you so much for coming."

He hugged Lilly and held her for a little longer than necessary.

"You are part of my history. Who knows what would have happened to me had I not met you," Lilly said

"We had a bit of fun down the way as well, didn't we?"

Lilly socked him in the arm.

"You're so bad. You're lucky Roger isn't the jealous type." Lilly grabbed Roger's hand, and they went out the door together.

Zander turned to Danny, and Audrey joined them.

"I've got two bedrooms in my cabin so Danny, you and Ingrid, can stay with Audrey and me."

"That has already been settled," Jo interjected. "They will be staying with us. Besides, I think you have other things that need to be taken care of tonight."

"Ingrid and I are tired from the flight, and we need some sleep. It might be too noisy at you place."

Zander didn't know how to respond. Sexual thoughts concerning Audrey had been filed away. She needed to give him some kind of cue.

"While I've just met Jo and Bert, I think you will both be in good company tonight," Audrey said, standing behind Zander while wrapping her arms around his neck.

"Ingrid thanks for coming. I know it was a pain rushing out here," Zander said

"Danny and I are together because of you. You saved me."

"If I remember right, you pretty much took care of Quentin Stryker all by yourself."

"That wasn't what I was talking about," Ingrid said with a twinkle in her eye.

Zander knew exactly what she was talking about. The sex they had together was historic. At least it was for Zander. It made him think about all the women he had relationships with over the years, and how he managed to screw every one of them up.

He knew the answer. Now, he could face it without all the denial he used in the past. Sara Jane, or whatever her name was at the moment, had been the cause of all his dysfunction.

The actual truth was far more complicated. She was the catalyst, but his flawed character was of his own doing. There had been no reconciliation until he met Aubrey Moreno, now Audrey Wood. It was his awakening. There was life after Sara Jane, but then he messed up and slept with her again. Now everything was more complicated because of his daughter, Sandra.

He was still a million miles away when Audrey shook him.

"Hey, where were you just now?"

"Just took a little vacation," Zander joked.

"Well, next time take me along," Audrey joked back.

Danny stood.

"Ingrid and I have to go back tomorrow afternoon. We have a flight into Sioux Falls." He hugged Audrey first and ended with Zander.

Ingrid joined the hugs and gave Zander a kiss on the lips.

"You're the best, Zander."

"Tell her," he said indicating Audrey.

"She knows."

"Breakfast will be at our place tomorrow at 9:00. Hopefully you'll be caught up by then," Jo said. "Fran and Fats are invited as well. See you all then."

Jo herded everyone out the door leaving Zander and Audrey at the table.

"You've got some great friends," Audrey said.

"Way better than I deserve."

" Can't argue. Let's go help Fats and Fran," Audrey said.

"You two just need to leave. Fats will give you a ride to your cabin. We'll see you at Jo and Bert's for breakfast," Fran said.

Zander noticed Fats locking the front door to keep out late-night stragglers.

"Thanks for everything, you two. It was a great night."

"No charge," Fats said. "I should get you home. Sounds like you have a lot to do."

Zander said nothing. He didn't know if Audrey was ready to participate. He needed to take his cue from her and not push.

Fats dropped them off, made a U-turn, and headed back to the bar. Zander was surprised to see the cabin lit up. When they entered, there was a banner that said "Welcome Home Zander and Audrey."

Zander went to the refrigerator and noticed it was well-stocked. Audrey walked around and poked her head into the different rooms.

"This is really nice. I could live here," Audrey said.

"That's the plan," Zander said.

Audrey smiled, took his hand, and looked him in the eye.

"It's been a long day. I'm going to take a shower. Why don't you fix us a nightcap?"

"What would you like?"

"Whatever you decide to pour," Audrey said and went into the bedroom.

"There are towels in the closet next to the shower," Zander yelled in after her.

Zander went over to the cabinet above the refrigerator where he kept the liquor. There were the usual vodkas, whiskeys, rums, and tequilas. He was looking for something sweeter to end the evening.

After pulling out a number of bottles, Zander was disappointed at not having better stuff to offer Audrey. Finally, he settled on a bottle of Peach Schnapps. He wondered how long it had been up in that cupboard. No matter, it was all he had. After finding two glasses, he filled them half full. There was no ice, so they would have to drink it neat.

Zander tried a sip and decided it wasn't bad. He took another swallow, filled his glass up to the same level as before, and waited for Audrey to join him.

It was quiet in the cabin, so he decided to put on some music on his stereo. He still played the vinyl. He liked how it sounded with all its pops and sputters. Zander never felt the need for a television. He hadn't been home enough to watch it anyway. In the past, the cabin had been his retreat for eating and sleeping only. He could see that it was about to change.

He made sure to play some Beatles. His favorite album had been *Rubber Soul* but it was too steeped in Sara Jane history, so he selected *Abbey Road* and cranked it up. He was singing, "Here Comes the Sun," loudly and quite badly when Audrey entered the room.

Zander stopped singing. Audrey was wearing one of his button-down shirts.

"We didn't get to go shopping, and I don't have anything to wear as a nightgown."

"You look amazing," Zander said. "Here's your nightcap."

Zander gave Audrey her drink, and they both sat at the table listening to the music.

"What is this?" Audrey asked indicating the drink.

"It's peach Schnapps. Sorry. I'm not very well stocked."

"It's not all that bad. I've never had it before."

"Schnapps was popular and like everything else, fell out of favor."

"So you are telling me it's old."

"Sorry. I've never been much for stocking a bar."

"Just another thing we can both do together to make this into our home, Audrey said."

Zander liked what he heard. When he looked over at Audrey, he also liked what he saw. She was sitting cross-legged in the chair across from him. The shirttails rode up her leg just far enough to make Zander look and never want to stop looking He wondered if she was doing it on purpose.

Audrey tossed back the remainder of her drink and held it out to Zander for more.

Zander filled her glass.

"My turn for a shower," he said and stood.

Audrey took his glass.

"I'll fill your glass and have it ready for your return."

Zander smiled and went into the bedroom. As he got into the shower, he heard the stereo turn off and then a bit later heard some Jackson Brown playing. He liked Jackson Brown and knew Audrey really liked his music. It made him feel bad. He should have played that for her instead of playing what he liked. He needed to be more vigilant. He needed to realize it wasn't just him living here now. Audrey's needs would come before his own.

When he opened the shower door, Audrey handed him his filled glass. He was dripping wet and failed to grab his towel. He was standing completely naked in front of the woman he loved. He felt embarrassed until he realized that Audrey was completely naked as well.

Zander didn't have time to finish his drink.

13

Kevin Grienne took Elaine Taggart to dinner. It was the least he could do for her. She was putting herself into jeopardy by doing research for him. Her superiors would fire her if they knew what she was doing.

Kevin decided on a hotel restaurant in South Beach for dinner. If things worked out, they wouldn't have far to go to share a room. Kevin didn't think it would happen, but one never knew. "Always be prepared" was his motto, even though he had never been a Boy Scout. He called the restaurant and made reservations for two at 8:00.

Kevin kept busy the rest of the day opening mail and shuffling appointments. At precisely 5:00 he scribbled something on a sticky note and put it on top of a few files. He put the file folder Elaine had illegally obtained for him into his shoulder bag. He addressed Elaine as he approached the main desk.

"Elaine, here are the files I needed. Thanks. You can put them back." Kevin handed her the files.

Elaine saw the sticky note and removed it as she moved the files to her desk. She glanced at it and turned and smiled. Kevin smiled back. The note went directly into her top desk drawer. The date was set. They would meet at the hotel. It suited Kevin. He hated to pick up his marks if things didn't go according to plan. There were too many variables to leave to chance and transportation wasn't one of them.

Kevin brought his rental car back to the airport. He took a cab back to his condo. Before he went in, he thought it prudent to check on his car in the garage. He had a set of keys hidden and started the car just to make sure it would run for his evening performance. "Leave nothing to chance" was his other motto. He didn't know where it came from, but it served him well.

The car started without any problem. Things seemed to be working out. He put the extra set of keys back into the hiding place and went into his condo. It was on the second floor. It was an older building that might have been a motel at one time. The condos had been remodeled and two rooms were made into one unit. It served Kevin just fine. He spent little time here other than to sleep.

Before he looked at the file Elaine had given him, he decided he needed a drink. He pulled the freezer door open and saw some freezer-burned ice. He threw it into the sink and took out a beer instead. It was some kind of craft brew. Kevin never drank any of that light shit. It had no taste, and he wanted something with some kick. If he wanted a watered down drink, he would just drink water.

The beer was cold and he finished half of it before he sat down to look at the file. He noticed the name on the top, Sander Van Zee, a.k.a Zander. Last known address Frisco, Colorado. There were a number of paragraphs that traced his life from his teenage years until the present. Even though Kevin wasn't much interested in those details, he was always amazed at how much the branches of the government knew about ordinary citizens. It was why Kevin was careful about any trail he left, and he was good at it. The only thing that people would ever see in his file was what he wanted them to see. It helped to have a job that allowed him to have more access to information than the average person.

He skipped the parts that had no significance and read on, until he found a relationship with a woman named Audrey Wood. Kevin sat up. Something didn't add up. There hadn't been any mention of someone named Audrey Wood. He thought the name had been Aubrey something or other. He couldn't remember her last name.

Kevin sat back. The file already had been sanitized. Someone with some juice had pulled some strings. He would be careful not to stir up that hornet's nest. He was just a small cog in the big wheel of covert government meddling into people's lives. It was a dangerous business, and he wanted no part of that aggravation.

Near the end of the file was a photocopy of a card with Zander's name and number. Kevin assumed he was some type of private investigator. This was very helpful, and he could only hope, that other than the woman's name, everything else was factual. He jotted down the information from the card on the back of a piece of paper and put it into his billfold. He would read the rest of the file later, when he had more time. There could be some information that he could use when dealing with this Zander character. Kevin knew he was smarter than this private dick. Anything else he could find might be the Achilles' heel he needed.

Kevin finished his beer and cracked open another. He took it into the bathroom and drank it while he showered. It had been a long day, and he was tired. He knew it would not be a good idea to take a nap. He might oversleep and miss his date with Elaine, so he got dressed and made sure he looked presentable.

The note he had given to Elaine listed the hotel, restaurant, and time of their reservation. Kevin decided to be early. He wanted to scope out the area to be sure nothing was out of order. If Connie McGill got her hooks into Elaine, Kevin knew he wouldn't be safe. He would wait at some inconspicuous place where he could keep his eye on the hotel entrance.

Kevin's vehicle was a white midsize SUV. It was like thousands of others. It would never draw attention like so many of the flashy rides notorious for the South Beach area.

He was at a coffee shop across the street from the hotel at precisely 7:15. They had an outdoor seating area, but Kevin bought a small coffee and elected to sit inside at a table near the window. He could see everything without being seen. He had 45 minutes before he needed to meet Elaine. He assumed she would be early, so his wait probably wouldn't be that long.

Kevin was on high alert. He watched for anything out of the ordinary. It was difficult, because this was South Beach. Everything was out of the ordinary. He had lived here long enough to wade through all that crap and trust his instincts.

Nothing jumped out at him. It was craziness as usual. At 7:50 he saw Elaine get out of a cab and head into the hotel. Now would be the time for something to happen. He would be late on purpose, making sure Elaine hadn't been followed. Nothing unusual happened. After twenty minutes, Kevin was satisfied that things were fine. He decided not to keep Elaine waiting any longer. There was always a chance of diminishing returns if she felt slighted.

Kevin slipped into the opposing chair and picked up Elaine's hand.

"I'm so sorry I'm late. The traffic was crazy. When I finally found a place to park, I realized I was late. Thanks for waiting, and I promise it won't happen again."

Elaine smiled, because Kevin had just pushed the right button. He had said, "It won't happen again," which was code for this was not just a one-time thing.

"I didn't have to wait that long. You're here now, so all is good."

"Thanks, Elaine. You are so understanding, and I think that's what first attracted me to you."

Elaine was embarrassed, but Kevin could tell she liked what he had just said. The awkward moment was shattered, when the waiter came over to take their drink orders and place the menus.

"Do you drink red wine?" Kevin asked.

"Yes, I do," Elaine said and looked at the menu.

Kevin could see she was still embarrassed at his "understanding" comment.

"I want to make sure I order what you really like. Would you prefer a white?"

"I like reds the best. I especially like something dark and dirty." She smiled.

The reference was not lost on Kevin. It was all about dark and dirty for him. He selected a pricey cabernet that was rich with a dark purple color. He looked at the menu and then up at Elaine. He knew he would need to carry the conversation, or the evening would turn out being awkward for them both.

"Is there anything that speaks to you this evening?"

"I don't know. I've never been here before. Is there a signature dish I should know about?"

"The fish is always great. I would stay away from the red meat. I've never liked their steak presentation. I don't know where they get their meat, but it isn't from the Midwest. That I can tell you."

"Were you from the Midwest?" Elaine asked.

Kevin realized he had just made an error.

"Spent some time in college there. It was long ago, but I remember the steaks." He smiled. "They usually have a nightly chef's choice, so we could see what that is before we make up our minds."

Kevin was good at deflection and was relieved when the waiter returned with their wine. As he poured the wine into their glasses, he gave them the special for the evening. The entrée was a rendering of golden tilefish. Kevin stopped listening as the waiter explained everything. He looked at Elaine and realized she was quite attractive. She dressed plainly and wore little make-up. Kevin decided that he wanted to see what was under the loose-fitting dress with the high collar. He wanted to see what she looked like with her hair down around her shoulders instead of pulled back. He wanted to know if she was a true blonde. He was still fantasizing when he realized the waiter was looking at him.

"I'll have the same as the lady," he said and snapped his menu closed.

Elaine smiled, and Kevin could see he made the right call. She was flattered that he took direction from her. Things looked good for later.

The food was excellent. The wine was even better. After two bottles, Kevin decided to order an after-dinner drink. He was careful to ask Elaine what she would like. Elaine was feeling the wine and most of her shyness had evaporated with her empty glass.

"This is all new to me. You order for us," she said.

Kevin saw that there was a honey whiskey listed on the drink menu. He selected two over rocks. He knew the taste would seem harmless, but the kick would help him over the next hurdle. He had to be careful about how he approached his effort at seducing Elaine. The tricky part would be getting her to agree to finish their date in an upstairs room at the hotel.

Elaine loved her drink. She told Kevin a number of times. She was getting giddy and laughing at all of Kevin's little jokes. Kevin knew the window of opportunity was opening, and he didn't want to lose her vulnerability. He ordered another double for them both. Halfway through the second drink, Kevin made his move.

"I have to use the restroom. I'll be right back. Don't go away." He stood, and put his hand on her shoulder letting it trail down her back as he left.

"Don't be too long, or I might need to order another drink," Elaine said.

Kevin went toward the restrooms. He made a detour toward the front desk when he was out of Elaine's sight. He booked a room and paid cash. The desk clerk wanted a credit card for incidentals. Kevin was happy to comply and gave her one of his many credit cards with a name other than his own.

When he got back to the table, he noticed that Elaine had finished her drink. They had been sitting for a long time, and he could see she was getting restless. As he sat, he took both her hands from across the table.

"When I go out for the evening, I usually book a room. If I've had a lot to drink, it keeps me from driving."

"Like tonight," Elaine said letting his hands lightly squeeze her own.

"Exactly. I don't want you to think I'm being too forward, but I'd like to invite you up for a nightcap. I don't know if the minibar has this particular alcohol, but I'm sure we could find something you might like."

Elaine looked at Kevin for a moment.

"I'd like that."

Bingo, Kevin thought. His night was about to be made.

14

Audrey awoke smelling coffee. It had always been a comforting part of her life. Her parents were huge coffee people. After all, they were of Cuban decent. She put Zander's shirt back on from the night before. She left the top three buttons open as a tease and walked out into the kitchen.

Zander was rummaging around in the refrigerator and turned around to see Audrey posing for him.

"You know, I want to take you back into the bedroom when you do things like this."

"I know," Audrey said and sat at the table. "What's for breakfast?"

"You get coffee and my world-famous microwave eggs."

"Ew." Audrey pulled a face.

"Just wait. Don't judge until you've tried them."

"Fine. Can I shower while you are killing yourself over this amazing breakfast?"

"That should give me enough time to wow you with my cooking skills."

"Huh. We'll see." Audrey went back into the bedroom.

Zander could hear the shower running, and soon Audrey was singing. Zander loved her voice, but she only sang in the shower. He knew she was too shy to sing publicly. He had tried numerous times to get her to join him singing karaoke in some bar. She always turned him down.

Breakfast needed to be prepared. Zander needed to have it ready for Audrey when she came back into the kitchen, or she would never let him hear the end of it. He cracked four eggs into a Pyrex bowl and poured in a quarter-cup of milk. He beat the crap out of the mixture until it was yellow. Next, he threw in a package of shredded cheese, followed by chopped spinach, and an orange chopped pepper. He thought about including a jar of mushrooms but didn't know if Audrey liked them. He put the mushrooms back into the cupboard. He finished his mixture with some coarse ground pepper and sea salt. The trick to good microwave eggs was cooking for a few minutes and then stopping and stirring the mixture.

Zander followed his own directions and six minutes later the eggs were ready and steaming in the bowl. He put it on the table with a serving spoon and two plates and forks. Both he and Audrey took their coffee black, and he filled two large mugs and placed them on the table. He was almost ready to call Audrey when she walked into the room. Her hair was wet, and she was pulling a comb through it.

"Let's see this concoction of yours."

She sat at the table, and Zander was happy to serve her. When the plates were filled, he sat back and waited for her critique.

Aubrey drank coffee from the mug and smiled at Zander. She was in no hurry and was enjoying his discomfort. Finally, she took her fork and tested the eggs. She chewed a forkful and swallowed. She put down her fork.

"Well?" Zander asked.

"Not fair. These eggs are full of cheese. Everything is always better with a ton of cheese on it."

"What's your point? You didn't ask how I made them. You decided that you weren't going to like them because all you heard was microwave eggs."

"That's not true. I heard that you were going to make them. That made me think they wouldn't be good."

"So, what's your opinion, now that you actually tasted them?"

"They are excellent. I could eat the whole bowl."

Zander dished out half the eggs onto her plate and took the remainder for himself. They ate in silence, and when they finished, Zander poured more coffee. When he filled Audrey's mug, she grabbed his wrist, almost knocking the coffee pot to the floor. Zander caught it just in time.

"Sorry. I didn't mean for that to happen. I wanted to tell you how happy you've made me. I love everything about this place except the altitude. I had a hard time breathing last night."

Zander laughed.

"I don't know. You seemed to be breathing pretty heavy for a while there."

"Very funny. I thought you were going to pass out," Audrey said.

"It's been a while," Zander said, and then realized he still needed to tell Audrey about his daughter.

The thought put a damper on his conversation. He turned and brought the bowl and serving spoon to the sink. He ran water into the bowl to loosen the eggs, before he washed the bowl.

"Come back here, and sit down. Let's finish the coffee and decide what we're going to do today," Audrey said.

Her attitude was catching, and Zander buried his previous thought somewhere back in his mind. He would consider it later, when the time was right. He hoped there would be a good time to break news like that. He was afraid of how Audrey would react, but he also knew that secrets between the two would never keep their relationship intact.

"What would you like to do today?"

"I want to see the area. I want you to show me places you think are interesting, and I don't want us to come back until we are both exhausted," Audrey said.

Zander could see she was excited to explore what was going to be her new home.

"That's a great idea. Why don't you finish getting ready, and I'll clean up the breakfast dishes. I'll make some plans while I wait."

"Who says you're going to wait for me. I might be the one waiting for you," Audrey said, and got up and went back into the bedroom.

Zander knew her well enough to know that would never happen. Audrey would never be seen in public until she was satisfied that she looked perfect. He thought she wouldn't have to do a damn thing and still look perfect. Women had such a burden compared to men, but he was quite happy with this arrangement as it was.

Audrey came out looking stunning. Sometimes Zander wished she wasn't quite so put together. She always turned heads when they were together, and it could get annoying. He decided it was a burden that he would have to carry.

"I think we should stop at the Branchwater and see what's going on before we head out for the day."

"What are we going to use for wheels?" Audrey asked.

"Look out the window." Zander had brought the yellow T-Bird up from the shed while Audrey was getting ready.

"Is that yours?" Audrey asked.

Zander nodded.

"I love it. Let's go." Audrey was out the door.

Zander had to hurry just to keep up. It was turning out to be a fine day indeed. It was a fine day, until he realized that Audrey was behind the wheel.

"I'm driving."

Zander was trying to think of something to say that would put him in the driver's seat. He knew there was nothing he could say. He took his place in the passenger's seat.

"Well played," Audrey said, and started the T-Bird and put it in gear.

Zander was amazed at Audrey's perception. She seemed to know what he was thinking even when he said nothing. It was a bit unnerving. He heard that couples that were meant for each other could read each other's feelings before they had a chance to communicate them. The thought made Zander happy, because he thought it might mean they were meant for each other. He needed to work harder on understanding Audrey's feelings. He wasn't sure his perception was as strong as hers.

"Take a left at the stop sign," Zander said.

"I know how to get to the bar," Audrey said.

"Sorry. I guess I'm just used to driving," Zander said.

"Oh, stop pouting. I know. You can drive after we stop at the Branchwater."

"Thanks," Zander said relaxing.

Audrey laughed.

"You are such a dork."

"Thanks," Zander said again.

When they got to Frisco, Audrey turned into the alley behind the bar. Zander looked puzzled.

"I thought you would want to enter the same way you usually do. I also didn't know if the bar would be open. It's only 10:00."

"Fats and Fran usually open early. The doors are always open after 8:00. Most of the time they're here by six."

"It's a bar. Why would they open so early?"

"We get a lot of regulars. They come for coffee. Someone always brings donuts. All of life's problems get solved in there between 8:00 and 11:00."

"Does Fats help to solve those problems?"

"Much to Fran's chagrin."

"What happens after 11:00?"

"The locals go home. The lunch crowd starts arriving, and they come and go until about 1:30. Then the bar gets ready for the evening crowd."

"Do they serve dinner?"

"Just bar food, like lunch. The drinking crowd starts filing in around 5:00, and it goes until the last dog dies or Fats kicks everyone out. It's always a guessing came when it comes to actual bar hours."

"It's my kind of place." Audrey smiled.

"It's mine as well. We have that in common."

"That, and countless other things. Let's go." Audrey got out of the T-Bird and was inside the back door before Zander could unfold his long legs from the passenger seat.

When Zander entered the bar through the back room, he saw that Audrey had already joined the morning group. Someone had given her a cup of Fran's coffee, and she had a long john poised in her hand. Zander sat down at the bar.

"She makes herself at home doesn't she?"

"She's a hard one not to like," Fran said.

"I know. It won't be long, and she'll have those guys falling all over her."

"You know the worst of the bunch will be Fats, right?" Fran asked.

"I know, but he's basically harmless. He'll try to talk her to death. She'll chew him up if he tries to use that hippie speech on her."

"We could all be so lucky," Fran said and took the coffee pot over to the morning group and filled cups until the pot was empty.

Zander took a break from watching Audrey play nice with the boys. It was good to be back. This was his environment and was as close to home as he ever thought it could be. Audrey's enthusiasm about Frisco, and the surrounding area nestled in the heart of the Rocky Mountains, made this even better.

He looked back at Audrey. He knew he would need to tell her about Sandra, his daughter. It needed to be sooner than later. It needed to come from him, and he couldn't risk someone else telling his secret before he could explain. Explaining it would be the problem. There was no good explanation. He would hang everything on his stupidity. Maybe, if he went back and explained how he got to that point with some personal history, it might soften the blow.

If Zander could weather this storm, he would need some direction from Audrey. They would need something meaningful to take up their time. He already knew that she didn't want anything to do with marriage. He would have asked long ago if she had agreed. It was not the case.

Fats walked over with Fran after she filled the patron's coffee cups. Fran went to the back for some water to make another pot, and Fats sat down next to Zander.

"Magnificent and luscious bores into this man's cranium."

"I hear you. It seems like she's always on my mind."

"Have you explained the conundrum involving the comingling of your genetics with the person of your painful history?"

Zander looked straight ahead and realized he couldn't trust Fats to keep his mouth shut. He would need to tell Audrey about Sandra very soon.

When Zander looked back, it seemed as if Fats was reading his mind.

"My significant other and myself were speaking in a lively conversation during a long-needed and unrequited celebration of our honeymoon."

"You aren't married to each other."

"Just a minor detail that is of little to no concern."

"Where is this conversation going?"

"It will play out only with the two females that are closest to us at our sides. I will procure Fran and you roundup your requisite Miss Audrey." Fats went to the back to find Fran.

Zander walked over to where Audrey was sitting and whispered in her ear.

"Fats wants to talk to us at the bar."

Audrey nodded and stood. She followed Zander back to the bar and sat on the stool that Fats had vacated.

"What's this all about?" she asked taking Zander's hand.

"I have no idea. Fats was talking in his usual way and said something about a honeymoon."

"I didn't think they were married."

"They aren't. I'm thinking this might just be another one of Fats' harebrained schemes."

They stopped talking when Fran and Fats walked in and sat across from the couple.

"I want you to know that this has been something Fats has been talking about for quite some time. I told him if he wanted you two to hear him out he needed to get rid of his irritating lingo."

Zander began applauding.

"You are a funny man, Sander Van Zee. Don't push your luck," Fats said.

Zander thought it best to follow his instruction. He had too much to lose at the moment.

"I don't know how to explain this, so I'll just come right out and say it. I want to take Fran to Hawaii."

"Honeymoon?" Zander asked.

Fran hit Fats in the shoulder.

"I told you to stop saying that."

"Okay. I want this to be a vacation."

"That sounds wonderful. I think you two should go and make it an adventure," Audrey said, smiling.

"I think we're in agreement. There's just one little nagging detail that needs addressing."

"Here it comes," Zander groaned.

"We need you two to work the bar while we're away."

"How long do you think you'll be gone? As if it really matters, you're gone when you're here." Zander said. He thought for a moment and then blurted out, "Not you Fran. You're the one that makes this place work."

"Nice recovery," Fran said, smiling.

"Well, let's see. There are four main islands and two smaller ones that we need to explore, so I think four weeks ought to do it."

Zander stood immediately.

"Four weeks. Are you insane?"

Audrey pulled Zander by the shirt and sat him back down on the stool.

"I think it's a wonderful idea, and Zander and I would be happy to help out, no matter how long you want to be gone."

Fran went around the bar and gave Audrey a huge bear hug.

"You are wonderful. We've been working this bar so long I hardly know anything other than work. I think I really need some time away."

"When would you be going?" Audrey asked.

"Well, I've been working on the planning over the last few days, and we can fly out the day after tomorrow. It's a direct flight right from Denver to Oahu. Bert and Jo said they would take us to the airport. So, you wouldn't have to do that."

"Well, that's something, I guess," Zander said out loud but barely audible.

"That will be enough out of you. You owe your friends a great deal, and this is one way to help pay them back." Audrey's words were kind but firm.

Zander knew he had no say in the matter. He was screwed.

15

The rest of the day was spent going over the duties at the bar. Zander didn't need to be told, but he was patient for Audrey's sake. Audrey followed Fran around and kept detailed notes of everything that needed to be done on her end. Zander could see she was enjoying it. He was acting like this was a huge burden but in reality, he knew it would be good for both of them to get back to a normal routine.

Audrey started to work in the kitchen with Fran, and Zander tended bar alongside Fats.

"You know you're going to owe me big time for this," Zander said.

"Let's just admit that this is payback for all the things I've done for you," Fats said, as he polished a wine glass with a dry towel.

Zander rolled his eyes. He knew it would be impossible trying to point out what it cost when Fats interfered with his life. He knew Fats would never be able to see it. Zander looked at him. He knew his heart was in the right place, and Fats was his best friend. He saved his life that time west of Paxton, Nebraska, so, it was true that there was something owed. Zander thought he had more than paid him back, but friends never kept score, did they? Friendship needed never be tallied, no matter how lopsided it seemed.

"Have you made all the arrangements for your Hawaiian adventure?" Zander asked.

"Just need to pack. We'll do that tomorrow while you two immerse yourselves in the finer business of bartending," Fats said, as he looked at Zander for a response.

"I guess it makes sense. It might give us us a reason to decide not to do this."

"Exactly."

"Well, before you leave us in the lurch, please check in tomorrow before you abandon us."

"Later in the afternoon, Fran and I will make an appearance to see that everything is running smoothly. If you have any pressing questions, you can save them for that moment in time."

"You know that this used to be my bar as well, right?"

"Haven't forgotten," Fats said, and then got serious. " You know, we would never have asked you to do this if I didn't think you could handle it. Hell, I know you can do a better job than I could ever hope to do. Fran didn't want to leave Audrey with questions and feelings of inadequacy."

Zander laughed out loud.

"You don't know Audrey. She'll have this place running like a Rolex long before you get back."

Fats looked over and stroked his chin.

"Just remember, Fran and I want this place back when we return."

"We'll see."

Fran and Audrey came back into the bar from the kitchen.

"I think we've got everything covered. Audrey is a quick study. I'm feeling much better about leaving Zander in charge."

"You are very funny. Let's have a drink to celebrate a month without seeing Fats."

Zander poured four beers, and they sat at the bar. The conversation pivoted around the places Fats and Fran planned to see.

Since Zander had never been there, he paid little attention. He was content to watch Audrey interact with his friends.

The evening crowd was sparse, and Fran let Audrey work the kitchen under her watchful eye. Zander was content to let Fats run most of the bar business. It would be his turn soon enough.

There were a few drinkers left at 11:00, and Fats decided to call it a night. He went over and checked on the two men at the table. They had been drinking heavily, and Fats was concerned about them driving.

"You two can't drive. Do you want me to call someone?"

"Nope," one of the guys replied. "We walked, so we'll just stumble home."

Fats knew they had it covered, but he always checked. He felt he owed it to his customers. The two men got up and left through the front door. They weren't staggering all that much, and Fats knew law enforcement would leave them alone to find their way home.

"That was a good thing you just did," Zander said to Fats.

"It's something I've tried to do with those that stay too long."

"Are you concerned that the sheriff's department might pick them up for public intox?"

"Nope. We've got an understanding. They will let them alone if I keep them from driving. Quid pro quo."

"That's good. I'll continue the practice while you're AWOL."

It took another half-hour to clean up, and at 11:30 the two couples parted ways. Zander got behind the wheel of the T-Bird before Audrey even had time to think about driving. If she noticed she never said anything.

"I'm happy we agreed to help them out. I think it will be good for the both of us."

Zander smiled and said nothing. Audrey was right. It would be a good thing for both of them.

Zander dropped Audrey off at the door to the cabin, and he put the car back into the shed. He knew he was fussy with the yellow T-Bird, but he loved the car. When he opened the front door, Audrey was there with drinks in hand.

"Cuban rum and Cokes gets the nightcap nod this evening."

"Thanks. This will take out the stink of disappointment for not being able to show you around," Zander said and took a drink.

"There will be time for that later."

"You know, I'm not much of a Rum drinker but this is good. Thank you."

"You are very welcome, but you're not much of a drinker no matter the alcohol served."

"When I worked at the Glass Onion, Jasper always said 'that shit's meant to be sold.' I guess I learned from the best."

Audrey put her glass down.

"I'm going to get ready for bed."

"I'll wait for you, and I might just have another drink."

"Don't drink up all your profits," Audrey said, and touched his hand.

Zander thought it was a provocative move on her part, and he suddenly was feeling lucky. He finished his drink and heard the shower start up. He poured another rum and Coke but made sure it was a light one. He wanted to be able to perform.

Twenty minutes went by, and Zander finished his drink. The ice had melted in Audrey's glass, and he threw the remainder in the sink and placed the two glasses on the counter.

He thought Audrey said she was coming back out. Maybe he anticipated she would come out and finish her drink. He decided to check on her and went into the bedroom. Audrey was in bed, and Zander could hear her purring. He experienced immediate disappointment, but he had to smile. It had been a big day, and Audrey had processed a great deal. He could see how she would be tired.

He got undressed and turned out the lights. He slipped into the bed as quietly as possible so as not to wake this sleeping beauty. He was thinking about how lucky he was when his own tiredness kicked in and he fell asleep. All dreams that night were good for them both.

When Zander awoke, he could smell bacon. He got up and stumbled into the kitchen. He looked at the clock on the wall.

"What the hell? Why are you making breakfast at 5:30 in the morning?" Zander asked, and then noticed Audrey was fully dressed, and what was worse, she looked like a million bucks.

"We've got to get to the Branchwater and open up. The regulars will be waiting for their coffee."

"Just because Fats is nuts doesn't mean we have to be. What's wrong with 8:00?"

"We have people who now rely on us. Get going. Breakfast should be ready by the time you are."

Zander turned around pretending to be irritated and headed for the shower. When he was ready, Audrey had the table set and was patiently waiting for his return. He sat down and looked at the spread. Eggs, bacon, and coffee were the only items.

"Where are the hash browns and the toast? Seems kinda skimpy if you ask me."

"Who's asking you anyway?"

"This will be just fine. You know, there will be donuts, and if we don't eat one or two the regulars will be offended."

Zander realized Audrey already was fitting into the bar business far better than he ever did. When he finished, Audrey poured more coffee. They sat looking at each other. Zander drank his coffee and enjoyed just sitting, not having to speak.

"I want to thank you for being so understanding last night," Audrey said.

"You were tired. We had a big day. Truthfully, I fell asleep immediately after I realized you weren't coming back out to finish your drink."

"I haven't slept that soundly in a long time."

"Maybe it's the company you're keeping."

Audrey smiled.

"Let's go to the bar."

"Let me take care of the breakfast dishes," Zander said.

"We'll worry about that tonight."

"Let it be said. Let it be written."

Audrey was opening the front door.

"Where's the car?"

"It's in the shed," Zander said smiling at Audrey's disappointment in not beating him to the driver's seat.

"Give me the keys. I'll go get it."

"Not a chance. You couldn't get the door open anyway. There's a little trick to it, and I'll show you later. Maybe after you do the breakfast dishes."

Zander walked out to the shed, and he knew Audrey would be right behind. She was going to be sure to learn everything, and there wouldn't be any bargaining on his part. Zander showed her the top latch that needed to be pulled on both doors. Audrey could reach them. He let her open the doors, and after she swung the first open, Zander went into the shed and got into the T-Bird and started it up.

"That might be the last time you ever beat me into the garage," Audrey said.

"I don't doubt that one bit," Zander said. "I've been thinking that maybe we should get you some wheels. I don't think one car is going to be enough for us both. Unless you'd want to drive the old white van."

Audrey saw it parked next to the shed. It looked like it hadn't been driven for quite a while.

"Why do you have that old thing anyway?"

"You've seen my car. Sometimes my P.I. work demands it."

Audrey thought for a moment.

"I've been thinking about that. I think that after Fats and Fran come back from Hawaii we should go into that business together. We would need new business cards printed though. You could still have top billing, but I would need to be listed."

"We'll talk about it." Zander thought it was a terrible idea. He didn't want Audrey anywhere close to any similar people that he had dealt with in the past.

Audrey wanted to move forward with their relationship, but Zander needed to tell her about Sandy. He decided he would talk to her after work. The bar was a neutral place and perfect for the discussion after everyone left. Talking about it at the cabin would be bad luck for their relationship. The bar was a temporary thing, but the cabin more permanent. He didn't want it to be a place of bad karma.

He drove the rest of the way in silence. He didn't know what Audrey was thinking but hoped she was concentrating on he role at the bar. He drove to the back of the Branchwater and pulled his keys from the ignition. He kept the backdoor key on the same ring. As he was putting the key into the lock, he heard a vehicle drive through the alley. Audrey put her arm through his, and they turned around to see what was going on. It was after six and too early for action.

It was light enough for Zander to make out a pickup. He couldn't see who was driving, until it stopped in front of them. It was Fats. He gave them a thumbs-up and drove away. Zander realized immediately that he was checking up on them.

Zander dropped his key ring, as he gave Fats the finger with both hands.

16

As always, the regular old bastards were waiting at the front door. One of them had a big box of donuts. Zander was firm and wouldn't let them in until the coffee was started. He stuck to his guns with Audrey pecking at him.

He finally gave her the cue, and she ran to the door. The old guys shuffled in and found their regular table. Audrey sat with them, and they shared their donuts. After the coffee was ready, Zander brought the cups on a tray. When everyone had their cups, and Zander collected their dollars, he went back for the coffee pot. The first pot was emptied, and Zander went into the back to get the water for the second. When the second pot was ready, he poured himself a cup and went to join the boys and his girl.

After fifteen minutes listening to the old boys talk, Zander was bored. He knew he could leave their conversation, be gone six weeks, return, and never miss a beat. Maybe that's what happened in the aging process. Eventually, all you have left are the stories from your past. Zander decided to make sure he made countless stories from this point forward.

He got up and motioned for Audrey to follow. She shot him one of those looks that told Zander he had better be careful.

"Audrey, maybe we should get the kitchen ready for the noon lunch."

Audrey smiled and nodded. Zander knew he was no longer in charge, and he had better communicate with his words. There would be less chance of misconstruing what he was trying to say.

Audrey snagged another donut and followed Zander back to the bar. They both went into the small kitchen. Zander turned and grabbed Audrey before she had a chance to react. He pulled her close and kissed her. She kissed him back. When she pulled away, Zander kept her close.

"Have I told you lately how much I love you?"

"That's from some song isn't it? You are so cheesy."

"It's all I've got. I want you to know exactly how I feel about you."

Audrey put her open hand on his cheek.

"You've got nothing to prove. I owe you my life."

"At least twice if I remember right," Zander said.

Audrey socked him in the arm.

"Don't push it, buddy. What's the special of the day?"

"We just do sandwiches like burgers, tenderloins, chicken, and whatever else is in the freezer. Throw in some fries, and you've got our menu."

"I might want to give them some other options."

"That's entirely up to you. You've got the kitchen duty."

Audrey screwed up her face.

"Why is this just my deal with the food?"

"Remember who volunteered for this gig? It wasn't me. Besides, you know I'm not much good in food preparation unless I can barbeque."

"That's a thought. Once a week you can run the grill outside, and I'll do the duties at the bar," Audrey said.

Zander considered what she had said.

"Okay. I think that might be a good compromise."

"Sure. If it is successful we can switch off every other day."

"Let's not get ahead of ourselves," Zander said trying to sound stern.

"You need to step up. These are your friends we're helping out."

"I think you'll be doing the stepping up for the both of us. Now, how can I help you get ready?"

Audrey thought for a moment and then charged ahead.

"Today, I'm giving people a chance for either fries or a house salad. You need to get the lettuce from the cooler and put it into a big bowl. Do they have dressing around here?"

"Sure. Ranch and French, I think."

"That's pretty limiting. I'll make some kind of balsamic for people who want some taste."

"Don't get your hopes up. This is a bar. Just be sure you have enough fries."

Zander found the lettuce in the cooler. He was happy to see there was a huge bag of lettuces and other vegetables ready to serve. He put a large amount in a stainless steel bowl and returned to where Audrey was standing at the counter. He put the bowl next to her.

"My work here is done." He took the opportunity to get back into the bar before she found something else for him to do.

The bar was busy in the mornings. Mostly, it was just the coffee drinkers. They started filing out around 11:00, when the lunch people started to show. Zander usually used the time to get ready for the day. He made sure the beer coolers were stocked and the hard liquor bottles were replenished. Lemons and limes needed to be cut and put on a tray along with cherries for the "old fashioned."

He was busy cutting up limes, when he felt a presence at the bar. Turning around, he saw a large man sitting on a barstool. Wiping his hands on his apron, he approached the customer.

"Can I help you?"

"Sure. I see you've got tap beer. What's a local beer that you might recommend?"

"You can't go wrong with the Breckenridge."

"I'll have that."

"Do want twelve or sixteen?"

"Pardon?"

"Twelve or sixteen ounces?"

"It's pretty early. Lets just do a twelve-ounce glass."

"Coming right up."

Zander took a beer glass and ran it under the tap. He made a mental note to check the keg beer. He had forgotten about that in his preparations.

As he walked over with the beer, Zander had a chance to look at the customer a little closer. He almost dropped the glass. This man looked way too familiar. His face looked like the woman he and Fats had shoved down the copper mine air vent.

Zander set the beer glass down in front of the big man.

"Do you want to run a tab or pay cash?"

"Cash," the man said and peeled off a five"

Zander turned to get him some change.

"Keep the change. I just want to ask you for some information."

Zander didn't like what he was hearing. He turned around, trying not to show his concern.

"I don't know if I can help you. I've just returned to the area myself. So, if it involves something local, you might want to try someplace else."

"I think I'm exactly in the right place."

"What information are you looking for exactly?" Zander asked, trying to distance himself from the conversation.

"My name is Vernon Bullock. People call me Vern."

Zander was pleased Bullock never said my friends call me Vern. He knew for certain that they were never going to be friends.

"Your name isn't familiar to me. You must not be from this area."

"The name Bullock has quite a presence in the Hills area of South Dakota. The name has quite a history, even before this country of ours was settled."

"Not much of a history buff, I'm afraid. I was more into music and the arts," Zander said, trying to sound apologetic.

"No matter. I'm here looking for my twin sister, Vera. Her car was found abandoned in a parking lot at Copper Creek."

"That's a ways away. What brings you to Frisco?"

"Just following up on some information. Vera told me she was going after someone named Fats, so I've been asking around to find out if anyone around here goes by that name. It's quite unusual, so I didn't think I would have much trouble locating him. You don't fit the description Vera gave me, however."

"My name is Zander. What do you mean, Vera was going after Fats?"

"Vera is a handful. She had a relationship with this man, and it didn't end on a very positive note. She told me that this Fats character ran her off the road and tried to kill her. She found him in a little town in Nebraska, but he left before she could do anything. I didn't speak with her after that, but she is relentless. I was sure she would find this guy. She has a great many resources. Our family has always been wealthy, and money can buy many things."

"So, how did you end up at this bar?"

"A bartender at one of the hotels in Copper Creek told me that a man named Fats owned this bar in Frisco. I really need to talk to him to see if he can shed any light on Vera's disappearance. This is her picture." Vern held it up to show Fats. "Maybe you've seen her?"

Of course Zander had seen her. The last time Vera was disappearing into a hole in the ground.

"Nope. Can't say I've seen her. I would have remembered someone like that. I can tell you two are twins. I haven't been back all that long, so she could have easily come and gone while I was away."

"Where have you been?" Vern asked.

It was an innocent enough question, but it pissed Zander off. His life was no one's business but his own and now Audrey's, of course.

"My whereabouts have nothing to do with you."

"I've got time. Just waiting to talk to this Fats character. Where is he, anyway?"

"Not here. You missed him. He and his friend left for a long needed vacation."

"That's some bad news. I don't suppose you would have an address or phone number where I could reach him?"

"Sorry. I'm sure he'll check in once he gets settled. He left today." Zander wanted to get this man away from the bar as quickly as possible. "Maybe if you left me your phone number, I could call you when I get more information."

Vern used the back of a cocktail napkin and jotted down his cell phone contact. Zander picked it up and looked at it. He placed it under the cash drawer.

"Thanks for your help. I really would like to talk to this man."

Zander was always good at reading people, and although this Vern Bullock seemed fine on the surface, there was an undercurrent that Zander's radar picked up. It made the hairs on the back of his neck stand straight out. It was a bad sign.

"Are you certain that nobody at Copper Creek has seen her? It doesn't make sense that her car was in a parking lot and no one saw her anywhere. Of course, it's mostly tourists up that way. Someone might have seen her, but they would be long gone."

"I've exhausted my search there. I even looked at the hotel footage of the front desk. I assumed she would have checked into the hotel at some point, but there was nothing. Things just aren't adding up."

No, they were not, and Zander knew why. If he could stall Vern Bullock, Fats might have time to get out of Frisco early and avoid the confrontation altogether. He needed to get Vern out of the bar, so he could make a phone call to Fats and Fran.

"Well, Vern, it's been nice meeting you. I hope you find your sister, and if I hear anything from Fats, I'll be sure to call you." Zander stuck his hand out for Vern to shake, even though it pained him to do so.

"What's your relationship to Fats?" Vern asked.

There it was. He knew something, and he wouldn't be satisfied until he found out exactly what happened. Zander was not about to let that happen.

"He's my good friend. Saved my life once or twice."

"Good to know." Vern slid off his stool and turned to leave.

Zander thought that Fats' incredible lack of timing might have reached a new low when he walked into the bar just seconds before Vern had the chance to leave.

"All packed and ready to go. Hawaii here we come."

17

Zander's look of doom must have been evident in his face.

"What's the matter? Something wrong?" Fats asked.

Vern turned and looked at Zander.

"I thought you told me he had already left."

"That was my understanding. That's why I'm working the bar and not down the road with my girlfriend doing something adventurous." Zander's effort to make light of the situation wasn't playing well with Vern.

"I think there are things going on here that you haven't been forthright about."

"I have no idea what you are saying. Just leave me out of this whole matter." Zander knew it was impossible at this point.

"Zander who is this guy?" Fats asked the question but already knew the answer.

This had to be Vera's brother. They looked alike but he didn't have Vera's best attribute, her breasts.

"My name is Vernon Bullock. I go by Vern. You must be Fats."

"Well, I'll be damned. You must be Vera's brother. She told me she had a twin."

Zander couldn't believe how easily Fats transitioned into the situation. He was much smoother than Zander could ever hope to be. It was probably because Fats was so full of bullshit.

"She told me much more about you," Vern said.

"All good, I would hope to think."

"Not unless you call attempted murder good."

"Whoa. Back that horse down. I would never purposely cause anyone's death."

"You pretty much destroyed her car on a lonely stretch of road in the Hills."

Fats realized Vera had shared a great deal more with her brother than he would have hoped.

"Vera did that to herself. She was trying to run me off the road and miscalculated."

"Did you stop to see if she was alive? Maybe you just left the scene of the accident."

"I no longer wanted to be under her spell. Escape was my only hope."

"How did that work out?"

"You already know that answer."

"She found you in Nebraska."

"Yes, she did, and threatened me again," Fats said looking right at Vern. "She's a crazy woman."

Vern laughed without any mirth.

"She has her peculiarities. I can't argue that point. You've been truthful, so far. Now I need to know what happened to her."

"How would I know that?"

"Because she came to find you. She told me she had some information that you were in the Frisco/Breckenridge area."

"I can't help you."

"You mean you won't help me. Her Bentley was found over in Copper Creek, and I believe you know exactly what happened to her."

Zander was listening intently and watching Fats at the same time. He thought Fats looked like he was going to break.

"Maybe she met someone else who wasn't as understanding as my friend here," Zander said trying to take the pressure off Fats.

"Vera was nothing if not relentless. She would never stop until she reached whatever goal she set for herself," Vern said to Zander. "I would appreciate if you would stay out of this. It has nothing to do with you."

Zander only wished it were true.

Fats had enough.

"You might be right. Her goal was quite obvious to even the most uninformed. I took offense at her extreme willingness to kill me. Her unyielding persistence became unnerving and finally unacceptable." Fats took a step toward Vern.

Zander didn't like where the conversation was headed.

"Let's all just relax. Maybe we can work together on this."

"It's highly doubtful. Vera and Vernon are of the same bloodline and therefore unable to react within societal norms. Violence is their outlet. If I were to do a study, I would presume it would be because of always having everything they desired. When someone tells them no, or doesn't do exactly as they say, they can only resort to violence," Fats said.

"That's enough. I'm tired of listening to you. My ears hurt," Vern said.

"It is my deep-seated talent."

"Enough," Vern shouted. "What happened to Vera?"

"She disappeared. I don't believe anyone will be hearing from her anytime soon."

Zander was dumbfounded. There was no doubt he had just told Vern that he had something to do with Vera's disappearance. He knew Vern understood all too well, when he saw him remove a knife strapped to his leg. It was almost as big as the corn knife Zander used to swing when he walked beans in his youth.

"There's been enough conversation. You now have to pay for your sins. Do you like my knife?"

"Not really. I prefer something more manageable."

"It's from the Mideast. They use weapons similar to behead their enemy. It will be a pleasure beheading you in your own place of business." Vern swung the blade.

Fats was too quick and leaned back just as the blade whistled past his neck. Vern switched hands and moved in for the kill.

Fats regained his balance and tossed a chair at Vern. Vern stepped around the flying seat.

"You won't escape your fate. I can make this a swift and painless death for you, or we can do the dance. Your choice."

"Let's dance," Fats said, and ran directly at Vern.

The move surprised Vern, and he raised the blade, at which point Fats dropped to the floor, and his momentum pushed him right into Vern's legs. Vern lost his balance and staggered back two steps. He regained balance and raised his knife as Fats was trying to get up off the floor.

Zander reached under the bar feeling for one of the hidden pistols. Before he had a chance to pull it out, he heard the sound of running feet. When he looked up, Audrey was racing toward the scene of the action, even though she didn't really know what was happening.

Zander called out.

"Hey asshole, look this way." He was trying to take focus off Audrey.

It worked for a second or two, and Vern looked at Zander. Out of the corner of his eye, he saw Fats getting up, but there was also a blur coming his way. There was just too much happening at one time. It confused him. Before he could clear his mind, the blur was upon him.

Audrey flew through the air and wrapped her left leg around the man's neck. Using gravity, she landed on her right but tucked her leg the moment she felt the floor. Her momentum took Vern and flipped him over toward the bar. The blade went flying, and his head hit the bar hard just above the foot rail.

Fats got to his feet and moved toward a stunned Vern. He grabbed the back of his head and whispered in his ear.

"It's time for you to join your sister. I'm sure she's just waiting for you." Fats beat Vern's head against the brass railing twice.

Zander ran from behind the bar and reached Fats just as he was going to give Vern's another head slam. He grabbed his arms and pulled him away. Vern's head fell between the railing and the bar. He was done. Blood was dripping from his right ear on the bar floor.

"Oh man, he's bleeding all over my floor. Is that all these Bullocks know how to do?"

Audrey went over to the man's body and felt for a pulse. She shook her head.

"He's dead."

"Not again. Fats fell to the floor."

"Get up. We've got to get our story straight for the sheriff," Zander said.

"What? We're not going back up to the mine? He would make Vera good company."

"What's he talking about?" Audrey asked.

"Long story. I'll tell you later."

Zander picked Fats up and sat him on a chair. It was lucky this was midafternoon and most of the morning customers had left. There were two witnesses, however, and Zander went over and talked to them. They nodded in agreement, and Zander returned to Fats. Audrey joined them.

"Where did that performance come from?" Zander asked.

"I've got a skill set, but it's a long story. I'll tell you later," Audrey said.

Her remark didn't go unnoticed. She was being subtle and mirroring Zander's own comment to her. Zander knew exactly what it meant. There could be no secrets between the two.

"I'm going to call the sheriff. Here's what we are going to tell him. This man threatened Fats with that knife. I came from behind the bar and tried to kick the knife from his hand but missed and caught him on the side of the head. He then fell and hit his head on the brass railing. Any questions?"

"What about me?" Audrey asked.

"You were in the kitchen and came out when you heard the disturbance. You are a witness to this account of what happened only. We don't need to have you involved in a police investigation especially in light of what you've gone through as of late."

"What about the witnesses?" Fats asked, and looked at the two remaining men in the bar.

"They are already on board. One more thing, when the sheriff arrives, let me do the talking. If he asks you questions just give him a simple answer. Do not volunteer information. Fats, are you listening? You need to keep your mouth shut."

"Understood," Fats said.

"But do you really? This is important, or you might just blow this whole thing wide open. There's too much at stake here."

"I can take direction," Fats said defensively.

"This is a mess. You caused it. Let me fix it."

"I've got it. Why don't you just keep beating the old dead horse?"

Zander went over to the bar phone and made his call. He explained some of the detail to the dispatcher. She said she would relate it to the sheriff. He was out, but she was on the radio before she hung up with Zander.

Zander went back to Audrey and Fats. He asked them to relate what they had just discussed so their stories would be straight. Satisfied, Zander went back to the two witnesses and discussed the story again. They were both Fats' friends and would do anything to back him up. Zander was amazed at how easily Fats made friends. It was a talent he wished he had cultivated over the years. He could still learn a few things from his friend, but Fats could learn some things from him as well.

The first to arrive was one of the deputies. He looked things over and whistled.

"What the hell happened here?"

"We've had a situation," Zander said.

"I can see that. Why didn't you call an ambulance?"

"He was dead. There wasn't a need," Zander answered.

"You didn't follow the usual protocol, did you?"

Zander hated that word. He was also getting irritated with the deputy's attitude. He was about to answer with some smart-assed remark, but the sheriff walked in.

"Well, look who we have here. Zander, I didn't know you were back."

"Just in time to stumble into something I could have done without."

"Looks to be the case."

The deputy decided to try and flex a little muscle.

"I've already started to interview the subjects of interest concerning this case."

"What you'll do right now is interview the two witnesses over there." The sheriff pointed at the two men sitting at the table near the pool table.

"But…"

"No buts, Dennis. Do as you are told." The sheriff dismissed the deputy by turning his back on him.

"Sorry about that. He's a real Barney Fife. I'm trying to knock it out of him. Why don't we have a seat, and you can tell me exactly what happened."

The interviews lasted thirty minutes. The sheriff took a few notes and didn't seem too concerned. The deputy removed the man's belongings from his pockets and brought his ID to the sheriff.

"Vernon Bullock from Lead, South Dakota. Does the name have any meaning with anyone?"

Nobody said a word.

"Well, I'll contact law enforcement up there. In the meantime, I'll need to do something with the body."

He told his deputy to get in touch with the coroner. The deputy left and seemed happy to be in charge of something so important. The sheriff shook his head as he watched him go. He told the witnesses that they were free to go.

"If I have anymore questions, I'll contact you," he said.

"I suppose that same thing goes for us as well?" Zander asked.

"Sure, you're not going anywhere. You just got here."

"I'm leaving for Hawaii in the morning," Fats said.

"Huh. I don't know," he thought for a moment, "I guess it's okay. If I have any more questions for you, I'll communicate through Zander."

"Thanks. Fran wouldn't be happy if we had to cancel because of me."

"Keep the place closed until the coroner removes the body. If I know my deputy, most of the people in town will know what happened by that time anyway."

"Thanks, sheriff. I'm glad we are dealing with you over this nasty incident," Zander said.

"I've got the feeling there's more to this than I care to know," he said, as he looked at Fats closely.

Zander decided to make a deflective move.

"I don't think you have met my girlfriend, Audrey," Zander said putting his arm around her.

"Very happy to meet you. I think you might be out of Zander's league. He's always been an overachiever." The sheriff shook Audrey's hand. "You add a whole lot of class to this place."

After the sheriff left, the three let out a collective sigh.

18

Elaine Taggart and Kevin Grienne took the elevator up to his room in the hotel. Kevin hated elevators, but he thought it would be tacky taking Elaine to the room using the stairs. He wasn't planning anything violent. All he really needed was some great sex. After his encounter with Zander in Cedar Key, he needed an outlet, and Elaine Taggart would fill the bill.

When they reached the room, Elaine found a seat on the couch. She sat in the middle, and Kevin took that as a good omen. The bar fridge had a number of small bottles of various alcohols.

"What would you like to drink," Kevin asked.

"Something sweet?"

Kevin moved bottles around and found two bottles of amaretto. There was no ice, and that pissed Kevin off. He hated to waste time and risk his prey changing her mind.

"There doesn't seem to be any ice. I can go get some."

Kevin didn't know if she read the reluctance in his voice, but Elaine said she would rather drink it neat. Kevin poured the contents into a small glass and handed it to her. Amaretto was far too sweet for his taste, so he looked for something else. A nice bottle of brandy was speaking to him, and he poured it into a similar glass. When he turned around, she was holding up her empty glass, apparently asking for another. He liked what he saw and took her glass and returning it with another serving.

"Thank you. I must be thirsty and ready for a good time this evening," Elaine said.

"There is absolutely nothing wrong with that." Kevin sat next to Elaine, allowing his hip to touch hers.

Elaine didn't move or try to pull away. She responded by pushing her own leg and hip harder into his. Kevin raised his glass, and they toasted to something generic.

"I haven't had such a lovely evening in a very long time. Thank you so much," Elaine said, and downed the rest of her drink.

Kevin took her glass and was ready to get up to get her another when she put her hand on his leg.

"Can I get you another?"

"I might have to slow down, or I might go down for the count. Why don't you finish your drink, and then maybe, we can both have another."

Kevin didn't like to down drinks. He preferred to sip and not risk losing control. He had no choice in this instance and gulped the remaining liquid. It burned going down, and he was surprised that he enjoyed the sensation. He looked over at Elaine, and she put her head on his shoulder. The glasses found the end table. Kevin wasted no time. He embraced Elaine with one arm around her shoulder and the other around her waist.

Kevin was surprised again when she kissed him with an open mouth. He returned the kiss and stayed in the position even after the kiss had waned. Elaine was breathing heavily, but Kevin didn't want to rush anything and lose the moment.

He kissed her neck in various places while she pushed against his body. Kevin could feel her breasts against his chest. She was bigger than he had imagined. Elaine always dressed conservatively, so there was no way of knowing what kind of body she had under all the layers.

Kevin cupped her right breast with his left hand. He knew this would be the test. She would either let her guard down, or the night would end abruptly. For a moment, he considered a violent ending to the evening if she balked. There was no need for such thoughts, however. Elaine melted into his grasp. Kevin could see his opportunity had revealed itself. He gently removed her sweater and kissed her gently as he did. When the sweater was safely in his hands, he placed it on the coffee table. He began kissing her chest and moving down to her ample cleavage, never removing his right arm from her shoulders.

Elaine reached back and unsnapped her bra, and Kevin removed it with his left hand. This time he threw it on the coffee table, not caring about a gentle placement. He was ready and pulled Elaine up to face him.

She began to remove his sport coat while Kevin worked on her skirt. Soon Elaine was standing in nothing but her black panties. Kevin still had on his pants, but she was working on the belt with determination. He decided to help her along and pulled down his pants and underwear together. He kicked them out of the way.

Elaine gasped. She hadn't been with a man in a long time. She had never been with anyone of Kevin's size. He was at full attention, and she couldn't help but take him in hand. Kevin pulled her close and pushed down her panties to her knees. Elaine moved them down to the floor and kicked them to one side. She was still holding onto Kevin. He picked her up, forcing her to lose her grip, and he carried her to the bed. Elaine had her arms around his neck and was kissing him on his cheek.

Supporting Elaine with his right hand under her ample posterior, Kevin threw off the covers of the bed with his left. They fell together on the sheet, wrapped in each other's arms. They remained that way for a time until Kevin tried to roll her onto her back. She resisted and instead pushed Kevin flat on his back. She was sitting on his chest and arched her back pushing out her chest. Kevin was enjoying the show.

He had always thought Elaine to be rather plain. How wrong he had been. He knew that he had never been with anyone with a better body.

Elaine moved down and soon found what was the center point of her evening. Kevin was inside her without any resistance at all. Elaine's orgasm was immediate, and Kevin had all he could do to contain his own. He didn't want this to be over so soon.

Elaine rolled off and sank into the opposite side of the bed.

"I'm so sorry. I haven't been with anyone for such a long time. I just couldn't contain myself."

Kevin rolled on his side, propped his hand under his head, and looked at her for a few seconds before he spoke.

"You are beautiful. I don't think I've ever been with someone so sexually desirable my entire life."

Elaine was embarrassed, but Kevin was happy she didn't try to cover herself. Seeing her naked kept him totally aroused.

"Don't worry about anything. We've got the whole night. I expect that experience will just be one of many."

Elaine didn't answer but rolled right back into Kevin's arms. It wasn't long before they were at it again. This time Kevin took control. He kissed her in places she had no idea even existed. It wasn't long before she had her second orgasm. Kevin moved back up to his pillow when she was finished.

"This is something women can only dream about. You are such a wonderful lover, and I'm sorry, but I don't think I can return the favor. I'm just not good enough."

"Nonsense. Just do what comes naturally. If something doesn't seem right for you, don't do it."

"You are so much more experienced. I've been pleasured twice, and you still haven't had the same."

Kevin smiled.

"I'm not nearly finished with you yet."

The third time was of mutual benefit for them both.

Sometime around 3:00 they both fell asleep. Kevin planned to make a retreat and leave after Elaine fell asleep. That plan didn't work out. When he awoke, it was 6:30 am and Elaine was gone. It took him a few minutes to process what had happened.

The night had gone much better than Kevin had ever dreamed. He had come off as a passionate lover. It was fortunate that he never had to resort to violence. He didn't mind violence. The fact was he enjoyed it almost as much as the sex. The time might come when he was through needing Elaine and her resources.

He was surprised by Elaine's early flight. She had been quiet, and Kevin never heard a thing. It was surprising because he was a light sleeper. He must have been worn out. The thought made him smile. Elaine had been the biggest surprise of all. He realized that her leaving was a windfall. He had no idea what he would have said to her in the morning. It was usually awkward when his prey woke, and the alcohol-fueled evening was just a memory. There was always some shame involved, and it was difficult for Kevin to try and be understanding. He would fumble through it, and that would be the end of any future relationship. This was much better.

Kevin got up and showered. He was in no hurry. His plan had been to get to the office by 9:00. He would have enough time for breakfast and still get home to change clothes.

He checked out and paid the bill with cash. The dining room had few patrons, and he was helped immediately. The breakfast was good but far too expensive for Kevin's usual taste. Today, however, he felt he needed to reward himself for the previous evening's performance.

Kevin drove into the parking lot at precisely 8:50. His mantra was "if you are on time you are late." He looked around for Elaine's car, and he realized he had no idea what she drove.

When he entered the building he walked past the reception area and paused long enough to give the women working the area a hearty "good morning." He heard a spattering of returns but kept his eyes on Elaine who was at her desk with her back to him. She made no effort to recognize Kevin's "good morning." It bothered him more than he could have imagined. It could have been because he still needed her as his information source.

He knew he would need to make a connection with her again. He thought about it for most of the day. He had a few clients, but his schedule was light. It gave him time to think about Elaine and how to proceed. Mostly it gave him time to consider Audrey Wood. He knew he would need to let more time pass. The Frisco people would be on high alert. He needed to give it time, so they would let their guard down.

Around 4:30 he got an email from Elaine "Frisco: Place Of Business-Branchwater." Kevin liked what she had done. If anyone were looking at the emails this would appear innocuous. It could be anything concerning a patient, and no one would look twice. If they did, he might be long gone anyway.

Kevin decided to wait near the reception area and follow Elaine out of the building to thank her. He was happy she was still doing research for him, so things might not be as bad as he first thought.

Kevin was disappointed to see that Elaine's desk was empty. When he asked about her, another receptionist told him she had left for the day. That seemed so unlike her. She was always the last one to leave. It made Kevin wonder if their relationship was over. He knew he needed to talk to her directly. He would try to do that the next day.

Kevin picked up Zander's file when he got back to his condo. He put Elaine's email into the folder and paged through it again to make sure he hadn't missed anything. There was nothing much in the condo for him to make dinner. He was trying to decide if he should go grocery shopping or go out. He decided to make a drink before making such a tough decision.

He poured himself a few fingers of Old Forester and finished with a few more. He decided to drink it neat but knew the 100 proof juice needed a splash of water. He had just finished making the drink when there was a knock at the door.

Kevin was immediately concerned. No one ever came to his condo. It was his safe place. He never had people over, and no one ever just dropped by. He put down his drink and went to the door. Wondering if it was someone selling something or maybe some Jehovah's Witnesses trying to save his soul. There was another knock and he opened the door.

Kevin's stomach dropped to his knees. It was Elaine, wearing a low-cut top and tight shorts.

As he stepped aside to let her into his condo, he knew this would not end well.

19

The sheriff left the Branchwater. Fats, Audrey, and Zander met behind the bar. Patrons would begin to come in for lunch, so decisions needed to be made.

"I guess I'll go back and tell Fran the trip is off. I'm not looking forward to that," Fats sighed.

"You'll do no such thing. You need to leave until this thing dies down." Zander was mostly concerned that Fats would run his mouth and get them all in trouble.

"Do you really think so? You heard the sheriff. He's suspicious."

"Of course he is. It's his job. There's nothing for him find unless you blab."

Audrey had been listening intently.

"Maybe you should have let me take the blame. Men have a way of forgiving women much easier than each other."

"Ain't it the truth," Fats agreed.

"Audrey, you don't need any more attention drawn to you. We're trying to make a fresh start here."

"Since I may have a propensity to be protrusive with my dialogue, it may be better to vamoose before I prostitute myself."

"Much too late for that. You need to leave," Zander said

"Say no more. My departure is immediate." Fats turned, and made his exit through the back door.

Zander shook his head but was smiling. Audrey looked at him.

"I thought my life was screwed up."

"You have seen only a small amount of Fats' life of bullshit, my dear."

"This just keeps getting better and better. I had no idea my life would be one adventure after another."

Zander wondered if she was serious or maybe just busting his ass. He decided not to try and find out.

"We better get ready for the noon rush. Maybe I should go over a few things with you."

"Just who in blazes do you think you're talking to?" Audrey turned, and made her way to the kitchen.

Zander looked after her for a moment realizing that with her experience at The Rod And Gun Club in Everglade City, she probably should be the one schooling him. Audrey stuck her head out of the kitchen.

"Come back here for a moment."

Zander walked into the kitchen. Audrey grabbed him and kissed him right in front of the grill. He didn't know who was hotter.

"You know I love you," Audrey said and kissed him again.

"Does this mean you are open for me to ask you to marry me?" Zander asked.

Audrey pushed him out the swinging door.

"Get to work."

Apparently, it was not the time for that question. Zander went to work behind the bar.

Neither Audrey nor Zander saw much of each other the rest of the day. It was not crazy busy, but they both had little time to sit down. If they did it was for a bathroom break. Audrey would be sitting in that position more than Zander, of course.

At 11:00 Zander announced last call. There were only two drunks left, and they went without incident. Audrey closed the kitchen at 9:00 and was helping behind the bar whenever she could. When Zander locked the front door, she came out from behind the bar.

"I haven't been on my feet for that long in a very long time. I'm out of shape." She sat at a table, and Zander sat beside her.

"You'll never be out of shape," Zander said.

Audrey made a weak gesture of hitting him in the arm but it amounted to very little. She was too tired.

"Let's just go home and wind down," Zander suggested.

"Why don't you fill me in on all this stuff between you and Fats first. Let's get the crap out of the way here rather than take it home. Home should be our refuge, and we should never take the nasty things with us."

Zander agreed and began to tell the Fats story. Some of it he had already shared, but he started from the beginning anyway. If that bothered Audrey, she never showed it. She listened intently until Zander was finished.

"Looking at you two, I would never have expected such a story."

"Nobody is more surprised than me. Mostly, this is Fats' doing, and I'm blaming him."

"Sounds like you may be the reason for what happened. Don't you think this goes even further back than your meeting up with Fats?"

Zander thought about it and realized she was right. Everything that happened was a direct result of his decisions concerning Sara Jane. When he thought about her name, something struck him right in the middle of his forehead. He needed to tell Audrey about his daughter. He needed to do it now because Audrey didn't want the bad stuff to go home with them.

"Audrey, there's something I need to tell you, and it's serious. Before I do, I think we're going to need a strong drink."

He went behind the bar and took two rocks glasses and filled them with ice. He poured each full of Old Ezra bourbon.

"This is going to be massive by the look of that drink," Audrey said.

"Please, let's just sit here and drink this. It may help both of us."

Audrey was wary of what she was hearing but took a drink to appease Zander. It burned going down but warmed her right up. It actually felt pretty good. She was surprised. Audrey had never been much of a drinker unless it was good Cuban rum, but that was hard to get. She took another drink and glanced over at Zander. He was taking his last swallow and clearly nervous.

"Why don't you fill that back up? You look like you need it."

There was no argument. He took the bottle and filled up the glass again. Some of the ice had melted, but Zander felt no need in watering down the second glass. He took two big gulps and set the glass back down on the table. He just looked at Audrey not knowing where to begin.

"This must be beyond serious. I've never seen you drink like that in the past."

"You're right. I don't usually drink like that, but this is serious."

"Maybe you should just throw it out there and see where it lands."

Zander thought about it and scratched his head. The booze was beginning to mellow him out a bit. Audrey was right. He should just put it out there and hope Audrey could make sense of what he had to tell her.

"Before I met you, when I was down in Key West, I made a huge mistake."

"That was when you met Max and he helped you with problems with your ex-girlfriend?"

"Exactly."

"You told me that story."

"I didn't tell you everything. I made this mistake, and I was embarrassed."

"We all make mistakes. Lord knows I've made my share, as you well know."

"I didn't say anything. I thought no one would ever find out, and I could just forget about it."

"Things just don't go away, do they? What was this big mistake?"

Zander turned away. He didn't want to look at Audrey when he confessed.

"Sara Jane and I, well…"

"Let me guess. You hooked up."

Zander nodded.

"Just the one time, and it wasn't good for either of us. It was nasty, and I still don't know how or why it happened."

"You saw me with Corey Prescott. It couldn't have been even close to being that bad," Audrey said trying to give him a pass.

Zander looked at her again.

"Only you never got yourself pregnant." Zander said, and a huge weight seemed to lift from his back.

Audrey looked at him. Zander wondered if he had just sealed their fate. He had no idea what she was thinking and thought it best to keep his mouth shut. Audrey rubbed her head with both hands and then took Zander's hand.

"Why were you afraid to tell me you were a father? Do you think I am that shallow? This all happened before you met me. Is that correct?"

"Yes," was all Zander could say.

"Then you must tell me all about this baby."

Zander gave Audrey a puzzled look.

"I don't understand why you aren't angry with me."

"How could I ever be angry with you after all the things you've done for me? You've saved me from a terrible fate, and you've saved me from myself. If I couldn't show compassion as thanks for all that, I wouldn't be worth having around anyway."

Zander didn't know what to say, so Audrey said it for him.

"Of course, if you would do something like that again, I would need to cut your nuts off."

Zander laughed long and hard. Mostly, it was from relief. He knew their whole relationship could have gone either way. He just never expected what depth of character Audrey possessed.

"No problem on that front. I want to keep what I have between my legs."

"The bigger problem for you will be how you are going to balance all this with a child in the picture."

"I know. It's all I could think about since your rescue from Cuba."

"Tell me about this baby."

Zander told her everything. His voice mellowed when he talked about how he and Sandra, or Sandi as he called her, bonded during their daily walks around Amelia DePont's grounds. He left nothing out, even talking in depth about Sandi's rescue from the Harris family. Audrey appeared to be mesmerized and said nothing until he finally finished. It was 12:30.

"You spin quite a tale. I think you'll be a good storyteller for your daughter. You kept me on the edge of my seat even as tired as I actually feel."

"Unfortunately, it's no tale."

"I know, but you're a good man, and I love that you're honest and up-front with me."

"I'm suddenly very hungry," Zander said, realizing he hadn't eaten anything the entire day.

"I am too. Your story wore me out, and I need some fuel."

"Shall I whip you up something in the kitchen?" Zander asked.

"I'm sick of this place. Let's go out to that all-night truck stop by the interstate. I need something greasy."

Zander liked what he heard. Soon they were sitting in a booth looking at a menu. There were a few men sitting at the counter but otherwise the place was deserted. The waitress came over with waters, which they both thought might be better after indulging in the Old Ezra earlier. The badge on the waitress's uniform said "Mavis." Zander thought it was a perfect name for a truck stop server.

"What'll ya have, hon?" She asked them both.

They ordered cheeseburgers, fries, and chocolate malts. Zander hoped it wouldn't keep him up all night with acid reflux but threw chance to the wind. He had survived his greatest fear, which was losing the love of his life. Everything looked so much brighter, even though it was the middle of the night.

He took Audrey's hand.

"You asked me a while back if we could go into the private investigation business together."

"I think I said 'private dick' didn't I?"

"Yes, you did. But it's not very private anymore, is it?"

"You are so clever."

"Just following your lead."

"Well, have you thought about it?"

"I have. I have to admit that, at first, I was thinking about all the ways it wouldn't work. But after seeing you in the bar today taking that 250-pound asshole down, I've had to rethink that position."

"And?"

"I think it might work. There will be a lot to iron out before we hang out a shingle, but I think it's doable. You've got skills I didn't realize you possessed."

"When you work for the state department, they teach you some things before you are allowed to go out on assignment."

"That's why they were hunting you down. They didn't want to lose their asset."

"Something like that."

"Their loss is my gain. I intend to keep it that way."

"So, whatever I want in this business partnership?"

"Let's not get carried away. Like I said, there's a ton of stuff to sort through before we get to the partner point."

"Just don't ask me to marry you," Audrey said with a smile.

Zander was still trying to figure out what that meant when their food came.

20

No coupling happened that night. They were both too tired. Zander was content to spoon with Audrey until they both got too hot. Zander's sleep was sporadic because of the late-night meal. He was glad to have antacids on the nightstand. It beat getting up and pacing with a sour stomach. He enjoyed lying there listening to Audrey purr. She actually did purr and sounded like the cats he had heard in his youth.

Zander decided to get up at 6:15. There was no reason to stay in bed and stare at the ceiling. Besides, when he did that, his mind started racing, and he thought about weird shit. He didn't need any more weird shit in his life. The coffee maker spit out a full load. Zander was busy making microwave eggs, when Audrey came out of the bedroom.

"Smells good in here."

"Ready for some coffee?" Zander asked.

"Sure. What have you got to go along with those eggs?"

"Nothing. Need a grocery run today."

"Where did the eggs come from?"

"I'm sure Fran put them there. More than likely, they needed to clean out their refrigerator before their big trip."

"We need to get some avocados. I want to make it with toast and fried eggs. Have you ever had it?"

"Nope. Not much on avocados."

"You'll like this."

"I will?"

"Of course. You always like what I tell you to like."

Zander looked at her with a smirk on his face. She smirked back.

"Are you going to get the groceries before we open the bar?"

"Nope. You are."

"Okay. You better make a list," Zander said eyeing Audrey. She had something on her mind. He could always tell.

Audrey got up, found a pen and paper, and sat back down looking off in the distance. She was trying hard to think of all the items they needed. Zander interrupted her thoughts.

"You'd better tell me what you are planning."

"Why do you think I'm planning anything?"

"Audrey, I know that look. What's going on?"

She put the pen down and rubbed the sleep from her eyes.

"We need to have an office if we're going to be partners in this investigation thing."

"I thought we could work out of the cabin," Zander said.

"Bad idea. We can't have work and home life intertwined. It would be a disaster."

Zander thought about it.

"You're probably right. What kind of place are you thinking?"

"I don't know. I thought I'd check the want ads and see what's available."

"I've got a better idea. You go over to Jo and Bert's office. Just tell them what you want and about how much you want to spend. They'll help us out."

"You want me to buy a place?"

Zander almost choked on his coffee.

"Good God, no. Rent. Find some place to rent. We don't know if this thing will take off. We might not even see a profit. I can handle some months of rent, but I don't want to own anything."

"You know we'll be successful," Audrey said and went back to her grocery list.

After breakfast, Audrey finished her list and handed it to Zander and went into the bathroom to get ready. When he finished the dishes, Zander filled his coffee cup and sat back down at the table. He decided to give Audrey some space. The bathroom was spacious enough, but it only had one sink. He needed to wait for her to complete whatever women did to get ready in the morning. She had much more on her plate for the day than he did. There was plenty of time to get the items on the list and still get to the bar earlier than he needed to.

Audrey came out of the bedroom complaining.

"I need to go shopping. You never did take me to that outlet mall, and all I have to wear are these blue jeans and this top."

She looked fabulous. She poured herself into her blue jeans, and the top was low enough to show off the "girls" as Audrey liked to call them.

"I can't take you since I've got bar duty. But you can take the entire day and just do what you want. I'll take care of the bar."

"Who's going to cook?"

"We've got a gal who comes in sporadically. Fats hates to pay anyone, but I think I'm going to see if she'll come in until Fats and Fran get back."

"I would like that. It would give me time to get things done around here." She indicated the cabin.

"What's wrong with it?" Zander asked with a wounded voice.

Audrey rolled her eyes.

"It's just fine if you are a guy. It needs a woman's touch."

"You're the woman to do it," Zander said.

"Don't ever forget it. I'm taking the T-Bird." She grabbed the keys from the peg near the door and was out the door.

Zander knew his use of the car would be greatly limited from now on. It didn't bother him all that much. He liked his pickup.

He got ready for the day and went to the store for the groceries. He bought much more than what was on the list. Zander realized he did that most of the time. Everything always looked good while pushing the cart through the aisles. It was a good thing he owned a pickup. He realized he could never have transported the groceries home in the T-Bird. He would have had to make at least two trips.

He was smiling as he put everything away. They would have enough variety to make meals for the next three weeks. He liked to be prepared.

Everything was put away, and it was only 9:30. Zander decided to go to the Branchwater even though it was early. He needed to contact the lady to help in the kitchen, and since Audrey was looking for office space, he would be short-handed behind the bar. He would get all the grunt work out of the way before the lunch crowd came in.

The coffee drinkers were waiting at the front door when he arrived. He had forgotten about them. After parking in the back, he put on the coffee before he opened the door. The men poured in. Zander was expecting the usual group of five or six, but there were at least fifteen men sitting at the table. Audrey was already having an effect on the business clientele. It made Zander smile. They would be disappointed today.

"Sorry to be the bearer of bad tidings, but Audrey won't be in today."

There was a collective sigh from the fifteen. The guy holding the bakery box opened it.

"I had to buy way more donuts today just to feed these assholes."

"Tough luck," Zander said. "Why don't you give me your dollars, and I'll get the coffee. It should almost be ready."

The boys ponied up. One of the guys offered to help Zander bring the coffee cups to the table. Zander took him up on it. He would rather pour the coffee at the table than try to juggle the full cups on a tray. He could have made more than one trip, but the thought never crossed his mind. He was a guy, and they could not process that kind of mental challenge.

Zander was busy behind the bar when the front door opened and Audrey burst in. She saw the group of men at the tables.

"Good morning guys. I'll be over to see you, shortly."

Zander saw them all smile at Audrey's greeting. Audrey rushed over to the bar and went around the side. She grabbed Zander around the waist, and the lemon he was cutting flew across the bar and onto the floor.

"Easy there, mama. This ain't no wrestling match."

Audrey ignored Zander's comment.

"I found the perfect place for our office. Let's go see it."

Zander looked at her and could see she was excited. She was acting like a teenager, and he found it endearing.

"You realize I can't leave the bar, right?"

"Just for a minute. Somebody can watch the place for us."

Zander placed a hand on her shoulder and put her on the stool behind the bar.

"Why don't you just tell me about it."

"Well, okay," she said.

Zander could tell she was disappointed so he feigned some excitement.

"Where is this place? It must be special, seeing how excited you are."

"We looked at a bunch of places and either they were too ratty or too expensive."

Zander liked what he was hearing. Audrey had listened to his little speech about being successful before they bit off more than they could chew.

"But you found something you like?"

"We will like it," Audrey said sharply.

"Of course, I meant we. Whatever you like I know I'll like as well."

"I like Jo. She must be a good friend."

Zander thought before he spoke.

"I suppose Jo and Bert are my best friends in the entire valley."

"You mean after Fran and Fats."

"If you insist." Zander was joking, but Audrey gave him a look. "Are you going to tell me where this place is located?"

"Like I said, we looked at a lot of properties. I was almost ready to go up the road to Breckenridge, but Jo came up with a great idea."

Zander was starting to lose interest in the elongated story. He tried to stay on point, however.

"So, you found a place that Jo recommended. You think it might be within our budget? You are happy with the set-up, and it is conveniently located?"

"Well, it's going to need some work. But it has everything we would need."

That phrase about needed work was problematic for Zander.

"It needs work? Where is this place?"

"It's above Jo and Bert's office. There's an entire suite of rooms up there."

Zander groaned and took a seat next to Audrey.

"They used to rent that out as apartments, but there hasn't been anyone up there in years. I can't imagine what it even looks like."

"It's not that bad. Just some paint and floor coverings are all we would need. You could have your own office, and so could I. There is a large room we could use for a reception area."

"Wait a minute. We aren't going to hire any receptionist. We are on a shoestring here."

"Maybe down the line, when we're successful. We'll need someone to answer the phone and do office work when we're out on a job."

"Well, I can't dispute your enthusiasm, but I'm not sharing your eagerness to do any remodeling."

"I suppose it could be hired out," Audrey said.

Zander would have been blind not to notice the twinkle in her eye. He had just been played.

"Maybe we can look at it after lunch. I could lock up for a half-hour or so."

Audrey jumped off the chair and hugged Zander.

"I haven't even told you the best part. Jo and Bert aren't going to charge us any rent. All we have to do is fix it up on our dime and pay for utilities. Jo said she would rather have someone up there than have it sit empty."

Zander knew he would need to thank Jo later. There was no doubt she liked Audrey and was trying to keep her in Frisco. That was just fine with Zander. This was home, and it would be Audrey's home as well.

"You've got quite a bit accomplished this morning. I am impressed. There's one thing you haven't done however." Zander motioned over at the men sitting at the tables. They were all looking at Audrey.

"Oh, I forgot about my boys." She kissed Zander and then turned to the men. "I'll be right there, boys."

The men in the bar all applauded, and that included Zander.

21

The next four weeks were without Audrey at the bar. Zander was happy that he had help in the kitchen. Audrey was spending her days at the new office digs. A number of nights Zander beat her home after closing the bar at 11:00. He changed his routine by driving past Jo and Bert's office before going home. If he saw the T-Bird, he would stop and try to get Audrey to stop working. Sometimes it worked, and sometimes she put him to work.

Zander was never so happy at seeing Fats and Fran return home. Fats walked into the bar late in the afternoon of his return. He seemed to be appraising the place.

"Well, I perceive this establishment remains a favorable retreat, and you have not yet diverged this fine parlor into some dive."

"I mostly leave those kinds of things up to you, since you are so good at it," Zander said, not missing a beat. "By the way, it's great to see you."

Zander went over and grabbed Fats and hugged him. He lifted him off the ground.

"Get down boy. Not the time nor place for this lascivious behavior."

Zander put him down.

"Why didn't you call? Someone would have come to pick you up from the airport."

"I refuse to take the risk of you deciding to be that Good Samaritan. I can ill afford to lose business by your absence."

"So, you called Jo, and she picked you up."

"Precisely. Where is your beautiful woman?" Fats looked around and glanced into the kitchen.

"I'll explain later. Right now, put on an apron and let's get ready for the after- work crowd."

"I could not be happier to assist. The islands are beautiful and all that, but they are no Frisco. I missed my digs."

"Good, because tomorrow, you and Fran are in charge. My role here ceases," Zander said and threw him an apron.

"Are there any reports I should be aware of concerning law enforcement?"

"It's been quiet. Almost too quiet, I think."

"Do not utter such things. I am no fan favorite of the calm before the storm."

Zander laughed.

"Who are you trying to shit? Your whole life is a storm."

"I will not argue. I do not want this to be one of those times concerning what transpired four weeks past."

Zander had enough of his diatribe and told him so. Together, they went about their tasks. There was some harmless banter and good-natured ribbing. In between customers, Zander was able to explain what Audrey was planning. Fats showed little emotion when Zander told him they had an office above Jo and Bert's place, and that was where she was spending all her time.

When they finally locked the front door, they both sat at one of the tables. Fats had tapped a couple of Breckenridge beers. Zander drank half of his in one pull.

"Easy there Foster Brooks. You need to drive home without getting a DUI."

"Just a bit thirsty after four weeks of this bullshit." He took another drink. "Besides, I could very well end up working until the wee hours at the office. Audrey is a slave driver."

"Hey, I'd like to see the place. Let's finish up here and go on over," Fats said sounding excited.

"I didn't know how you would react to us actually starting this business."

"What could I possibly not relish? It merely points to your staying here where you belong. If there is anything I can do to make your transition acceptable, please do not hesitate to query."

"Well, there's still some painting to finish and some furniture that might need to be moved."

Fats looked at him puzzled.

"There is no desire to do physical labor on my part. I would be available for moral support only."

Zander threw his apron at him.

"You can lock up. Use the outside stairway if you want to see the place. I'm leaving now."

Fats gave Zander his middle finger as he left.

Audrey had done wonders with the upstairs office. It had been quite run-down when she started, but everything had taken shape. Zander knew she had an eye for decorating. His office walls were painted a dark green. A large desk was placed in the center of the room. The woodwork was white, and the entire room gave the feeling of control. There were shelves on the wall. Audrey told him it would be good to put things he felt were interesting to him. Zander thought a stereo with record albums would be a much better idea. He kept that to himself for the time being.

When Zander walked into the room slated to be the reception area, he spotted Audrey sitting on the floor and leaning on a wall. He thought she was sleeping. He hated to wake her, but she needed to go home to bed. He made his way to her as quietly as possible. He was about to put his hand on her shoulder, when she spoke.

"I'm awake. I needed to rest my eyes."

"You've been working your ass off. Let's go home and get you to bed."

"You might have to carry me. I'm exhausted. I didn't realize this would be so much work."

"I have some good news for you on that front. Fats and Fran are back, so I can spend all my time working on this project with you."

Audrey's eyes opened and looked at Zander who had taken a position next to her on the floor.

"That is good news. We can knock this room out in a week and be ready to open the doors the following."

"Maybe we should take tomorrow off. I could take you to do the shopping that still hasn't happened."

"I don't know. We still have to figure out some signage for the front of the building."

"This isn't going to be some walk-in business, so a huge sign is not necessary. Besides, Jo and Bert would never allow it. I think something at the foot of the stairs would be perfect."

"Literally, a shingle."

"That's right, and I'll take care of it."

Zander thought he noticed some relief in her eyes. He realized she had taken on quite a bit with this remodeling project, and he was sorry his help had been minimal. He would need to change that.

"So, tomorrow will be a holiday for you. You can decide where you want to go, but we are not shopping for the business."

"I need clothes, so that's what we will do."

"That's just perfect."

"You could use some new things. You're starting to look a little ratty."

Zander groaned. He hated shopping for clothes. He hated trying things on and mostly lost his patience. Then he thought better of the situation.

"Whatever you want. The day is yours."

"I plan to use all of it, so don't get any other ideas."

"Where do you want to go? Denver isn't all that far."

"Why would we waste time driving, when we've got perfectly good shops in Silverthorne?"

Zander was about to reply, when he heard Fats coming up the stairs. Audrey leaned forward. Zander could see she was alarmed.

"Don't worry. It's just Fats exposing his nosey self."

Audrey smiled.

"You know, I missed that goofball."

"I know. So did I, but let's not tell him that."

Audrey knew exactly what Zander was saying.

Fats glanced around as he entered the office, and he let out a whistle.

"I perceive the indomitable Miss Audrey Wood has distinguished herself as a gladiator of extreme force in the world of construction."

"Thanks, Fats. I can't say it's been all that much fun."

"Work never has that appeal, unless you are in the bar business," Fats said and wandered around looking at the two offices.

"Where's the biff? I drank copious amounts of beer and have to wiz."

"It's right around the corner. It's really meant for staff only," Audrey said.

"Count me in," Fats said and slammed the door.

"You need to start the exhaust fan. Sounds like you are taking a shower in there. It's grossing us out."

The fan clicked on, and soon Fats was drying his hands with paper towels pulled from the holder.

"At least you know how to wash your hands," Zander said.

"Too much sickness in the world. Keep the hands clean, and you avoid some nasty things."

"I keep washing my hands, and yet, you're still around."

"It is very difficult to distinguish between your satire and sarcasm."

"There is no satire," Zander replied.

"Are you two going to do this the rest of the night? If so, I'm going home."

"We all are," Zander said and pulled Audrey up with him.

"I, too, will take my leave. You have nice digs and are a credit to the species of women."

"Thanks, Fats. Maybe you can plan an open house when we get closer to opening."

Fats smiled and bowed.

"I shall begin the thought process on my way home this fine night. I shall present you with a plan within the week proper."

"Don't overspend. We need to keep this whole thing on budget," Zander said.

"I am deeply hurt at the prospect. Everything will be on my dime, and I shall not entertain anything less. I take my leave." Fats bowed again and left quickly.

On the way home, Zander told Audrey what a good job she had done on the office space. She sighed and slid over next to him.

"I didn't realize how much work it would entail. It's good work. Makes me feel good."

"That's the important part. We all need something to do to help us feel relevant."

"That's been something that has eluded me over the years. Then I met you, and it all changed."

Zander looked at her and pulled the pickup over to the side of the road.

"I am sorry for what happened to you over the course of your life. You shouldn't feel alone, however. We all go through things."

Audrey put her arms around Zander and pulled him close.

"I know. Here I am feeling sorry for my past and then realize you have had one as well. You still need to do some reconciling, I think."

Zander hugged her back.

"This office space thing and running the bar has taken my mind off this problem for the last month."

"But it's always hanging around in your mind somewhere. I can see it in your eyes."

Zander knew Audrey had more perspective on his life than he could ever possess.

"I'm just happy I have you for support."

"I'm happy you had the smarts to share this with me. I'm here to support you, and if you need advice, I'm happy to give that as well."

Zander laughed.

"You have always been good at that."

"Speaking of which, we need to change the business cards."

"I don't understand."

"I'm a part of this business now, and I need to have my name included."

"Which one?" Zander asked.

"Don't get cute with me." Audrey paused, thinking. "Damn it, I never thought about your T-Bird. It's parked behind Jo's office. We need to go back and get it. I can drive it home."

"You would fall asleep before you even got to the highway. It will be fine where it is. We can get it tomorrow before we head over to Silverthorne."

Audrey sank back into the seat beside Zander. She seemed relieved, and Zander thought he might have said all the right things for once. It was highly unusual for him not to put his foot into his mouth at some time during a typical day.

They drove the rest of the way to the cabin in silence. Zander was again trying to decide how to proceed with his new daughter. Audrey was considering their new business. She wondered how they would advertise to get enough business to make the whole thing interesting.

Zander dropped Audrey off at the front door and went over to park the pickup in front of the shed. When he got into the cabin the only light was coming from the bedroom. He threw his keys in the bowl by the door and walked over to ask Audrey if she wanted a nightcap.

She was lying on the bed in her paint clothes sound asleep. Zander realized she was indeed exhausted. He helped her out of her clothes and stopped when he reached her underwear. Mostly he stopped because Audrey, half-awake, called him a pervert.

He covered her up and got undressed himself and slid into bed next to her. She put her arm around his chest, and for a moment, Zander was encouraged.

There would be no lovemaking this evening, however.

22

Elaine Taggart expected she would be spending the night with Kevin. Her encounter with him at the hotel had given her the most pleasure she had experienced in some time. She wanted more, and it didn't hurt that she was attracted to Kevin.

Kevin's excitement came from the fact that Elaine knew where he lived. It subdued his sexual attraction. He did notice what she was wearing, and it did make some inroads on his libido. Normally, he would have not concerned himself with the outcome. It would have been easy to get rid of Elaine when he was through with her. This was different. He had been "shitting where he was eating", and that had come back and bit him right in the ass.

He had no idea who had seen them together or who she might have told about being with him. It would be risky trying to eliminate Elaine. His mind told him that he needed to take the high road, but his loins were giving him another message.

These thoughts were still being processed, as he let Elaine into his condo. It was the first woman to ever cross the threshold. Kevin was nervous and tried to calm down by offering Elaine a drink. The reality of it was that Kevin needed a double at the moment.

"I have some red wine opened. Would you like a glass?"

"That would be wonderful," Elaine said.

Kevin thought she might prefer something white, but he didn't keep whites in stock. He hated the sour taste it gave him. He poured her a large glass.

"Wow, what a generous pour. You could be my bartender anytime."

Kevin cringed at the thought. He poured himself a full rocks glass of Old Forester without the usual ice. He needed some courage to stop himself from doing something stupid.

"How did you find my place?" Kevin asked and realized how stupid the question sounded. Elaine had the entire work resources at her fingertips. Kevin used her to find out about Audrey Wood, so finding his place would be child's play.

"I checked your employment file," Elaine said. "I hope I didn't do anything out of line."

Kevin needed her to stay calm. He tried to make his voice sound at ease.

"Of course not. Actually, I'm flattered that you would want to look me up."

Elaine relaxed.

"We had a wonderful time at the hotel, and I just wanted to tell you how important last night was for me."

"It was important for me also," Kevin said, hoping he sounded sincere.

"I was hoping you would say that. I'd like to see where this goes, if you feel the same."

Kevin felt like he was being painted in the corner. He knew he needed to end the relationship, but it needed to be on good terms or life at work would be hell. This was going to take more planning, and he knew he would not be able to end the relationship that evening.

"Have you had dinner?" Kevin asked.

"I was nervous coming over here and couldn't eat anything."

"Would you join me for dinner?"

"That would be lovely."

"There's a little Italian place a few blocks from here. It's dark and quiet, and the food is amazing."

"I love pasta. It's my favorite."

"How in the world do you keep that amazing figure with all that starch?"

Elaine's cheeks flared red, and she looked down smiling. Kevin could see she liked what she heard.

"Let me call for a reservation. They know me there, so it shouldn't be an issue," Kevin said and went over to the phone.

Elaine finished her wine. Kevin thought she might need more of the same liquid courage. After he made the reservations, he came back with the wine bottle.

"They can seat us in thirty minutes," Kevin said and poured more wine.

"My car is out front. I can drive."

"No need. We can walk. It's just a few blocks."

Elaine nodded and took a drink from her glass.

"I hope I'm not imposing. Did you have other plans for the evening?'

"I did not. I was wondering what I was going to do for dinner. I was considering going grocery shopping. You saved me from that nightmare."

They finished their drinks and engaged in some small talk. They both had enough alcohol to eliminate any uncomfortable feelings either might have displayed earlier. When Elaine finished her wine, Kevin took the glasses and placed them on the counter next to the bar.

"We have just enough time for a brisk walk to the restaurant to make the reservation," Kevin said.

"That should help with our appetites," Elaine answered.

Kevin had taken his time with the drinks to insure they would need to walk fast. He didn't want to make this a romantic evening by lingering and talking about things that would lead to anything.

They were seated immediately, and Kevin ordered a bottle of house Chianti from the waiter. He brought it to the table in a large carafe. Kevin supposed the restaurant had a huge barrel in the back somewhere. He felt it was a good wine for the price and certainly didn't want this to be some expensive affair. That would not be the message he wanted to send.

Elaine ordered a Caesar salad and a bowl of minestrone. Kevin did the same and added a large plate of antipasto as an appetizer for both to share. He was pleased that the meal would be reasonably priced. Maybe they could share a desert as a good gesture.

Elaine chattered incessantly throughout the meal. Normally, that would have irritated Kevin. Since he didn't have to carry the conversation, he was actually enjoying seeing Elaine's nervousness. It was almost enduring, and he knew it would lead to more intimacy later in the evening.

As they strolled back to Kevin's condo, Elaine put her arm through his. It was such a small gesture, but Kevin found it very arousing. They talked about nothing in particular until they came to the condo. Elaine turned and spoke first.

"Thank you so much for a wonderful evening. This is something that has been missing in my life, and you have made me see that there is more to life than work."

"My pleasure. Would you like to come up for another cocktail or some more wine? It's early, and I so seldom have visitors."

"Do you think it's wise? They frown on interoffice relationships at work."

"That's true. Maybe we could see where this goes, but we need to be discreet. I don't think either of us want to lose our jobs over this." Kevin was overjoyed at being able to interject this little bit of information. It would be the catalyst he would need to break off the relationship.

"Maybe I could have an after-dinner drink. I certainly don't want to wear out my welcome." Elaine liked what Kevin had just said. It was nice being with someone. Spending every night alone and lonely was taking its toll.

Kevin smiled and took her hand. He knew she wouldn't be leaving any time soon. When they reached the front door Kevin inserted the key and opened the door. He stepped aside and followed Elaine into the condo.

"Would it be possible to use the restroom?" Elaine asked.

"Sure. It's down the hall to your left." Kevin pointed the way.

He took the time to make Elaine a drink. He had a bottle of bourbon cream in the refrigerator and thought it might be something she would really like. He filled a glass without adding ice. The cream was cold from the fridge. The more he could get her to drink the less inhibited she would become.

Kevin handed Elaine the drink when she returned.

"Ooh. What am I drinking?"

"It's called bourbon cream, straight from Kentucky. It's actually fairly hard to get. I guess they only make so much of it."

"I hope I'm worth all this attention you're giving me."

"You certainly have been so far." Kevin filled his own glass with ice and poured the remaining bottle of Old Forester into it. He sat next to Elaine on the couch.

"Here's to a happy evening with a wonderful guy," Elaine said and clinked her glass with Kevin's.

"You are too kind. You are so very easy to be with, and the pleasure has been all mine."

They drank in silence for a few minutes. Kevin finished his bourbon and was ready to fill both their glasses, when Elaine stopped him. She put her hand on his and took his glass and put it on the coffee table along with her own. She put her arms around Kevin's waist and pulled him over as she reclined on the couch.

Kevin wasted no time, and soon they were removing each other's clothing. Kevin stood and Elaine pulled down his shorts. He pulled her to her feet and removed the rest of her undergarments. He paused just long enough to admire her body. She was beautiful fully naked. Most people looked better with clothes on, but Elaine broke that stereotype. Kevin only could hope she thought the same of him.

He carried her into the bedroom and soon the air was filled with their passion. Elaine was very vocal, and it was a huge turn-on for

Kevin. He had all he could do to contain his climax, until she found hers.

Elaine paused for about six minutes after her orgasm, and then sat on Kevin's chest just daring him to continue. When he finally came to attention, Elaine slid down looking for a ride. This time Kevin couldn't contain himself.

They both collapsed with Elaine still on top of Kevin. When they both stopped the heavy breathing, Kevin spoke first.

"You are going to kill me. I haven't had sex like this in…well…ever."

Elaine kissed his neck.

"Happy to be of service." She rolled off of Kevin and put her elbow on the bed with her head on her outstretched hand. "Now what?"

Kevin was incredulous. "You want to do it again?"

"No, well, I would if you wanted to. I meant where do we go from here?"

Kevin was relieved. He knew he had completely spent whatever stamina he possessed. There was another opportunity here, however.

"We should go slow from here on out. I say that for two reasons. First, all this is going to give me a heart attack or a stroke. Second, we need to be vigilant about our jobs. We can't let anyone at work know what we are doing." He glanced over at Elaine and saw she still looked amazing lying next to him naked. It could be he had more stamina than he realized previously.

"What do you suggest?" Elaine's voice had a note of disappointment in it.

"I think we could see each other once a week, but we would have to be very careful. We can only be professional at work. We should avoid each other as much as possible."

"Once a week? Maybe we could find some more time than that," Elaine said, sitting up in bed.

"I don't think so. But we could make it count. If there is a weekend where we could do a getaway, that would also be a possibility." Kevin was being firm. He needed this opening to remain for the future. He would need to break everything off when he made his move on Audrey Wood.

Elaine was visibly disappointed and swung her legs off the bed.

"I know what you are saying is true, but I need more. Maybe I should just quit my job. Then this whole thing would go away."

The comment alarmed Kevin.

"Let's not be hasty. There is time to make plans in the future." He pulled Elaine back onto the bed next to him and put his arms around her.

Elaine noticed something immediately.

"It appears you're not dead, yet."

They had sex again, and this time both fell asleep afterward. Kevin woke around 5:00 am. He gently put his hand on Elaine's shoulder and moved it a little. She stirred and opened her eyes.

"Did we fall asleep?"

"Well, sure. No one can have that much fun and not be exhausted."

"What time is it?"

"It's five in the morning."

Elaine sat straight up.

"I've got to get going. It will be light soon. If we want to keep this a secret, we've got to be discreet. I don't want to be seen leaving your place this time of the morning."

Kevin watched her dress and thought he might get aroused again. A fleeting thought crossed his mind. He might have what he needed right here. Why would he go after Audrey Wood? He pushed the thought away. It wasn't a part of his protocol.

Kevin put on his shorts and walked Elaine to the door. He kissed her lightly as she left. Kevin watched her walk down the sidewalk toward her car.

Neither of them saw a vehicle down the block. Connie McGill was in her personal vehicle watching them both.

23

Zander and Audrey worked together getting the office ready. The work was enjoyable, when they were both together. Zander fashioned a sign out a piece of cedar he found in his shed. He got some screw-on letters from the local hardware store. It was a triple complete set of both letters and numbers. Zander knew he would need to consult Audrey before making a decision on the sign.

"I bought the letters for our sign. What do you want it to say?"

"I think we should keep it simple."

"And." Zander needed more detail.

"Should we have the name of the company listed?"

"Good question. What is the name of the company?"

"I haven't thought that far ahead."

"Well, if we're going to be open next week, don't you think that might be one of those important details?"

"Don't be a smartass."

"That's the only part of my anatomy that people recognize as smart. Don't make me give that up."

"I wouldn't even know who you were if that were gone. We need to make a decision on the sign and what details our business card will list."

Zander sat at the receptionist desk. Audrey followed and sat on his lap. She took some paper from the drawer and found a pen.

"Okay, let's brainstorm for some ideas."

"You realize we haven't made love in quite a while."

"Of course, I know that. What's that got to do with anything?"

"You're sitting on my lap, and Mr. Leonard is trying to stand at attention."

Audrey jumped up and sat on the desk facing Zander.

"Is this better?"

"Not really, Mr. Leonard wants what he wants. I have little control over him."

"Focus bucko. Let's hammer this out. Keep the little man in your pants for now."

Zander was both disappointed and yet heartened at her last two words. He decided to cooperate.

"Let's first decide on the company name. You keep the notes."

"I don't think first names are a good idea. I think Audrey in the title sounds weak."

"Well, I don't want Van Zee in the title, and I've never gone by Sander, ever."

"Do we want something without our names?"

"I don't think so. That's confusing. How about Wood and Zander, private investigators?"

"We don't have a license to call ourselves private investigators."

"That's true."

"I do like the Wood and Zander, though." Audrey thought for a moment. "How about Wood and Zander Personal and Discreet Investigations?"

Zander lied and told her he liked it. Personally, he thought it sounded too feminine.

"I'll put our address on the bottom of the sign for identification and delivery purposes. What about the business card?"

Zander pulled the old one from his wallet and handed it to Audrey. She took it and studied it for a moment.

"We could use the same title as the sign. I do like your 'Have Resources Will Travel' phrase. I can mess around with it and show you what I think might work."

Zander took a huge risk.

"That's not necessary. I trust whatever you decide will be perfect. You'll just need to get it to the printer, so we can have these things ready to pass out."

It was the right response. Audrey slid from the desk and put her arms around Zander.

"You're the best."

"I know." Zander realized that sometimes when you lost, you won.

They were in the middle of a long kiss, when they heard a throat being cleared. Zander stood up with Audrey's arms still around his neck. It must have been a comical picture, because the young woman with the throat clearing was smiling.

"I'm sorry to interrupt, but I was told you were the people to see to help with solving problems."

Audrey let go of Zander's neck and turned to greet their first customer.

"Please, follow us to the conference room, where we can have a private conversation and get more details." Audrey reached into the desk and pulled out a yellow legal notepad. It made what they were about to do seem more official.

Audrey placed the young woman in the chair at the head of the large walnut table, and she and Zander sat on either side of her.

"May I ask who referred you to us?" Zander asked.

"My parents were friends with Jo and Bert Williams who own the realty business in this building. I've known Jo most of my life, and she always seems to know the right people. Do you know what I mean?"

Zander knew exactly what she meant. He knew Audrey would soon enough as well.

"She's quite a woman. We are friends as well."

"She said I couldn't do any better than to hire the two of you."

"That's why we pay her," Zander said, and noticed the young woman startle immediately. "That's just my feeble attempt at humor. Sorry if it startled you."

Audrey threw one of the pens she was holding at Zander to try and lighten the mood. Zander ducked and the pen hit the wall.

"Hey, we just painted that wall. Be careful," Zander said.

Audrey turned back to the young woman.

"You must think we're a couple of juveniles. I'm sorry for the behavior, but we haven't actually opened the doors to the public yet. We're still a little goofy from all the pressure of getting this place ready."

"I'm sorry if I've overstepped. I assumed you were taking cases."

The young woman started to get up, but Audrey stopped her.

"Please sit. We have to start somewhere and get things rolling. You would be our first case."

"First case? I was under the impression you have experience."

"First case in this new office. Together, we have a wealth of experience, just not here. Zander has a whole binder full of past cases if you are interested. I'm sorry we haven't introduced ourselves. I'm Audrey Wood, and this is Zander. Our company is called 'Wood and Zander Personal and Discreet Investigations.'"

Zander cringed at hearing the new name but kept his composure. He was enjoying watching Audrey work. She was building a relationship with the client and doing a good job of it.

"I don't believe I caught your name," Audrey said to the young woman.

"Is it important?"

"Yes. If you want us to look into your situation, we'll need to know everything. That includes your name." Audrey was firm.

"I suppose so. My name is April McCauley. This is completely foreign to me, so you'll have to be patient while I try to work things out."

Zander decided to add to the conversation.

"That's why we're here. Take your time and fill us in."

Zander could see some panic in her eyes when he spoke. He realized it might be something that she would be more comfortable talking with Audrey without him present.

"Would you rather talk to Audrey without me being here?"

April nodded and looked down. Zander leaned over as he was getting up and put his hand on her shoulder.

"There is nothing to worry about. You will be in the best of hands with Audrey. When the time comes, I can also become involved, if that's your wish. There is no pressure here. We're just available to help solve your problem however you think best." Zander smiled and left the room.

April watched him go and then turned back to Audrey.

"I'm so sorry. He seems like a good guy. It's just that I have trouble talking about this in front of a man."

"You're right, he's a great guy. I could tell you what he's done for me in my life, but we would be here for the rest of the week. Don't worry about Zander. He's a big boy, and we're here to help our clients however we can. If that means you are more comfortable with just me, then so be it," Audrey said.

"Oh, thank you so much. You don't know how much that means to me."

"Do you want to tell me about yourself and what help you want from our firm?"

"Where do I start?"

"Why don't you include anything you think is pertinent? Go back as far as you need. We've got time."

April began her story, and Audrey was mesmerized from the start. April had a life that most children could only dream about. She was an only child. Her father was some sort of international banker, and her mother came from money and high society. She never worked and took little care of Audrey growing up. There were always nannies and tutors for that. Audrey was expected to be the best at everything she chose to do. They didn't force her to do things. They demanded perfection for those things she did choose, however.

They had an elegant condo in West Palm Beach, Florida, which they visited infrequently. April's mother preferred her Aspen palatial estate and all the social outings that went with it.

Their closest neighbor, across the valley, was John Denver. April was selected to be in the audience when he did his Christmas special outdoors in a glass bubble. From that day on, she loved his music and was devastated when he died in a single plane accident.

That was pretty much April's life until she was eighteen. She had been dating an older guy who was twenty-one and things became intimate. The second month she missed her period. She bought a home pregnancy test from the drug store in Carbondale, because she didn't want anything coming back to her parents.

When she found that she was pregnant, she went to the father. He called her a whore and told her it was all her fault. He left that same day, never to return.

Then she went to her parents. They were both mortified and disowned her. They threw her out of the Aspen mansion and wanted nothing more to do with her.

They let her keep the Jaguar they had bought her at graduation along with her clothes and personal items. Her father slipped her ten grand in cash to get her started, and that was the last April had contact with either of them.

Audrey had a hard time not showing her anger toward April's parents. She wondered how any parent could treat their daughter with such disrespect, no matter what she had done. April showed little emotion. It was almost like she had shut the past off and was going through a history lesson. Audrey could detect no frustration or anger in her voice.

"What did you do? Where did you go?" Audrey asked.

"I left Aspen. I knew I couldn't face either one of them. It would have even been worse carrying around a little baby under their noses."

"I don't understand this whole thing. You were their only child. You made a mistake, but they were still your parents. They needed to step up."

"And yet, they didn't. I don't hold a grudge. It was part of their culture, I guess. My father got his position from my mother's family, and my mother never had to do a thing except go to parties and live the life. I never really wanted that for myself."

"What about your grandparents?"

"They were both gone by then, and I never knew my father's parents. They never came around, and we never visited. I always felt my father was ashamed of them."

"April, I am so sorry for this. You have had one screwed up life. What happened to your child?"

April's eyes lit up.

"It was the only good thing that ever happened to me. Johnny is six now. He's a beautiful little boy."

"I can only imagine. If he takes after his mother, he would be perfect."

April smiled and stood up.

"I'm sorry. I don't know where the time has gone. I have to pick up Johnny from school. He's a kindergartener now." April said.

Audrey stood up with her.

"We haven't even come close to the part whether we decide if we can help you. You need to come back tomorrow and finish this story. This could be a novel."

"I can be here at 9:00 and give you until 2:00. Would that help?"

"Whatever works for you. We'll be here regardless." Audrey went back to the reception desk and wrote out the phone number of the business. She included both of their cell phones.

"If something comes up, call one of these numbers until you get someone." Audrey gave April a hug. "We're going to help you one way or another."

"Thank you. You are so kind." April found the exit, and Audrey could hear her padding down the steps.

"What's going on?" Zander asked.

"Let's go to the Branchwater. I need a drink. You aren't going to believe this girl's story."

Zander walked with his arm around Audrey all the way to the Branchwater. There were no coincidences. This woman had found them for a reason.

24

April McCauley walked back into Audrey's life precisely at 9:00.

"You are punctual. That speaks volumes about your character."

"Maybe, you should reserve that judgment until after I finish the story."

***

Audrey had dismissed Zander and told him to leave until she called. Zander didn't know exactly what to do without Audrey. He decided to go to the Branchwater and try to put up with Fats' bullshit as long as he could. He would wait for her call hoping it would be sooner than later. He was interested in the rest of April's story and wondered what she needed from them. One thing was for certain; he would not be working at the bar. Today, he would be drinking free coffee and sitting with the boys.

***

April and Audrey went back into the conference room with coffee. When they were settled, Audrey waited for April to speak first. She continued on from where she left off the day before.

"The ten grand my father had slipped to me gave me some breathing room at first. I could never afford anything in Aspen, and I really needed to get away from there. I bounced around I-70 trying to find work. I had some waitressing jobs in a few truck stops, but they didn't pay much. I was living in cheap motels, and I realized I couldn't do that much longer on what money I had left. I needed a decent job, but when the employers saw that I was pregnant, they wanted nothing to do with me."

"I can't even imagine how tough that had to be for you. Did you have anyone close to you that could help?"

"I had no friends left. They must have thought my pregnancy was some sort of leprosy. One of the other waitresses, who was older, told me about this motel owned by a little old lady who rented rooms by the month. It was off the beaten path, and she had turned the motel into rentals and no longer offered rooms by the night. It was the only way she could keep the place open. The workers in this area are always in need of reasonably priced lodging. There's not much available."

"That's what happens when you are in the middle of a skiing area. Most people don't realize the problem it creates. Some of these companies are starting to build dorms for these kids," Audrey said.

"There were a few around but not for a pregnant girl."

"So, did you go to this long-term rental?"

"I did, and it turned out pretty good. The lady was sweet, and I think she took pity on me. She was always making extra food that she gave to me when I got off work. Sometimes she would invite me over for Sunday dinner if I didn't have to work."

"What is her name?" Audrey asked.

"Her name was Delores Knobloch." April looked down and rubbed her eyes.

"Where is this place?"

"It's just north of Silverthorne on highway 9. It's a lonely spot in the road right out of the fifties. There was a row of 10 motel rooms facing the road and five or six small cabins behind in the trees. She let me have one of the cabins for a hundred bucks a month." April looked away.

"Sounds like she gave you a very good deal."

"She felt sorry for me, but she wouldn't let me feel sorry for myself."

"What do you mean?"

"She's a tough old cookie. She would come to visit me when I was off work and ask me what my plans were when I had the baby. I hadn't thought that far ahead, and she would remind me to start making plans. She took me to the doctor the first time and waited until I set up appointments. I never paid a dime. She took care of all the doctor bills."

"What about when Johnny was born?"

"She took care of that as well. She even drove me to the hospital and stayed with me while I had Johnny. I guess she was my coach. She took care of Johnny and me until I could get back on my feet. I had no clue how to take care of a baby. She showed me that, too."

"Sounds like you were pretty fortunate to find her," Audrey said.

"You just can't imagine, but I needed money and had to get back to work. She babysat Johnny every day. I wasn't making much as a waitress, and she told me to apply at the shops at Silverthorne. I got a job at a Nike outlet and almost doubled what I had been making. Still, I was living from hand to mouth and knew if anything ever happened to Delores, I was screwed, again." April smiled at Audrey.

Audrey caught her meaning.

"This time it wouldn't involve any pleasure, would it?"

"Exactly right. I needed something to do that could support Johnny and me. I also needed to put money away for a rainy day."

"So, what did you do?" Audrey asked.

"Delores was watching out for me. She would give me the wants ads from the weekly paper. The jobs she thought fit me were circled in red. I had no real experience, but she said I could use her as a reference. I imagine she would think of some story where I helped her with the motel business. She was pretty convincing."

"What did you find?"

"Not much at first. Most of the jobs were similar or worse than mine. I needed something that paid. That's when I found a company in Leadville that needed an executive secretary. I didn't know what that was, but it sounded important. It was a salaried position with lots of benefits. I was immediately interested. When I showed it to Delores, she told me to call immediately. I did and lined up an interview the very next day. Delores took Johnny, and all I had to do was ask for the day off. They weren't happy but let me go, because I had done so many double shifts. I think they knew I was a good worker. Maybe they didn't want to lose me."

Audrey looked at April while she was telling her tale. She really liked this young woman. There was no pretense, and she was as genuine a person as Audrey had ever met. She had no idea how she and Zander could help her, but she knew it was going to happen.

"I assume you got the job?" Audrey asked.

"Yes, I was hired on the spot, and I always wondered why. I had taken business courses in high school, but other than that, I had zero experience."

"Tell me about the company." Audrey was taking notes.

"The main business in Leadville, other than tourism, is mining. This was a trucking and shipping company. They brought in and took out everything the mining operations needed."

April paused and looked at Audrey before she continued.

"I suppose that included the copper ore. They loaded train cars with that. Everything else came and went by truck."

"Where you suspicious of anything? "

"I don't know what you mean?"

"Was everything being done legally?" Audrey sat forward.

"I doubt it. I couldn't get that close to the daily business."

"Well, what did they have you doing?" Audrey was writing everything April was telling her.

"Just the usual meaningless office stuff. I made coffee, answered the phone, handled the mail, typed letters, and…" April stopped and stared at the table.

Audrey could see something was wrong. She knew she had to proceed carefully.

"That doesn't sound like an executive position. Were you allowed to attend board meetings and keep records? I assume they had a board," Audrey said.

"They did, but it was all so secretive. I was never invited to sit in on any of their meetings."

"What is the name of your boss?"

"Anthony Ritz." April looked back down at the table.

Audrey knew she was getting close to why April wanted to hire them, but she also knew April was in a fragile state.

"Do you want to take a break?"

"I could use a bathroom break and maybe some more coffee," April said.

"You go use the restroom. I'll get the coffee."

When Audrey went to get the coffee, she saw Zander sitting at the secretary's desk.

"What are you doing skulking around here? I though you were going to the Branchwater."

"I did. I can only stand so much of Fats' bullshit, and I reached my limit. Are you almost finished?" Zander asked.

"I think so. Something is definitely wrong. She just hasn't had the courage to come out with it."

"I'll hang around if you need me. I thought I'd hang the sign at the foot of the stairs if that's okay with you."

"How are you going to attach it?"

"I bought a metal arm at the hardware store. It's ready to go. I just need to screw it to the siding."

Audrey laughed.

"You just can't get that word out of your mind, can you?"

"When you've been deprived of something for so long, it's human nature to dwell on it more than you should. It can't be helped."

"Poor boy. See you later." Audrey followed April back into the boardroom with coffee in a carafe.

She poured the coffee into the cups and took her seat.

"Let's continue. You were telling me about your boss, I believe. What kind of man was he?"

April shot a dark glance at Audrey. Audrey caught it immediately. It was uncomfortably quiet in the conference room. Audrey decided to wait it out. The story had to come to an end soon. If April was uneasy enough, she might blurt it out.

"He was really nice when I first started. He even invited to Sunday dinner. He has a wife and two kids. A boy and a girl, and they were both nice to me."

"Sounds like an all-American kind of guy."

"You might think so. He was at first, anyway. I was happy working there. They were paying me more money than I had ever made in my whole life. I got full insurance coverage for both Johnny and me and two weeks paid vacation. They even set up a 401K account for me. Get this, I was making almost 80 thousand a year."

Audrey looked up from her notes and whistled.

"That's a big chunk of change for someone with such limited duties."

"That's what I thought. I figured they must be doing something illegal, and they needed someone naïve in the front office."

"Something changed after that?"

"Remember when I told you I was never allowed in the boardroom?"

Audrey nodded.

"That was just when the board was in session. Mr. Ritz did some work at the big boardroom table at various times. It was a big table, and he needed room to spread out documents. The boardroom was on the second floor of the office building. It was the only thing on the second floor."

"Did you find it unusual for him to be using it as his office?"

"Not at first. He would ask for coffee and office supplies when he needed them. I would bring them up. A few times he asked me to take a break with him, and we shared small talk. It all seemed so harmless."

"April, what happened to change your situation?"

"It was late on a Friday evening and most of the other employees had left for the weekend. Mr. Ritz called me into his office and asked me to come in that Saturday for a few hours. He told me he had some items that needed to be collated for the following Monday board meeting."

"Was that unusual?"

"It was for me. It was the first time he'd ever asked me to come in after hours. I was salaried, so I suppose he had every right to do so. It just made me uncomfortable because of Johnny. Delores was so good to me that I didn't want to take advantage of her. It would be a lot to ask to watch Johnny on a Saturday."

"So, I assume you did what he asked."

"I had no choice. I had such a good job I just couldn't afford to give him any reason to terminate me."

Audrey didn't like what she was feeling. She put down her pen and looked April in the eyes.

"What happened that Saturday?"

"The only thing he wanted to spread out on that big boardroom table was me."

25

April finally had enough and broke down. Audrey got up and put her arms around her. When April's shoulders stopped heaving, Audrey let her go and sat next to her holding her hands.

"How long has this been going on?"

"It seems like forever."

"April, you realize this is rape?"

April nodded.

"That's why I came to you. I don't know what to do. I don't know how to make it stop."

"Did you think about quitting?"

"He threatened me. He said he would make sure I didn't work anywhere if I left. Then he showed me a pistol in his desk drawer and asked if I got his meaning. I've never been so afraid in my life."

Audrey stood and went to the conference room door and threw it open.

"Zander get in here." Audrey realized she shouted a bit louder than she should have.

Zander was sitting in a chair waiting for instructions. He heard them loud and clear, and in less than two seconds he was in the conference room.

"What's wrong?" he asked.

"Almost everything. April is going to need our help. We need to drop whatever else we've got going on and put this first on the docket."

Zander realized that Audrey was exaggerating for effect. He supposed it was because she wanted April to see how dedicated they were. He was not quite so quick to sign on.

"What do I need to know?"

April looked panic-stricken. Audrey knew she couldn't go through the story a second time.

"I'll fill you in later. What you need to know right now is that April is being raped by her boss on a continual basis."

Zander sat down next to April.

"April, we will do everything to make this stop."

"He threatened me, and I've got Johnny to think about."

Zander wondered if she was backpedaling or trying to work things out in her mind by speaking out loud.

"It's because of Johnny that you have to take action. How long do you suppose this will go on before your boss feels threatened and does something even worse?"

"I know. I've thought of that. I just don't know what to do."

"For right now, you will continue to go to work as if nothing has changed. We don't want to spook him into doing something we aren't prepared to handle. By the way, what is his name?"

"Antony Ritz. Everyone just calls him Tony."

"Is he connected?" Zander asked, noting the heavy Italian influence.

"I don't know what you mean," April replied.

"Never mind. Getting information is our job. Your job will be to act normal."

"I don't even know what normal is anymore."

"I don't mean to pry into your business, but we're going to need you to tell us everything concerning you and Tony."

"I understand."

"Have you taken any precautions?"

April looked confused.

"He's asking if you have used birth control," Audrey said, trying to show as much sympathy as possible.

"I'm on the pill. I have been since Johnny was born."

"That's good. At least we won't have to worry about him coming after you because you are pregnant."

"Once was enough, and that was consensual."

"Audrey and I are going to have to put our heads together and figure out how to proceed. We will keep you in the loop every step of the way, so there will be no surprises."

April looked down, and Audrey could see something was bothering her.

"April, is there a problem? Is there something else you aren't telling us?"

"No, I've told you everything. It's just that I don't have much money to pay you. I've used my salary to cover debts. I'm almost caught up, but you might have to wait before you get paid."

"Don't worry about that," Zander said taking her hand. "We'll work something out."

"Do you think I'll be able to keep my job after all this is over?"

The question took Zander by surprise.

"I very much doubt it. Why would you want to stay in a position like that anyway?"

"I don't know where I could find a job that pays as well with my limited experience."

"Did you ever consider that you are being paid well because Tony expects you to have sex with him whenever he wants?"

April looked like a whipped pup.

"I never really thought of it that way."

April was naïve. There was no doubt about it, and that made her entire situation even that much more appalling. Zander could feel the anger stirring in his chest and knew he needed to let it go or the whole situation would get out of hand.

"Zander and I will discuss this and get back to you," Audrey said. "We'll call you, or you can call us anytime."

"That will be true especially if you feel threatened for you or Johnny's safety," Zander added.

April got up on shaky legs.

"Thank you very much for your help. I feel a little better."

"Try to keep your distance from Tony as much as possible," Audrey said.

"I'll do my best."

"I know you will but so will we. We are here to get you out of this mess."

April nodded and left the conference room. Audrey and Zander looked at each other, until they heard her going down the stairs.

Zander was about to speak, when Audrey cut him off and gave him the Cliff Notes' version of what April had told her. Zander listened until she was finished. He got up and walked around the conference table and then sat back down on the same chair.

"Damn it. This is going to take some research."

"My thoughts as well. How are we going to get what we need?"

"I think I will start with Max. He would be able to tell us if there's anything in Ritz's background that would make us proceed with extra caution."

"Seems like you count on Max to do many things. Do you think we should maybe back off on that?"

"Max loves the intrigue. Besides, I'm just asking for info. It would just take him one call to get what we needed."

"Okay, that's a great place to start. Then what?"

Zander could see Audrey's wheels turning and was eager to share her idea.

"What do you think we should do?"

"While we're waiting for the information from Max, why don't we go over and nose around in Leadville. Let's see what turns up."

Zander knew there was more than she had just told him.

"Let's hear the rest."

"Well, I thought you might look around and ask some questions as a tourist. Maybe you could stop at the Chamber of Commerce office and tell them that you are looking for a place to expand your business. You could ask about existing companies."

"What kind of expansion?"

"I don't know. Do I have to think of everything?"

"Understood. What will your role be in this deception?"

"I think I will apply for a job at this shipping company."

"Do you think that's wise?"

"We need to get the lay of the land. What better way than have someone check it out from the inside?"

"What if he offers you a job?"

"Better yet."

"I don't think I like the direction where this idea is headed. This guy might be dangerous. We already know he has no regard for people who work for him."

"I know all that, and I can see your point. We just can't waste time when April's sanity is on the line like this."

"I know. Let me kick it off by calling Max. Maybe he can put a rush on the information if he's not busy."

"Good idea. I'll call April and let her know what we are thinking."

"Don't give her a time line. Just tell her not to be surprised if you show up at her workplace some day," Zander said.

"Why wouldn't we tell her when we are coming?"

"I don't know if she's strong enough to handle that kind of information without drawing attention to herself. I think it would be better to have it come as a small surprise. She would know we're coming but not exactly when, so there would be less pressure on her."

"I think she could handle it."

"She's young. She has no experience in matters like this. It would be wrong of us to put her in a situation like that. She's got enough stress in her life right now."

"I might see a stronger woman there than you do."

"I think you see some of yourself in her. She will be a strong woman someday, but that day has not arrived yet. She is not you nor will she ever be you. There can only ever be one." Zander reached over and messed up Audrey's hair.

Audrey knocked Zander on the head with her fist.

"Enough of this foreplay. You go call Max, and I'll contact April's cell phone."

Zander decided to go out in the lobby area and use the landline. He felt more comfortable with the old Bakelite phones. He liked that they had an earpiece and a mouthpiece. He didn't have to talk to a surface that looked like a small piece of glass. It was difficult for him to hear on cell phones, because he pushed it too tight against his ear. Audrey usually tried to get him to hold it away from his ear without much success.

Max wasn't available. For some reason, Mona answered his phone. Zander explained the dilemma and wondered if Max would be available to give him some information.

"I'm sure he would be happy to help. I've got him in Key West doing a grocery run. He needs something to get his mind off all these mundane things I assign him," Mona said.

"That would be great, Mona. We are in a tight time frame and need some info as soon as he could find the time."

"I'll see that he works on it immediately. He left his phone here on purpose, so I couldn't contact him. I would call him right now, otherwise. Give me the details."

Zander filled her in on what he needed. Mona wrote everything down and read it back to Zander when he was through. She didn't want to miss anything important.

Zander confirmed the information and told her she was a great stenographer. They shared a little small talk and then Audrey came into the room, and Zander told Mona he needed to let her go.

"Don't you and Audrey be strangers," Mona said and the line went dead.

Zander realized that Max had filled her in on Audrey's new name. There might be two better friends somewhere, but Zander knew there were none better in his life. He turned to Audrey.

"What did April say?"

"She's nervous, of course. I think we need to wait a few days before we go down to Leadville. It would give her time to calm down. She's going to be jumpy. I don't want us to add to the problem."

"No, you're right. We need a little time for Max to get back to us with the details on Antony Ritz."

"What did he say?"

"He wasn't there. Mona answered and she'll give him the details. We should hear from him in a day or two at the most."

"Good. I need to see your new sign, and then let's go to the Branchwater. We could get an early lunch."

"I like that idea. Hope you like the sign."

"After lunch we can come back here and put the finishing touches on the office."

Zander groaned.

"I thought we were finished."

"We're finished when I say we're finished. We need to add some decorative touches."

"I see. I have no idea about decorative things. You'll need to tell me what to do, and I'll follow your directive."

"I hope you do this with a positive attitude."

"I doubt if that's possible. I could always just stay at the Branchwater while you finish up." Zander looked at her, hopeful.

Audrey slugged him in the arm and after Zander rubbed away the sting, the two of them walked arm-in-arm down the stairs and down the street toward the Branchwater. They paused only to have Audrey give her opinion of Zander's sign.

It was passable, and Zander knew it was about all he could expect.

26

Elaine Taggart left Kevin's condo happier than she had been in months. After she thought about it, she knew it had been years since she had any kind of joy in her life. She drove her Toyota hybrid home without concern.

Elaine spent money on herself because she had no one else in her life. The hybrid automobile was important to her. She was worried about the environment, and trying not to leave a carbon footprint was important to her.

Connie McGill, who was following Elaine at a comfortable distance, did not share that same feeling. She drove a gas-guzzling four-wheel-drive Jeep. It was the biggest one the company made. She felt safe in the vehicle and knew that anyone who hit her would get the worse end of the deal. She would take safety over the environment every time.

Connie's mission was to head off this relationship before Kevin Grienne put another woman in harm's way. She had come to work at the office after Kevin and was quite familiar with his past before starting her employment. It was, after all, why she had taken the job in the first place.

***

McGill had been Connie's married name. The marriage lasted almost a year. Sean McGill was a bad drunk, and unfortunately for Connie, he was drunk most of the time. He had always been the life-of-the-party type of guy. Connie had been drawn to him immediately because he had a way of making her laugh. Sean never saw a pub he didn't like and frequented one almost every night. He would seldom come home without being rip-roaring drunk. If Connie made the mistake of confronting him, she would become his punching bag. It had always been her mission to change him. She realized after nine months that it would not be happening. Her mission changed, and she needed to figure out a way to get rid of him. He didn't work and lived off what Connie made. It was a deal worth taking and one not lost to his sober self.

Sean was a sweet man when he was sober. He treated Connie gently and with tenderness. Then he would get drunk again. Connie tried to get him to leave when he was sober, but his sobriety always included a terrible hangover. He would cry and promise to change if Connie would give him another chance. Before Connie could agree and talk about consequences, he would hug her and go out and get loaded. When Connie finally had enough, she knew she would need to do something drastic. Her sister came to stay for a visit and together they discussed what the two of them could do. Leaving and finding new employment never appealed to Connie. It would be admitting defeat and give Sean all the power. It was ironic in Connie's mind that her maiden name was Powers, and she had given it all away to this man.

Her sister, Margaret Powers, was a great sounding board. After the two talked about their options, the one they always came back to was the total elimination of Sean. Connie knew the possibility would be easy enough when Sean was passed out after one of his benders. The problem would be disposing of his body. That would take some planning and help from Margaret. Together they explored the area hoping to find some place to get rid of Sean's body. There was a road that snaked through an Indian reservation just off I-75 to the west of Ft. Lauderdale. After it passed the reservation a few miles, there were Everglades on both sides of the road. It was a perfect place to dump a body. They could weight it down with something and leave it for the gators.

Margaret waited for the call from Connie. When it came, she rushed over and found her sister had rolled Sean's corpse into some gardening plastic. Sean was of Irish descent and a small man like so many others of his ancestry. Connie tied two ten-pound barbells to a burial cocoon with some yellow rope she found in the garage. Margaret thought they would need more weight to keep the plastic and body from floating up. They found a half dozen bricks in the garage that were left over from the new pool apron Connie had installed. They decided to stuff them in the plastic before they put the body into the glades. Together, Margaret and Connie put the body into the trunk of the car and drove it out to the site they had agreed upon. Everything went as planned, and with the help of the headlights of Connie's car, they watched the body sink into the black water.

Margaret put her arm around Connie not knowing how she would react. Connie looked out into the Everglades.

"Well, that's done. I could use a drink."

Margaret reacted by dropping her arm.

"You seem a bit too comfortable with all this."

"You didn't have to live with him and put up with his abuse."

"Have you thought about what you'll say when people ask about him?"

"I'll tell the truth. I'll just say he went away." Connie smiled to herself.

"What about family. What will you tell them?"

"I doubt if he has any. I've never met anyone from his side. He never talked about family."

"Let's leave. This place is giving me the creeps. I think I see eyes out there."

"Could be gators or snakes or panthers. They've got a lot of things that can kill you out here."

"Including us."

They laughed at the joke, but the humor seemed hollow. On the way back to Connie's home, they talked about their lives and what was happening with each of them. Connie was speculating, because she was finally free of Sean's control. Margaret, on the other hand, was dealing with another problem. Her sister Demi was in trouble.

"Demi's got herself into a situation, and I can't talk sense to her."

"Now what?" Connie knew their little sister had a flair for the dramatic. She usually got herself into trouble. Connie and Margaret bailed her out of situations countless times. It was compounded by her deep depressions after her extreme highs. That's where the problems always ended.

"She's involved with this man. He's older and she thinks he's the one."

"The Powers girls are such good judges of character in our men, aren't we?"

"Ain't it the truth? I'm worried about this one, though. I've tried to check him out, and there is nothing out there. I can't find a thing."

"That's interesting. Maybe you could follow him and find out something about him that way."

"Good idea. I might just do that."

"Just keep me in the loop, and if you need my help, just call. I owe you."

"You certainly do."

The next time Connie and Margaret saw their sister, Demi, it was at her funeral. Margaret went on a mission after that, and Connie lost track of what was going on. Then, she got a call from Margaret saying she was hot on the trail of Kevin Grienne and thought that maybe she would need Connie's help soon. Nothing was planned, and it would take a great deal of patience.

Connie never took the time to go back to her maiden name. No one ever asked about Sean. She supposed they all thought he had left her. It was the perfect scenario, and it made a name change less important.

Connie had been working as a private counselor with some success. She had a small office in a building across from the hospital. There were friends at the hospital who were happy to refer patients to Connie. She wasn't getting rich but making enough to be able to live in southeast Florida.

Everything changed the evening she got a call from Margaret.

"I'm ready to make my move on Kevin Grienne."

"What do you need me to do?"

"He works at some federal place. I want you to check it out." She gave Connie the address.

Connie thought the place sounded familiar, but she said she would check it out and get back to Margaret by the next morning. She drove to the address and realized why it sounded familiar. It was indeed a governmental institution, and she had worked with people who had come from there and still needed follow-up counseling.

She called Margaret the next morning and told her about the place.

"He must be a counselor or psychiatrist or something. You need to be careful. He has many resources available to him."

It was quiet on the other end of the phone.

"He's responsible for our sister's death, and I plan on making him pay the ultimate price."

"You'd better go slowly. Think this thing through."

"I've thought it through, and I need to do something."

Connie thought her sister was not thinking clearly, and it concerned her.

"How can I help you with this problem?"

"It's something I need to do myself. But I may need your help with the body. I just haven't thought that through yet."

"You need to call me with exactly what you are planning to do. I'll need to be close in case you need help."

"He likes sex. I know it, so I'm going to be the bait."

Connie knew she had everything in all the right places. She was stunning from head to foot. She also knew it was uncharted territory.

"Discretion is the key word here. You don't know enough about this guy. He might be dangerous."

"Not as dangerous as me."

Connie was alarmed at her total disregard of any personal safety.

"When are you planning to make good on this threat?"

"I don't know. Soon, I hope."

"Call me with the details when you know more." Connie said.

"You know I will."

But she never did.

The next time Connie saw Margaret was when she had to identify her remains in the morgue. It was then she made Kevin Grienne her life's revenge. She would do what her sister had failed to do. She would be smarter and less emotional.

Connie never grieved for her sister. There was no time to grieve. Later, after Kevin Grienne no longer walked the face of the earth, there would be time enough.

Connie closed her counseling business and got a job at the same government facility.

***

Connie pulled into the parking lot and saw Elaine drive into her apartment garage. She parked in a space across from the garage and walked over as Elaine got out of her car.

"Elaine, we need to talk."

Elaine jumped and dropped her keys. She looked out and recognized Connie.

"Connie, you scared the hell out of me. Are you following me?"

"Yes, I am. I'm concerned that you might be in danger."

"What are you talking about? What danger?" Elaine asked.

"Are you seeing Kevin Grienne?" Connie knew she was but wanted to give her the chance to tell the truth.

"What do you know about that? I don't like people prying into my personal life."

"You might be glad I did when you hear what I have to say."

"What's that?"

"Not here. Can we go somewhere? This might take some time, and I want to be sure you know the exact nature of this danger."

Elaine was uncomfortable inviting Connie into her apartment.

"There's a sports bar over a block. We could go there."

"Perfect. We could both use a drink. Let's walk, just in case."

"Just in case of what?"

"You might be followed."

They walked toward the bar in silence. Connie never liked prolonged silence. She felt it had a negative effect on future productivity.

"You've done a very good job of keeping your relationship with Kevin Grienne a secret."

"We were pretty much told that it was frowned upon when we were hired."

"I remember, and yet here we are," Connie said.

They sat at the bar and ordered drinks. Connie wanted to fill in her story without some wait staff coming around. When they got the drinks, they went to the far side of the bar and found a booth.

Connie finished most of her drink before she felt loose enough to tell her story. It was a long rendition and took the better part of the rest of the evening. Connie could only hope that when she finished, Elaine would see that Kevin Grienne was a psychopath that needed to be eliminated.

27

Audrey and Zander worked at finishing the last of the office details the next few days, and things were almost perfect. At least that's what Zander thought. Audrey would never be satisfied, he figured. He needed to get her to focus on something else so the office would become less of a problem.

Zander suggested they put together an ad that could be listed under "Services" in the paper. They could keep it in the paper weekly for a year and see if it paid off. Audrey liked the idea and began to sketch out want she wanted in the ad. Zander made the coffee, and they were badgering back and forth when his phone rang. Zander looked at the caller ID.

"It's Max."

"Hurry and answer it. Put it on speaker," Audrey said.

"How do you do that?"

Audrey rolled her eyes and grabbed the phone from Zander's hand. She punched a button and put the phone on the desk. She motioned for Zander to say hello and rolled her eyes again.

"Hello, Max," Zander said finally.

"Back at you."

"Hi Max, it's me Audrey."

"I'm happy to hear your voice. You sound good."

"She is and feisty like always," Zander said.

"And you are the same old asshole," Audrey countered.

"I can't argue with that logic," Max said. "I have some information that might be of interest to you, Zander."

It sounded to Audrey like she was about to be dismissed so the men could speak privately. She was having none of it.

"Before we go any further, Max, you should know that Zander and I are now partners in this little investigation venture."

"I see. So, what you are telling me is to proceed carefully with how I relay information from now on," Max said.

"Exactly. We both need to be involved."

"Maybe, I'll just tell you. Seems like the safer move."

"Very funny," Zander said. "What have you found…for us?"

"This Anthony Ritz has been on the radar of a few government agencies. He's small-time but has connections. From what I could tell, it has been mostly drug-related. He uses his company as cover for some cartels to ship product. He's very careful and never been charged, as far as I can tell. Oh, and he changed his name to Ritz from Ritzerelli. I guess he wanted it to sound less Mafioso and more American."

"Thanks, Max. It's good to have intel on a subject whose life we're about to disrupt," Zander said.

"There's more. Lately it seems he's branched out and is under suspicion for human trafficking."

"Whoa. That might change things. We need to know more. Maybe we shouldn't get involved with this thing," Audrey said.

Zander didn't say anything but caution reared its head for him, as well.

"There's been a crackdown on the Mexican border. Illegals wanting to get into the country are trying to find other ways to enter. Ritz is providing that service for huge fees. The cartels are also using his service to get their prostitution rings staffed. Unfortunately, most of these are young women and some boys."

"Why haven't they shut him down?" Audrey asked, incensed.

"He's slick. Just when they think they have him, he has a totally legitimate load crossing the border."

"Somebody on the inside giving him information?" Zander asked.

"That's the theory. ICE needs to clean up their act before they can shut this down. Maybe you are the answer here. No one knows about your little operation, so you could get around undetected."

"We aren't looking at this guy for any of that stuff," Audrey said.

"I know. Zander filled me in earlier. It could be that your interference on the part of the young woman could yield the bigger prize. You two need to shake the tree and see what falls."

"This is bigger than anything I have ever tackled before. I don't know if either of us is equipped to pull it off."

It was quiet on Max's end. Zander was ready to ask if he was still on the line, when he spoke. "I've been thinking about a vacation lately. Mona and I could use a change of scenery. What would you think if we came to Colorado for a visit?"

"We think it would be a wonderful idea," Zander said, with relief in his voice.

"You will be staying with us," Audrey said.

"No. That's not a good idea. We need to work this independently. Mona and I will find a hotel someplace. The less we're seen together, the better. Especially if this thing blows up, and it will blow up."

"I've got just the place. There's this hotel in the middle of everything in Breckenridge that will be perfect for you and Mona. It's close enough to Frisco and yet far enough to keep your anonymity intact."

"Great. We'll be in touch. I better run this by Mona before we get too far ahead of ourselves."

"I hear you, man," Zander said.

Audrey socked him in the arm.

"We can pick you up at the airport if you give us your flight details," Audrey said.

"We won't be flying. I have too much equipment to take with me. I could never get it on any airline, and it would be a hassle to try to have shipped privately. Mona and I will be driving."

"Better give yourself four days unless you're are planning to drive straight through."

"I need to sell this as a vacation to Mona. We'll be taking it easy and maybe taking in some of the sights along the way. Don't look for us before a week from today," Max said and clicked off.

Audrey hadn't realized he was gone and was making some small talk when Zander took the phone, shut it down, and put it in his pocket.

"What did you do that for? That was rude."

"Audrey, he was already gone after he told us he wouldn't be here for a week."

"That's weird. He didn't say goodbye or anything."

"That's Max. It's how he operates. He tells you what he thinks you need to know and keeps everything else to himself."

"I don't like that approach."

"Get used to it. You are here because of Max's peculiar methods. It took me a long to time to accept it. When I realized that his results were always spot-on, I decided to do what he said and worry about all the other stuff later."

"What are we supposed to do, sit on our asses and wait a week?" Audrey asked.

"No. Max told us to shake the tree. We just need to do that without getting involved with the smuggling end."

"Don't you think that will all be a part of it?"

"Not if we play it right. Max needs to be here to help before we venture into something from which there might be no return."

Audrey sat in the office chair at the receptionist desk, while Zander sat across from her on the desk. They were both in thought. Audrey broke the silence first.

"Should I contact April and tell her we're ready to get started?"

"I think that would be a good idea, so she isn't startled when she sees us at the business. Call her after work tonight."

"No, I think I'll go up to her place after dinner and talk to her in person."

"Always a better idea."

"What are you going to do?"

"Surveillance. I'm going to take a ride over to Leadville and get the lay of the land."

"Okay. I'll finish up the ad and get it to the paper. Maybe, I'll rework our card and get it to the printer's, so we'll have something to hand out with our number. How many should I have printed?'

"A couple hundred ought to do it."

Audrey nodded in agreement. Zander got up and moved toward the door.

"Why don't we meet up at the Branchwater later. I don't think either one of us will have time to make dinner this evening. We can pick something up at the bar."

Audrey frowned.

"I'm kinda sick of bar food. Why don't we go up to Breckenridge and find a nice place to eat for a change."

"Sure. Let's still meet at the Branchwater and grab a drink before we go. I'm going to have to let Fats in on some this."

"Do you have to? The fewer people in on this the better, don't you think?"

"I would agree, but you know how Fats is. He'll stick his nose into everything and probably screw it up if we don't include him."

Audrey realized he was right and waved goodbye. She looked back down at the ad.

Zander took his leave and bounced down the stairs. He had one leg in the pickup before realizing he hadn't spoken to either Jo or Burt in over a week. There was no hurry in getting to Leadville, so he decided to have a visit.

Burt was out, and Jo was sitting in her office with the door open.

"Anybody here?" Zander asked.

"In my office," Jo said.

Zander went in and sat down without being invited. He usually did that, and Jo didn't seem to mind.

"I haven't seen you and Burt around for almost a week, so I decided to stop in and say hello."

"It's about time."

"I know, and I want to thank you for this office thing upstairs. It's really given Audrey something to hang onto. She needed the diversion."

"Happy to help, but it's always better to have an entire building occupied. So you're doing us a favor as well."

"You gave it to us for a song, and I thank you for that as well."

"Burt and I discussed it, and we decided we wanted you to stay. We didn't care about the money, and you are just starting out. We would like you to succeed, and we know you are smitten over Audrey."

"We could pay more rent to be fair to you and Bert."

"How are you going to do that? You've got to have clients before you can generate income. We're just happy you're paying the utilities."

"Well, promise me that if the business takes off, you'll make adjustments in the rent. I've got money to pay more right now, and I don't feel right about it."

"No promises. We know you've got money. That's not what this is about. We want this to be something for you and Audrey to share and make productive."

"Like you and Bert?"

"Exactly like us. What do you suppose kept us together all these years? We worked together and made this a profitable business. By doing that, we developed a deeper respect for each other. If anything ever happened to Bert, I would close this place in a heartbeat, because I couldn't do it without him. That's what I want for you and Audrey."

Zander stood, went around Jo's desk, and gave her a hug.

"Thanks for the human relations lesson," Zander said.

"God knows you men need to be reminded now and again."

"I'm out of here. We've got our first client, and I need to do some background work."

"Sit back down. You aren't leaving until you tell me all about it."

Zander did as he was told. He always followed Jo's instruction and today was no different. The story lasted fifteen minutes before Zander had a chance to stop talking.

"You need to nail that bastard," Jo said, and then stopped to think. "She will lose her job over this one way or another, right?"

"We've already told her that was a given."

"When the time comes, bring her around. I think we are going to need some office help, and by the sound of it, you will too. Maybe together we can do something for this poor girl and her son."

"I like the way you think."

"Somebody has to think around here or we would all be sunk. Now you need to take care of the reason she hired you."

Zander left the building careful not to disclose the other part of the problem. Jo didn't need to know about Max's inclusion, at least not yet.

Zander thought about it all the way to Leadville.

28

Connie and Elaine had hunkered down in the booth at the sports bar down the street from Elaine's apartment. Connie could tell by the look on Elaine's face, that she wasn't a believer. Kevin Grienne had his hooks far too deep into her.

Connie reached into her purse and brought out the pictures of her two deceased sisters. It was difficult but something that had to be done. Elaine needed to see what a dangerous situation she had gotten herself into.

"He killed my sister, Margaret, but he could just have well done the same to Demi. He broke her heart and then tossed her away. She wasn't strong enough to recover from something like that."

"What happened?"

"She killed herself that's what happened. Then Margaret tried to hold him responsible, and he killed her. I'm sure it wasn't his first and won't be his last."

Elaine was trying hard not to believe, but Connie was making it difficult.

"I just don't see him being violent. He has never done anything to me to make me leery."

"He uses people to get what he wants or what he thinks he needs. Then he discards them. Sometimes it's emotional and sometimes it's physical. I think he gets off on it. It's his need for control."

"Seems bizarre to me. Why would he need to do things like that?"

"Because he's nuts. You can't find reasons for what people like that do. You just need to stay away from it."

"He hasn't done anything like that to me. I'm the one who has been pushing this relationship."

"Oh, my God, Elaine. This isn't a relationship. He needs something from you." Connie knew exactly what Elaine had been doing for Kevin. She had been checking her computer.

"I don't think so. He hasn't asked for anything."

Connie looked at her, until Elaine had to drop her eyes.

"Don't bullshit me, Elaine. I know what you've been doing for him," Connie said.

Elaine was hot.

"You've been spying on me? How could you do that?"

"I'm trying to save your life. Why do you suppose he wants information on my client, Audrey Wood? Didn't you think it was odd that he came on to you and then almost immediately asked for this favor?"

"He was actually more interested in this Zander character. He wanted more information about him." Elaine paused to think. "I just thought that he was being protective of Audrey Wood by making sure that this guy didn't have anything bad in his background."

"Sure you did. That's what you told yourself. You've worked at the job long enough to know that should have sent up a bunch of red flags."

Elaine knew what Connie had been saying should have made her wary. She also knew that she enjoyed Kevin's attention and would have done almost anything for him. She was beginning to have a few doubts, however.

"I may have let his charm cloud my better judgment. What do you think he's planning to do?"

"Well, he's stalking her for sure. After that, I have no idea. I only know that it can't be good. Audrey Wood is in danger and perhaps her friend, Zander, as well."

"What do we do?"

"You do nothing. I've got someone to work on this, and he is in contact with the people in Frisco. Kevin Grienne has to think that everything is normal, and he's in charge. You need to carry on like nothing has changed."

"I don't know if I'm a good enough actor."

"Listen Elaine, this is probably the most important thing you've ever done in your entire life. You made a mistake in stalking and finding Kevin's address. He doesn't take his conquests to his home, ever. That's the reason I'm telling you all this right now. You just gave him a reason to eliminate you. He doesn't like loose ends. Believe me, I know. I've been following him for some time now, and his protocol never changes. You could gamble your life savings on it."

Elaine sat back in the booth. Her very core was shaken. She should have known things were wrong from the beginning. It was so far out of her character to be the aggressor in any relationship, and yet here she was doing everything that was completely unnatural to her. Her life could be in jeopardy because of a few stupid decisions. The thought made her sit up.

Connie could see the change in her demeanor.

"What are you thinking?"

"I was thinking that this whole thing was my fault. Now, I'm sure it is not. Why should I take the blame for this psychopath? I just wanted to have some relevance in my life, and Kevin Grienne took advantage of that fact. I need to rectify it."

Connie smiled.

"Work with me on this. Together, I think we can put this guy away."

Elaine eyed Connie.

"When you say 'we' can put this guy away, what's your meaning?"

"What do you think? We're not going to worry about getting the law involved."

"Do you mean kill him?"

"Not necessarily, but I'm not opposed to the idea. We'll need to be very careful and see how everything plays out."

"I'm supposed to pretend that nothing has changed between us? How in the world can I do that?"

"Is the sex good between the two of you?"

"Better than good." Elaine was surprised the comment didn't embarrass her.

"Concentrate on the sex, then. You'll be too busy with that to concern yourself with the other details. That will be my job."

"I think that might be a possibility."

"There's just one thing. You need to stop being the pursuer, because he needs to take that role back. It will be safer for you, and never go back to his condo. You'll need to find other places to meet."

"You want me to take him to my place?"

"I wouldn't do that unless it was during the day and people saw you together. He likes to remain anonymous and keep his comings and goings away from prying eyes. Don't let yourself get caught in positions like that."

"This is making me nervous. What if I need help?"

"I'll give you my cell number. I think you should let me know whenever you are planning to meet. That should give us a way to keep him tracked whenever you're involved."

Elaine leaned back into the booth.

"I though that my life might actually turn around for the better. How could I be so naïve?"

"Your life will turn out for the better when we eliminate this bastard from the face of the earth."

Elaine realized at that moment that Connie would never be satisfied until Kevin Grienne was dead. She was somewhat surprised that she had similar feelings.

***

Kevin closed the door to his condo after he watched Elaine walk up the sidewalk toward her car. He disliked people in his home and now realized that Elaine Taggart would need to be eliminated. Since there would be some downtime before he could get going on his Frisco plan, he would need to continue to seek the comfort of Elaine's sexuality until everything came together. He had to admit, it was quite pleasurable, and she was more than willing. It just would never happen at his condo again. That was too risky.

He went back inside and fixed himself a nightcap. He sat at the table and reread the file Elaine had prepared for him. She did good work. The file was detailed. Kevin had to have as much information as possible if he was going to have any luck extracting Audrey from the Frisco area. He had no idea how he would do it and what would eventually happen to Audrey Wood. That was something he needed time to consider.

Kevin finished his bourbon. It was early by his standards, and he was wide-awake. He glanced at the file once more and then had an idea. He found a name and shut the file. It was time to make a call.

He got into his car and drove around, trying to decide where to look for a pay phone. They were hard to find, but he had a nagging thought that he had seen a bank of them somewhere. He remembered when he passed a billboard advertising the Dolphins football team. There had been a number of pay phones in the arena when he attended a game with a few co-workers. Kevin had never been a sports fan, but he tried to fit in by faking it. He was smart enough to keep his mouth shut when everyone else had his or hers open.

He needed to find another option. He thought about a convenience store or a gas station. He made a left turn and saw a strip mall. On the street side of the parking lot he saw a phone-from-car pay phone sign. The phone had a glass bubble around it, and it was lit up with signage and a security light. Unfortunately, it was in use. There was an old Chevy parked in front of it, and a guy was just hanging up the phone when Kevin pulled in behind him. The guy held up his finger to signal that he had one phone call left. Kevin waved him off and put his vehicle into park. He turned up the music on the radio and sat looking out over the strip mall.

There were ten businesses listed on the sign at the entrance. It seemed that most of them provided a service. There was an insurance agent, fitness center, satellite dish television seller, hearing aid business, and business-printing company. They were all closed for the evening. The remaining shops included a pizza delivery place, a liquor store, and a woman's clothing shop. The shop was closing, and Kevin saw the sales clerk turn the open sign around.

Kevin was amazed at the array of businesses trying to make it in Miami. Some of them did, but many had "out of business" signs posted on their front door. Retail was hard work, and Kevin had no interest in it. Liquor stores were interesting to him, however. He thought he could do a good job of marketing the products. The problem, as he saw it, was that there was a liquor store on every block of the city. The market was saturated. He felt lucky he didn't have to make a living in the business.

There was a knock on his driver's side window. It startled Kevin out of his reverie. He pushed the button and the window went down.

"Hey man, thanks for your patience. I'm planning a surprise party for my wife's anniversary, and I don't want her to hear me use the phone."

"No problem. I'm not in a hurry," Kevin said, trying to sound friendly.

"Well, thanks, anyway. I left a couple of bucks in quarters on the tray in front of the phone as a way of saying thank you. You have a good day."

Kevin watched as the man got back into his car and drove away. He was surprised when he said "her anniversary." He had heard that same line from other men over the years. It might be a comment concerning marriage, but Kevin was clueless.

He drove ahead and found the stash of quarters and put one into the slot. He dialed the operator and asked for the number of the Branchwater Bar in Frisco, Colorado. The operator said to wait one moment. Kevin waited more than a moment. She finally came back on the line.

"Would you like me to ring that number for you?"

"Yes, that would be fine."

Kevin waited a few more moments and heard some clicking sounds. The phone was ringing, and someone picked up the receiver.

"The Branchwater is located in the heart of the beautiful Rocky Mountains. This would be your prized and beloved libation server. How may I be of assistance on this magnificent and glorious eventide?" Fats asked in his usual vernacular.

Kevin hung up. He had talked to Zander and knew his voice. This voice was not his. He might be an employee. It made no difference. The Branchwater existed, and he knew that Zander had some role to play in it. It was the first step in making some kind of plan.

Kevin thought he might be able to step up his timeline. He was getting restless just thinking about it.

29

Zander made a few trips through Leadville over the years. The key word was through. There wasn't much to entice tourists to stop. Leadville was an old copper mining town and much of that had dried up. The environmentalists were happy about it. Coming down off the mountain one could see the scars left by the mining companies. Zander didn't like what he saw and usually went through town as fast as the speed limit would allow.

He needed to do some scouting and decided to drive around the community. He was happy he did. Leadville looked like it was reinventing itself. There were all kinds of shops that catered to visitors. Zander realized he was hungry and decided to stop at one of the restaurants. It might be possible to get some information on the Ritz Shipping Company in the process.

He found a place called Wild Bill's Hamburgers and Ice Cream. It sounded perfect. There were quite a few cars around the front, so

Zander thought it might be a good place. It was busy inside, and Zander found a seat at the bar.

A cute little server handed him a menu and asked him what he wanted to drink. Zander considered a few suggestions and settled on iced tea. He handed back the menu without looking at it.

"Give me your best hamburger."

"That would be a double burger with cheese," the server said.

"What kind of cheese?"

"All kinds." She took the menu and went over to the kitchen to place the order.

Zander wondered what she meant by the comment. He decided not to question someone whom he told to give him the best.

The server returned with his tea, and Zander thanked her. She looked him over and decided he was someone who might like a bit of conversation.

"Are you visiting or just passing through?"

"I am visiting and hoping to do some business."

"What's your line of work?"

Zander had to think quickly. He needed information on the shipping company so he needed to come up with something plausible.

"I market and sell equipment for ski resorts." He felt good about that lie. It was vague enough to be boring and most people wouldn't think twice about it.

"Why would you be trying to do business here? We don't have any ski resorts."

"What I'm looking for is a shipper that has access to all kinds of delivery systems. I heard about a place called Ritz Shipping."

The server stopped and stared at Zander before answering.

"They've got their company off the road about a mile north. It's in a reclaimed strip mine. There's a small sign at the entrance."

"That's the way I came in. I didn't see anything."

"You can't see the place from the road. It's easy to miss the sign. Where are you from?"

"My business is in Denver."

"I would think you'd have a better choice there."

"What do you mean?" Zander could see she wanted to make a comment.

"I would stay away from them."

"Why would that be?"

"I guess what I know is mostly from gossip, but where there's smoke there's fire. You know what I mean?"

Zander decided to try and get the young woman to tell him everything she'd heard.

"Why don't you tell me?"

The server went into detail about the rumor of drugs and smuggling humans from Mexico. She stopped when Zander's order came up and came back with his burger.

Zander looked at the sandwich and saw what she had meant about all kinds of cheese. There were at least five slices of cheese between the two patties. Not one of them was the same. Zander thought there must have been at least four thousand calories lying in ambush. He looked at the server, and she was smiling.

"We get that kind of reaction all the time. If I were you, I'd use the knife. It would be easier to eat."

Zander did as she suggested. He took the first bite, and it was delicious. Without a doubt, it was the best burger he had ever had.

"This is excellent. What a great suggestion. Thank you. Would there be anything else I should know about Ritz Shipping?"

"I may have said too much. It's all rumor, and I don't think they've ever been in trouble as far as I know."

"But…"

"Tony Ritz is a real creep. He comes in here sometimes, and I'm always happy when I don't have to wait on him."

"Why's that?"

"It's just the way he looks at me. I think he's a perv. I know of a few women who tried working out there and quit in just a few weeks. None of them will talk about it, but they stay away from there."

Zander knew why they had quit, and he knew why no one talked about it. Tony Ritz was good at intimidation. Zander realized he had a good source of information in front of him even though it came from the unsubstantiated rumor mill. Zander had no need to prove anything since he was not involving law enforcement.

"Is he married?"

"He has a wife and a couple of kids I think. They don't live here. I heard they have some kind of big estate up in Vail."

Zander filed that little fact away for future use.

"You've been very helpful. I may have to rethink my involvement with this company. I'd hate to get wrapped up with anything illegal."

"That would be a good choice. The guy is bad news." She went back to the register and added Zander's bill.

Zander finished the burger, and he was stuffed. He had planned on sampling the ice cream, but he left a third of the burger on his plate and had no room for anything else. The server dropped his ticket off as she went around and filled coffee cups of the other customers.

Zander looked at the bill and saw it was under ten bucks. He left the server a ten-dollar bill for the burger and another twenty for a tip. She was a nice person and had been very helpful.

As he was leaving, the server called out.

"Thank you so much. You made my day."

Zander was happy when he made someone's day. He was too preoccupied today, however, to dwell on it. He got back into his pickup and drove back north. He found the sign for the Ritz Shipping Company just before Route 24 split off with Route 91. Zander had come in on 91 and could see how he missed the sign. He paused at the entrance and decided to go in and try to negotiate some shipping deal. It was a change in plans. Originally, he and Audrey had decided to only do background work. Zander wanted to kick it up a notch. Things were going too slowly to suit him. Patience had never been one of his virtues.

He followed a curvy road into a fenced-in compound. It was huge, and there were a variety of trucks parked around the grounds. What caught his attention was the office building. Zander had expected to see some kind of doublewide trailer or a repurposed shack of some kind.

What he saw instead was a huge brick structure. It was two stories and had a carport-type entrance. The place looked more like some mansion one might see in the Hollywood hills.

Zander drove under the carport. It was similar to some he'd seen at swankier hotel entrances. He turned off the ignition and got out of the pickup. The door opened, and a man in a suit came out to greet him. Zander saw he had a firearm in a holster strapped to his side. He knew it was odd that a trucking company would need to hire muscle.

"Good afternoon. How can I help you?"

"I would like to visit about doing some shipping business."

"Do you have an appointment?"

"No. But I heard your company has resources. I'm from Denver, and I need to be able to rely on a company that has multiple means of getting product to my consumers." Zander thought he did a fairly good job of bullshitting.

"You need an appointment. Mr. Ritz is a busy man."

Zander wondered what he was busy doing. He hoped April was at her desk and not in the boardroom with Mr. Pervert.

"I came all the way from Denver. Could you just see if he could see me for a few moments?"

"I'm sorry. You'll need to make an appointment." He handed Zander a card. "Call that number during business hours and someone will set something up."

Zander looked at the card.

"You mean I've got to come up here and make another trip?"

"That's exactly what I mean. Now, before you waste any more of my time, I would suggest you be on your way."

Zander got the hint and got back into the truck. He had come for information, and he had enough of it to make a plan. He looked over at the entrance and saw April coming down the steps from the second floor. Her hair was disheveled and her eyes looked terrible. He knew why Tony Ritz was too busy to see him.

Zander was pissed. He reached for the door handle thinking he might rush the guy at the entrance and give him a shot of "Old Sparky." He reached for his boot and saw the guy looking at him. He had his hand on the holster at his side, making no effort to hide that he was packing a firearm.

"So much for the element of surprise," Zander said to himself.

"Old Sparky" was no match for a pistol, and Zander had a change of heart. Even if he had taken the guy by surprise, there was no plan about how to proceed after that. Zander took his hand off the door handle and started the pickup. He dropped it into gear and saw the hired gun go back into the office area.

As he drove back toward Frisco on Route 91, Zander had time to think. He had got what he needed from his trip to Leadville. He had something nagging at him, however. There was going to be more to this job then he first realized. He had no idea how many other men were Ritz's bodyguards. The place was huge. They would need more than luck to get to Tony Ritz.

When he got to Copper Mountain, Zander was ready to turn right and return to Frisco. Something jarred his brain, and he turned left instead. Vail was a mere twenty miles up the road. It would be good to find out where Tony Ritz stashed his family. It would come in handy to have that piece of information. Zander was certain he would need to move fast once the ball got rolling, and he needed the information for the sake of saving time and effort.

He stopped at the city office when he arrived in Vail. He talked to a woman and told her he was looking for the address of an old friend. The woman checked her computer and gave him the address of the Ritz family. It was almost too easy.

Zander took a little tour of the area and drove past the house. He slowed down enough to see that it was more of palace than a house. It had three or four acres surrounding the structures. It pissed Zander off. No one needed a place like this. Zander thought that Ritz might have servants and that pissed him off even more.

Tony Ritz figured that, since he didn't shit where he ate, his family was safe enough in Vail. His business would never cross over to them, and he would be free to do whatever he needed to do in Leadville.

Zander realized as he drove back to Frisco that Tony Ritz made a huge miscalculation, and he and Audrey would be using it to bring him down. Zander would no longer be content to just help April. Tony Ritz needed to be destroyed.

30

Audrey was waiting for Zander at the office, because it was too early to meet at the bar. He saw his T-Bird parked in front of their new office. It was almost 4:00 when he climbed the stairs.

"Well, what did you find out?" Audrey asked, before he closed the door.

"Nice to see you, too."

"Oh, did I hurt your feelings?" Audrey gave him a short kiss on the lips. "Now, tell me everything."

Zander explained what he had learned. The most important thing was the high security.

"Did you see April?"

"I did. It appeared that things have remained the same. She looked very unhappy when I saw her."

"We've got to do something."

"I thought that's what we were doing."

"No, I mean we have to do something right now."

Zander thought about it.

"Maybe we should get her out of the situation immediately."

It was Audrey's turn to think.

"That won't solve the bigger problem, will it?"

"The bigger problem?"

"The next young girl that takes a job there will be in the same predicament. It looks like once you're in it's impossible to get out."

"I see what you mean. Tell me what you want me to do."

"Let's go to the Branchwater and talk about it."

Zander agreed, and they decided to walk over. Audrey took his arm, and they talked about other things. Zander was happy about that. This job was getting too intense, and there was no plan for a remedy. It always made him nuts when there was no solution at hand.

The Branchwater was busy. Fats' mission was to run around and try to keep the customers satisfied. Audrey and Zander took the two empty stools at the end of the bar. Fran came over and greeted them.

"You look busy. Do you need help?" Audrey asked.

Zander kicked her foot trying to keep her from volunteering their services. Audrey paid no attention.

"No, we're handling it. I look at it as a win. If we can keep Fats busy, he has less time to pontificate."

Zander laughed.

"Good luck with that."

He barely got the words out before Fats was at his side.

"What discourse do I need to be aware of this fine day?"

"There is nothing here that concerns you. There are customers that need your service," Fran said.

Fats turned around and went back to his job. Zander thought he saw his shoulders drop just a bit. He made a mental note to let him in on what was going on. That usually seemed to placate Fats and put him in his usual good mood.

Fran brought them both tap beers without taking their order. Zander looked at her questioningly.

"The keg is almost empty, and I need to change it. These are on the house, but you'll need to pay for your food if you are eating," Fran said, and went back to her other customers.

Audrey and Zander both took sips of their beers. Neither of them cared much for beer, but it was free, so they drank it.

"Should we order food?" Zander asked.

"Let's talk first. I want to know how we are going to approach this situation with April. I don't want it to get out of hand and put her in danger."

"I agree totally. That's why we need to wait until Max gets here."

"Do you think that's wise?"

"What does your gut tell you?"

"I hate it when you ask me things like that."

"I know, but sometimes your gut is all we have to go on."

"When will Max be here?"

"A couple more days, I think."

Zander could see that Audrey was struggling with the April issue.

"If you feel that strongly, we could get April out now. It would complicate things, but it might be another option."

"What would she do? She wouldn't have employment at that company any longer."

"I talked to Jo earlier, and she thinks she could use some part-time help. She suggested that we could use some receptionist time as well."

Audrey thought about what Zander had said.

"We couldn't pay her what she's making now."

"You let me worry about that problem," Zander said.

Audrey looked at Zander.

"I might have another idea."

"What's that?"

"Too early to talk about. I'll check things out tomorrow. You'll need to stay in the office while I do this."

"No problem. I need to get things into some kind of order."

Zander could tell by Audrey's look that the comment was not appreciated. She had been working on her own system, and Zander knew there would need to be much compromising if their partnership would be successful.

"Let's order food," Audrey said, changing the subject.

When they finished eating, it was almost eight o'clock. The evening crowd had thinned out considerably, and Fats was able to join them.

"I'll wager you have mixed emotions when you perceive the amount of green Fran and I are purloining from this beautiful Branchwater."

"I'm happy you are busy and making money. I'm sure with your personality we have only Fran to thank for it. You would have chased away the bulk of the people a long time ago."

Zander knew it was bullshit. Fats had a great personality for the bar business, and people liked him. It had always been easier for him, and more of a struggle for Zander to keep customers happy.

"Why do you think she is a partner in this business with me? I know my limitations, and she makes up for all those." Fats knew what to say and when to say it.

Fran smiled and rolled her eyes, but Zander could see she loved this goofball. He decided to tell them what was happening with April. He told Fats to sit, but before he could start the discussion, Audrey stood and leaned over and gave Zander a kiss on the cheek.

"I've had enough of this day. I'm going home."

Zander stood, intending to go with her. She pushed him back down.

"No, Fran and Fats need to hear all of this from you. Come home when you're finished." She walked out the front door.

"What is this necessary dialogue she speaks of?"

Zander took more time than he wanted explaining the latest happening with April. He also told them about Max and how he was coming to address the bigger problems of drug running and human trafficking. There were entirely too many questions from Fats to suit Zander. He tried not to be short with him, but Fran could see that Zander wanted to leave.

"Thanks for sharing all that with us, Zander. If we can be of any help just let us know," Fran said, giving Zander a chance to make his exit.

"I have a few more questions that need to be addressed," Fats said.

"Save them for another time. Can't you see your friend needs to go home?"

"But…"

"Goodnight, Zander," Fran said, and pushed Fats toward the back.

Zander took the opening and left. He sprinted toward their office, got in his pickup, and went back to their cabin. When he reached the cabin, he saw the T-Bird parked in front and noticed there were no lights on. It disappointed him. Audrey had gone to bed without him.

He parked the pickup and went into the cabin. He tried not to make any noise. He went to the sink for a glass of water without putting on the lights. He was about to take a drink when the lights went on. He turned and saw Audrey wrapped in a Packers blanket.

"I'm sorry. I tried to be quiet. Did I wake you?"

Audrey said nothing. She dropped the blanket, and Zander saw nothing but her beautiful body. She smiled and went into the bedroom. Zander had no time to finish his glass of water.

***

Zander was dreaming about something the next morning when he woke up to the smell of coffee. He looked at the clock and saw it was after 9:00 and wondered if he had ever stayed in bed this late. He got up and put on some gym trunks.

When he opened the door, he could see he was alone. He poured himself some coffee and noticed a note next to the coffee maker.

"I'm off on the errand we discussed yesterday. I'll see you this afternoon. I hope you had a good night."

Audrey was such a tease. Of course it had been a good night. It was the best. She was the best. He drank his coffee and wondered what she had up her sleeve.

He finished his coffee and got ready for the day. He would do what Audrey wanted and stay at the office. There was enough work to keep him occupied. He could always bother Jo if he got bored.

***

Audrey left the cabin after she made the coffee. She started up the T-Bird and backed out onto the highway and headed north toward I-90. She would be going to Aspen with the goal of finding and speaking with April's parents.

April had discussed them when they first met, but Audrey knew very little about either. She knew the father's name, John McCauley, but had no idea about the mother's first name. She felt certain the Chamber of Commerce would have some type of directory.

The ride to Aspen was pleasant especially when you were able to leave the interstate. There was more money in Aspen than in any other ski area in the entire state. People with means had homes with the bulk of them being part-time residencies. Audrey had been to Aspen twice with Zander since they had arrived together in Colorado. It was hard for her to justify the cost of living there. Movie stars, musicians, corporate bigwigs, and anyone with money seemed to have a place there as a status symbol.

Audrey had to admit, that she enjoyed all the high-end shops in the downtown strip. She enjoyed them right up until the time she saw the prices. They were insane, and it soured her. Still, it was an interesting place to visit.

She stopped at the chamber office to look for an address for John McCauley. The woman behind the desk looked up at Audrey and appraised her in one glance. She looked back down at some pretend work. Audrey noticed a wall of brochures and went over and grabbed a few. The woman noticed.

"Perhaps I could help you with something?"

"Perhaps you could," Audrey replied in the same tone of voice. "I'm looking for the address of a John McCauley."

The woman looked at Audrey but said nothing. Audrey stared back at her until the woman became uncomfortable.

"I'm afraid we can't give out that kind of information."

"Then we're going to have a problem. I'm here on official business," Audrey handed her one of her new cards.

The woman looked at it and pushed it back.

"It changes nothing."

"Well, of course it does. You can deal with me on an informal basis, or we can call in the state police. You see this is a matter of their missing daughter. I was hired to find her, and I'm bringing them the information they paid me to get," Audrey lied but felt it was a good lie.

The woman looked at Audrey for a moment. She decided that it would be better not to involve anyone else in the matter. She pulled out a directory and paged through it, until she found the address. She took out a pen and a sticky note and wrote something down. She handed it to Audrey.

"Your heavy-handed tactics are not appreciated in this community."

Audrey looked at her and decided to have some fun with the snooty woman.

"Well, kiss my ass if you aren't some hoity-toity bitch. You're working in a chamber office. Does that make you one of these rich assholes that think everyone owes them some kind of adoration? Maybe, you're just one of those wannabes. I am not buying it, sister. But thanks for the address. You just saved yourself a whole shitload of problems."

Audrey was quite satisfied at seeing the look on the woman's face, as she left the building.

31

The ride to the address of John McCauley was a pleasant one. It was a beautiful day, and the pines smelled like a glass of gin. The houses were on acres of land and not feet. It was almost too much to process in a single moment.

Audrey stopped at the driveway's entrance. There was no gate, and that surprised her. The house was big but not ostentatious like so many surrounding the property. Audrey couldn't help but think there might be some hope for these people. She hoped, for April's sake, it would be true. The sign on the mailbox read: John and Margery McCauley. Audrey made a mental note of her name as she proceeded up the drive.

The house was a simple two-story with four or five different rooflines. Audrey supposed there was something about it in the building code. The front door had a doorbell stuck into the brickwork. Audrey pushed it once and then again for good measure. She was ready to knock on the door in case the bell was out of order when the door opened a crack.

"Can I help you?"

Audrey decided to take a chance.

"Would you happen to be Margery McCauley?"

"Yes, and who are you?"

If there was a chance at shocking the woman, it might not get any better than this, Audrey thought.

"I'm here concerning your daughter, April."

The door slammed shut, and there was a moment when Audrey thought she had blown the chance to talk to April's parents. Then, she heard the chain slide out of its track, and the door opened wide.

"Come in and keep your voice down."

Audrey stepped through the door into a room. It was small and had one chandelier hanging from a ten or twelve foot ceiling. There was no furniture. Audrey turned and looked at Margery. From the information April had given, Audrey calculated that Margery was somewhere in her middle to late sixties. She looked much older. Time had not been good to her.

Audrey put out her hand.

"I'm Audrey Wood."

Margery ignored the gesture and motioned for her to follow. They moved to the left and entered a small sitting area that looked to be a reading room. The chairs were winged-back and massive. The room was small but quite comfortable. Audrey thought she would like a similar room in her new home if she ever got one.

Margery closed the door, trying not to make a sound.

"Please sit."

Audrey took a chair, and Margery sat across from her so they could speak quietly.

"What's happened to April? Was there an accident? Is she alive?"

The questions surprised Audrey. She had assumed there was little concern for her daughter, since they had been estranged for so long.

"April has hired my firm to do something for her. Physically she's fine, but emotionally she's in trouble."

Margery appeared confused at what Audrey had told her.

"Why are you here?"

"I think you know why I'm here. I need information about why you would turn your daughter out into the world when she needed you the most." Audrey wondered if she had come on too strong.

Margery dropped her head and sat motionless for a few minutes. Finally, she spoke:

"I never wanted it to be this way."

"And yet, here we are."

"I wasn't strong enough to stand up to John. He made his mind up, and that was the end of it."

"You could have stood up to him."

Margery shot Audrey a glance.

"Then what? I would be out on street along with April. I had no means of support. What was I to do?"

Audrey tried to brush away her feeling of disgust for this woman.

"You could have done what was right. April needed your support, and instead, you just threw her to the wolves."

"I tried to help her in secret. I even hired someone to help me give her support. John found out and went through the roof. He told me that if I ever tried to contact April again he would be through with me."

"I don't understand why you would want to stay with him. He threw your daughter and grandson out. You haven't even mentioned him. His name is Johnny, and he's a nice boy."

"She named him Johnny?"

"I suppose she named him after her father. April is a lovely, caring, young woman. She is a way better person than I would be under the same circumstances."

"I can't disagree. John came from a strict Irish background where weakness wasn't tolerated. He was a devout Catholic. When April came home pregnant, he couldn't get past the fact that she had premarital sex, let alone a baby out of wedlock. It was too much weakness for him to handle."

"That kind of thing has been happening since the beginning of time. Maybe it's time he came out of the Middle-Ages and into the here-and-now."

Margery stopped and looked at Audrey.

"Maybe you could talk to him? He's not the same man that April knew."

"Are you trying to tell me he's mellowed in his old age?"

"He's still unwavering and strong-willed. On the inside, I believe, he's had a change of heart."

"What makes you think that?"

"Little things he does and says to me. He's never been demonstrative with his feelings, but lately, he has said some things to me and...."

Audrey realized Margery was uncomfortable talking about the relationship she had with her husband. It was the old-school approach to life. Zander had a bit of it from his Dutch background, but he had worked hard at overcoming it.

"I understand. I came here to speak to both of you. April is in trouble and needs help. My partner and I will work at getting her free from that trouble, but she will need outside support. That's something that will need to come from someone other than us."

"Can you tell me what is happening to her?"

"I can, but I only want to tell the story once. If your husband is around I could tell you both."

"He's in the garden. He raises flowers and is quite good at it."

"Seems like an unusual pastime for someone of his ilk."

"Like I said. He's not the same man."

"What did he do?" Audrey looked around. "It appears he's done quite well for himself."

"He's always been a good businessman and provider. He was a big investor in the computer industry. Did you ever hear of Gateway computers?"

"Didn't they have the black-and-white box that looked like a cow's hide?"

"That's the one. When they sold out, he made a great deal of money on all the stock he owned."

"Did he have a position with the company?"

"He worked in the distribution end of it. He set up quite a network and made the company money by cutting transportation costs. It was one of the best systems in the country until the owners lost interest and sold out."

"Then what?"

"He didn't have to work. This all happened in North Sioux City, South Dakota. Iowa Beef Processors in South Sioux City, Nebraska, hired him to do for them what he did for Gateway. It worked out fine until they sold to Tyson Foods."

"Welcome to corporate. What happened then?"

"He retired, and we bought this place."

"So, April was mostly Midwestern-raised, until you moved here?"

"That's right. We had a good life, but John always wanted to live in the mountains. We should have waited until April went off to college before we moved here. She was lost without her friends and fell into the arms of the first boy who showed her any affection."

"That explains quite a bit. Thank you for that. We should find your husband and talk to him."

"He will try to intimidate you. You'll need to look past that."

"I can handle it, believe me."

"I do." Margery stood and gave Audrey a hug. "I'm so happy you are here. You may be the catalyst needed to get April back into our lives." She paused. "And Johnny."

Audrey was happy Margery said Johnny and needed no correcting. She followed Margery out to the garden behind the home. It looked like something out of Better Homes and Gardens.

"John, we have a visitor."

John looked over at the two women and got up from his knees. He brushed the dirt from his pant legs frowning all the while. Audrey decided to preempt any response he might have.

"My name is Audrey Wood, and this is no doubt the most beautiful garden I have ever seen." She put out her hand, and he looked at it. He took it, and Audrey thought she saw the makings of a smile somewhere deep down.

"What brings you here?"

"I have a story to tell you, and your wife and I think you'll want to hear it."

"Very well, why don't we sit over in the gazebo? The sun is warm today."

Audrey could tell he was trying to be civil, but it was difficult for him.

"Why don't I get us something to drink?" Margery offered.

"Just sit," John barked.

"Audrey decided to ignore his comment.

"Thank you, Margery, but that won't be necessary. I'm on somewhat of a time constraint."

"What's this all about?"

"This is about your daughter, April."

"What's she done now?"

"It's what's being done to her that should be of concern."

"I don't believe I need or want to hear any more," John started to get up.

"You sit your ass down, and hear me out." Audrey gave John a shove, and he fell back onto the bench.

"Who the hell do you think you're talking to?" John exploded.

"The biggest asshole in Aspen and probably all of Colorado. Sit there, and keep your mouth shut until I'm finished."

Audrey began April's saga and stopped only when she came to the part where she met Margery at the front door. The rest of their conversation from there on was privileged, and John would never hear of it from her.

Both Margery and John were quiet. It surprised Audrey. She was expecting him to explode and probably kick her out of the house. It never happened.

John looked at Margery and put his arm around her. She began to sob.

"Margery, I'm so very sorry. This is entirely my fault. My pride has ruined this family." John hugged her with both arms.

"It's not too late for this family. You can still do something to salvage what time you have left," Audrey said.

"What can I do?" John asked.

"You can give April and Johnny support when we get her out of this mess. Your grandson needs a grandfather."

"And our daughter needs a father and mother."

At that moment Audrey could see that Margery was taking back some of the power that she had lost over the years. It made her smile. Life in the McCauley household had just changed forever.

"Do I even have a chance of reconnecting with them? It's been such a long time."

"All you need to do is ask. You may need to stop being such an asshole though."

For the first time since she saw him, John smiled. He looked old right up until that moment. There was no doubt that April and Johnny would bring life back into this family. Now all that was needed was to solve the bigger problem.

John stood and walked over to Audrey. He grabbed her hand.

"I need to be involved in the solution as well as the aftermath. It's who I am, and I can help."

"Why don't you explain that to me."

"This guy is in transportation and shipping. It's what I did for years after I got out of the investment-banking merry-go-round. I still have credentials and can help you work something out. You need to infiltrate their business, and it doesn't sound like your partner has any idea on how to get that done."

"What's your idea?"

"Let me get started and work something out. Give me your card, and I'll contact you when I have a plan."

"As I said, we don't have much time."

"I'll have something by tomorrow afternoon at the very latest. I'll need to call in a few favors, but that shouldn't be a problem."

Audrey handed John a card with their phone number and other information listed. She liked that he might be another option but was hard-pressed to see how it would work.

"I can't promise that we can use you, but we'll certainly listen to any ideas that could possibly help."

"That's all I ask."

"I need to get back to Frisco. We've got someone else coming in who can help us if we need firepower."

"One more thing," John said.

"What's that?"

"Tell April I'm sorry, and that we will see Johnny and her soon."

"No, tell her that we're both sorry," Margery added.

Audrey liked what she heard.

On the way back to Frisco, she realized what a coup she had made with the McCauley family. She thought she might actually be pretty good at this investigative work. She would be sure to remind Zander of that fact when she got back to the office.

32

When Audrey drove the T-Bird in front of the office, she could see a note taped to the door. She got out of the T-Bird and grabbed the note. It was from Zander.

"I'm at the Branchwater. Come over when you get back."

She was mildly irritated. It was too early to close the office. She wondered if Zander was taking this business venture seriously. She decided to walk over to the bar to give her some time to cool off. She had great news, and she wanted to share it immediately.

When she opened the door to the Branchwater, she saw Zander sitting at a table with two people. She was on a mission and never bothered with recognizing the other people at the table.

"I thought you were going to wait for me at the office. It's too early to close the doors. We might have clients trying to contact us."

Zander responded by standing.

"You remember Max Kuhn, and this is Mona Kane."

Audrey was embarrassed at her rude behavior. Max had literally saved her life. He had become a close friend during her recovery. He was the only outsider that the doctors and counselors had allowed to visit. His warm and caring personality had done more to encourage Audrey's recovery than anyone would ever know. Audrey knew, however, and needed to correct her bad behavior.

"Max, I'm so sorry. My behavior was unforgivable. It's so good to see you." She gave Max a huge hug.

"I see your recovery has been complete and then some," Max said with a grin.

"I've got to keep my thumb on Zander always. You know how he is."

"Of course I do. It's a full-time job, and I'm just happy he has someone in such capable hands."

"Hey, I'm standing right here," Zander said.

Audrey ignored his protest and turned to greet Mona.

"Hi Mona, I'm Audrey. I've heard so much about you. Sorry I wasn't very cordial when I first walked in."

"No worries. I've heard much about you as well. Max shared what happened to you. Sounds like you've had quite a life."

"More adventures than most people could even dream about, I'm afraid."

"I've had my share as well. It makes us stronger, don't you think?"

"I think about it most every day. You need to tell me about your adventures, and we can compare notes."

"It's a deal. Why don't you both sit down and have a drink before the rest of the bar gets involved in all the theatrics," Max said.

Audrey ordered a beer, and Fats brought it over. Uncharacteristically, he turned and went back to the bar after he delivered Audrey's beer.

"What's wrong with him?"

"He's feeling left out. I'll get him up to speed later." Zander said.

"Zander's been telling me that there is a second issue besides Kevin Grienne that might need our help," Max said, changing the subject.

"I have some news in that regard." Audrey said, and explained what happened with her meeting with April's parents.

"Wow. That was some meeting," Zander said. "You always amaze me."

"You say that like you are surprised," Audrey shot back.

"Now kids, let's stop the bickering," Max said, putting his arm around Mona. "You should pattern yourselves after Mona and me."

"You mean that I should do everything she tells me just like you do with Mona?"

"Exactly. I've been around a long time, and life gets easier when you understand the pecking order."

"Aren't these boys just a scream?" Mona asked Audrey.

"They make us scream, alright."

"Well, I think that's enough of this pitter-patter. We may be able to use this John McCauley. It may be our ticket into the place." Max was thinking out loud.

"I've got his phone number. He's eager to help. I think he wants to show April he realizes the error he made and is here to make amends."

"This all has to happen quickly. We don't want to have loose ends when we have to deal with Kevin Grienne."

"What have you found out about him?" Audrey asked.

"My sources tell me they think he's almost ready to make a move."

"Sources?" Zander asked.

"Two people I believe Audrey may know."

Audrey looked at him questioningly.

"Connie McGill and Elaine Taggart."

"I know Connie. She was my counselor. I'm not sure about Elaine Taggart."

"She is a receptionist there. Quiet mostly. She has dark hair and a knock-out figure."

"Oh, I remember seeing her. She was always pleasant, as I recall."

"Another woman taken in by Kevin Grienne's tactics, I'm afraid. They're both ready to help us in any way they can."

"Is that such a wise thing?" Zander asked.

Max told them about her sisters, and what Kevin had done to them.

"There is such an extreme hatred that I think she may handle the whole problem for us if we let her. It would mean we would need to involve her directly. We would need to get both women here on short notice." Max said.

"I like that idea. Women scorned are a force to be reckoned with, for sure," Mona said.

"As soon as Kevin makes his move they'll inform me. I'll share what we've talked about and get them on the first plane here. It will need to be on your dime, however. Are you okay with handling their expenses?"

"Whatever you think. I just want Audrey to be safe. If this guy needs to be eliminated, then that's what we'll do," Zander said.

"Great. I'll deal with them later. Right now we need to deal with the Anthony Ritz situation." Max stood. "Let's go back to your office and make some calls. If we stay here we might drink too much and plan stupid things."

The four stood simultaneously, and Zander looked over at Fats. Fats tilted his head and raised his shoulders.

"I'll fill you in later. We'll be back."

The comment seemed to placate Fats, and Zander waved at him as they left the bar.

When they got to the office, Audrey went to the receptionist area and made her call to John McCauley. They agreed to meet at the Copper Mountain Golf Course parking lot at 7:00 the next morning. She gave him the watered-down version of what they were planning to do. She told him they would fill him in on the details on the way to Leadville. When she finished the call, she joined the other three in the conference room.

They were discussing the easiest way to infiltrate the Ritz office building. Everyone agreed the best approach would be stealth. There was too much muscle in the immediate vicinity. The trick would be to get inside and request a meeting with Tony Ritz. That would be John McCauley's job.

"Do you think he'll be an asset or detriment?" Max asked Audrey.

"He was an important guy in his day. He still has that aura about him. His daughter's future is at stake, and he wants to be a part of it once again. That is a huge motivator."

"It certainly is. Now what about April? What does she need to know?"

"She needs to know we're coming and that her father is involved, or she might blow the whole thing," Zander said.

"I agree, but Zander and I need to talk to her personally. We need to drive up to the motel."

"We can stay here and get things ready."

"No, you need to come with us. She needs to see you and know you are working with us. The more people she sees the more comfortable she'll be when we arrive. Zander and I will talk to her, and when we're finished, we can make your introductions. You can stay in the vehicle until then. She's quite shy but knows we're doing all we can for her."

"Let's go. We can take my Jeep."

"We'll take the pickup. She knows that vehicle and should keep her level of concern at a minimum."

The trip took just an hour. April was more at ease than either Audrey or Zander had expected. That was good. It was also good that the execution, of whatever was going to happen, would be the very next day. It gave April less time to worry about things she couldn't control.

Max gave her a .38 revolver that she could slip to Zander after he and John were searched. April said it would be no problem getting the pistol into the office building, because she was never searched. Audrey was not happy. She thought April should stay out of whatever mess they were about to create

Once they were back at the office, they decided to meet again at 6:00 the next morning. Zander asked if he needed to bring any weapons. Max assured him that he had everything they needed. It was a good thing, because the only weapons Zander had access to were the two chrome-plated Colts from under the bar at the Branchwater.

Max and Mona went back to their hotel for the night. Zander decided to go back to the bar and give starving Fats the information he felt he needed. Audrey was tired and went back to the cabin.

The bar was almost empty when Zander walked in. The bar business changed when laws became stricter. Revelers and bar flies went home earlier to avoid being charged with an OMVUI. Fats had seen the changes coming and added food at a crucial time. He was also smart enough to put in a number of televisions and call the place a sports bar.

"So good of you to return," Fats said.

Zander thought that he might be mocking him by the tone of his voice. He decided not to ignore it.

"Do you want to hear what's been going on, or are you going to bust my balls?"

"This must be of some serious nature," Fats said, ignoring Zander's outburst.

"We're making our move on April's behalf tomorrow morning."

"Do you need my expertise to be involved?"

"Absolutely not. We've got too much skin in the game the way it is. I don't need you and your pistols to screw things up. I think we've had enough of that anyway, don't you?"

"Most definitely so. I will serve as moral support only. Please inform me of the plans."

Zander was happy that Fats agreed, on his own, to keep out of the situation. He seldom had such an epiphany.

"How about we have a few beers? It should be worth the story I tell you."

"It's on the house for my friend and confidant. How did I comprehend such a transaction? I must be clairvoyant." Fats ran two beers and sat across from Zander behind the bar.

Zander told Fats everything. He learned a long time ago, that Fats was less trouble if he felt included in all details of whatever Zander was working on. When he finished, Fats sat quietly and appeared to be contemplating the information.

Zander finished his beer, and Fats took his glass and ran another from the tap. He put it in front of Zander and looked at him saying nothing.

"I didn't need another beer."

Fats said nothing.

"Why don't you say something? You're starting to creep me out," Zander said.

"I am concerned about all the things that could go wrong with your plan."

"We've got an ace-in-the-hole."

"Max is no superhuman."

"He's as close as you will ever meet."

"I want you to promise me that you will stay out of the fray."

"It may not be possible. There are just too many unknowns once we get inside the building. If things don't work out, Max will come in blazing."

"How will he know?"

"We'll all be wired. He and Mona will be monitoring our conversations from a short distance away."

"What is this guy, James Bond?"

"He's bigger than Bond. How do you think he's stayed alive all these years?"

"I don't know. I really don't know or understand the gentleman."

"And yet, it's because of you that he met Mona Kane."

"Wait. Are you telling me that was Mona sitting with you guys earlier?"

"The very same."

"I didn't even recognize her. She looks good. This guy must be good for her."

"She is, and she's good for him."

"See? My great timing always works out for everyone."

Zander got up and left shaking his head. Six o'clock would come too quickly to listen to any more of Fats' bullshit.

33

Audrey and Zander were up early. Audrey made the coffee after she got ready for the day. Zander took his turn in the shower and came out to a full pot. Audrey filled two "go" cups and gave Zander a piece of peanut butter toast.

"Is this supposed to be breakfast?"

"It's all we have time for. We need to get to the office. If what you tell me about Max and Mona is true, they will already be waiting for us.

Zander decided not to argue and ate his toast on the way out to the pickup. He took a sip of the coffee and burned his lip. He hoped the rest of the day would go better than the last few minutes.

True to form, Max and Mona were waiting in their Jeep in front of the office. Max rolled down his window and motioned for Audrey to do the same when they parked next to them.

"Let's go around back. I need to transfer some equipment, and I don't want prying eyes taking in anything that might delay or jeopardize our mission."

Audrey nodded and raised her window.

"Sounds like a James Bond movie to me."

"He knows what he's doing. We just need to trust him."

"I know all that. This whole thing makes me nervous. So many things could go wrong."

They both got out and met Mona and Max behind the office building. Max opened the back of the Jeep and took out a huge bag. Zander had seen it before.

"I have some weapons that you will need in case things go wrong," Max said, as he unzipped the bag.

He pulled out a long gun and handed it to Zander.

"Seems pretty large for an office building," Zander said.

"It's a shot gun and has ten rounds loaded with another in the chamber."

"I can't shoot a gun like that," Audrey said.

"You won't have to worry about that. You and Mona will ride with me in the back seat. I am going to say this only once. You will stay in the back seat until this is over. If shooting starts, you will both get to the floor and stay there until I tell you different. Do you understand?" Max was firm.

Both Mona and Audrey nodded.

"I want to hear you say it."

"We understand," they both said together.

"Zander and John McCauley will enter the compound together. Zander, you will take the .38 I gave to April, and put it in your waistband. I assume you'll both be frisked, so don't take the gun until after that. If things go wrong, and you are in the office with Ritz alone, shoot him in the head and wait until we get you out."

"What if we can't get in to see him?" Zander asked.

"Go back to your pickup and get this." Max handed him a 9mm with a suppressor screwed to the barrel. "If you don't need the shotgun for multiple bodyguards, use this to take them out singly. It should be quiet enough to get you to Ritz. Give the .38 to John just in case you need a little backup."

"How far away will you be parked?" Zander asked.

"Just down the road. We will monitor everything you say, and if things look problematic, we'll come in a-blazing."

"What are you planning?"

"Better if you don't know," Max said smiling.

Max went over exactly what Zander needed to say to Ritz to get him to back off April. The key would be to make him see how costly a venture it would be if he were to exact any retribution.

"This whole thing could have a number of different endings, so be vigilant. The object here is to eliminate the threat. If that means killing the target, then that's what we'll do. I want you all to understand the stakes here. This is not a man to be trifled with."

"What about all the other things he's doing? Are we going to ignore the smuggling and the trafficking?"

"You let me worry about that. That's not anything you need to be involved with. There are a number of agencies that will be contacted when we're finished here."

"Good to know. Let's move," Zander said.

He moved toward the driver's seat of his pickup, but Audrey stopped him. She put her arms around him and pulled his face next to her mouth.

"You need to be very careful. I need you to come back to me. I don't think I could go on without you." She kissed him, moved quickly to the Jeep, and got in the back seat with Mona.

Audrey's comment surprised Zander. He knew how much she meant to him, but Audrey had never really shared her feeling about him. He knew she loved him, but she kept her feelings private. Her comments made him realize how dangerous their plan had become.

Zander got into the pickup and found his way to I-70. He saw the Jeep following and decided to make sure they could hear him. There would be no voice communication from Max, but he was wired so they could hear Zander.

"Hey, if you can hear me, flash your lights three times."

He looked in the rearview mirror and saw the headlights of the Jeep flash three times.

"Great. Let's go." Zander moved the speedometer to 75 until he reached the turnoff to Copper Mountain.

He met John at the agreed spot, and the Jeep followed. When they got to John's car, both Zander and Max got out. Zander made the appropriate introduction, and John shook Max's hand. Zander saw his puzzled expression, and he told him he would fill him in on their way to Leadville.

It seemed to satisfy John, and he took out a briefcase from his car.

"Paperwork and some permits to make this all legal," John said, after seeing questioning looks from Max and Zander.

"Do you have any weapons in there?" Max asked.

"Just a small .22 pistol."

"Hand it over. You will be frisked, and we can't afford any surprises. We don't need people going off script."

John fished out the pistol and handed it to Max. Soon, they were on their way to whatever fate had in store for them.

Zander explained what they had cooked up the night before and what John's role would be in playing out their charade. By the time he finished, they were at the entrance of the shipping company. Zander looked at the rearview mirror and saw Max pull off the road into a small turnout. He flashed his lights three times.

Zander drove the pickup into the compound and found a spot to park away from the front door. He didn't want anyone to look into the truck and see the weapons. The pair got out of the pickup, and Zander stretched, trying to indicate a long drive. John reached back into the pickup, retrieved the briefcase, and slammed the door. They were both trying to be as relaxed and nonchalant as possible to avoid suspicion.

Zander was surprised that there wasn't a bodyguard or two lurking around the front entrance. The pair opened the front door and entered the building. They walked to the reception area and found April sitting at her desk. She got up when she saw them at the counter.

"Can I help you?"

Zander was pleased that she seemed calm.

"We're here to see Tony Ritz," Zander said.

"May I ask your names, please?"

Zander made up two names on the spot, and April wrote them down. She showed the paper to Zander, while avoiding any contact with her father.

"Would this be the correct spelling of both names?"

Zander looked and saw the note she had written about a camera above her head. Zander nodded and returned the paper.

"Mr. Ritz is in the yard at the moment but should return soon. If you'll have a seat, I'll try and contact him."

Zander and John went over to a seating area and sat. April turned and typed something on her computer. Zander assumed it was some type of paging device. A few seconds later the phone rang, and April picked up and told someone on the other end about the visitors wishing to talk to Tony. April waited a few seconds before getting up. She fumbled with something in her desk and then walked over to Zander and John.

"Mr. Ritz will be here in a few minutes. I think he's busy with some cargo in one of the trucks."

Zander knew it was code for either drugs or smuggling humans.

"Thanks. We can wait."

"Can I get you something to drink? We have coffee, soft drinks, and water," April said while she pulled up her shirt to reveal the .38.

"I think that maybe I would like that later," Zander said, knowing they would be searched before being able to talk to Ritz.

"I think I could use a cup of coffee if it isn't too much trouble," John said.

"Certainly." April turned and went into a side room.

Zander looked around the office and was impressed at the artwork on the walls. It might be something you would see in a big city on the walls of a large company. It seemed out of place for a small trucking and shipping company.

April returned with the coffee and handed it to John.

"Are you sure I can't get you something right now?" she asked Zander.

"Maybe a Coke or Pepsi. Either would be fine."

April went back into the room and returned with a soft drink. She handed it to Zander and returned to her desk. Zander looked to see if he could detect the .38 in her waistband. The gun was small and her blousy top covered the weapon well. There was nothing bulging to catch the eye.

John and Zander tried their hand at small talk. Mostly, it was about the business John was in and why he needed help with shipping in Colorado. It sounded convincing, and if anyone from the company were listening, it would be typical conversation from two businessmen.

Five minutes turned to fifteen, and fifteen turned to thirty. Zander was getting antsy.

"How much longer do you think we will need to wait?" Zander said, with some irritation in his voice.

"I'm sorry. Mr. Ritz is on his own time schedule. It won't do any good to try and hurry him along," April said.

Zander's motive was to make sure their behavior was typical of businessmen who were kept waiting. In truth, he was irritated, because he wanted this confrontation to be over.

Five minutes later, the door opened and in came the same goon that Zander had confronted in his reconnaissance mission.

"What the hell? I thought I told you to make an appointment," the goon growled.

"I did. Check with the receptionist."

The goon looked at April, and she held up a ledger sheet with the two made-up names.

"Mr. Ritz will be with you in ten minutes."

Zander groaned.

"We've been waiting for almost an hour as it is."

"Tough shit. If you don't like it, you can leave."

"Crazy way to do business, if you ask me," Zander said.

"Nobody asked you. Both of you stand up. "

"What for?"

"Mr. Ritz doesn't allow weapons in his place of business, so I'll need to search you both."

Zander knew that was a lie. There were all kinds of weapons around the compound. Ritz just didn't allow weapons on anyone but his employees. Zander wondered if he had received many threats on his life. He smiled when he thought of how he was going to get a large one today.

They stood, and the goon did a once-over. Satisfied they had no weapons, he went to work on the briefcase. Seeing nothing of interest, he handed it back to John and went over to April's desk.

"Tony will be in his office shortly. He'll call down when he's ready. You show these two to his office. Make sure that's the only place they go."

April nodded and watched the goon leave through the back. Zander could see she was afraid of him. He hoped the goon had not taken advantage of April as well.

No one said anything for the next ten minutes. All three jumped when the phone rang. April answered and hung the phone back up.

She stood and walked over to John and Zander.

"If you would follow me, please."

She put her hand on the handle of John's briefcase. He started to protest.

"Please, it's my job," April said.

Zander watched her slip the .38 from her waistband into the briefcase. It was done with such ease that Zander doubted that John had even noticed.

April turned and led them up the stairs to Tony's office.

It was game on.

34

April opened the door and announced the visitors. Tony never looked up. He motioned for the two to sit in chairs arranged in front of his desk. April left them and closed the door.

Zander and John sat down and waited to be recognized.

"What do you want?" Tony asked.

Zander thought it was a ruse to intimidate them, and he would not be playing along today.

My client is in need of a shipping company to move his product. Your company seems to have the resources he needs.

"What is the nature of your business?"

"Why does that matter?" Zander asked.

Tony finally looked up.

"You need to be very careful how you talk to me."

Zander smiled.

"I was wondering why you would care about what our business involves. Rumor has it that you just aren't all that concerned about what you transport as long as there's a profit in it."

"I don't know either of you. I won't be involved in any illegal activities. If you can't tell me what you need to be transported, I can be of no help. We might as well terminate this meeting." Tony stood up.

Zander could see that he was a small man. He thought he could take him with little effort. Zander was contemplating his next move, when John took over the conversation.

"Let's try and start over here. Seems like some egos are at play, and we can avoid all that." John reached in the briefcase, took out a stack of papers, and slid them across the desk to Tony.

Tony looked over the paperwork and nodded to himself.

"I've heard of you. You seek out alternate shippers to keep your fleets small while making sure everything gets to where it should go. Is that about it?" Tony asked, as he returned the paperwork.

John opened the briefcase and put the papers into it. If Zander thought John hadn't noticed April slip the .38 into the case, he was wrong. John's hand came out of the briefcase holding the gun in his right hand.

"No, it's not about it."

Tony recoiled, and Zander took the opportunity to add to the conversation.

"Keep your hands where we can see them. Put them both on the desk."

Zander figured Tony had some kind of button to push somewhere that would get his guards to his side in a moment's notice. He was almost certain he had a firearm located in a desk drawer.

Zander reached for the .38, but John pulled away, holding onto the gun and aiming it directly at Tony's head.

"What do you want?" Tony asked.

Zander was surprised that Tony showed no fear. Most people would be nervous when someone held a gun to their head.

"I want you to stop raping my daughter," John said, keeping the gun pointed at Ritz's head.

Tony's mouth dropped a bit. Zander could see that John had finally struck a nerve.

"Or what?" Tony asked with challenge in his voice.

Zander saw an opportunity to try and defuse the situation before John ran out of patience.

"Or we tell your family what's been going on here. I believe you have a nice place up there in Vail. We have a woman watching the house, as we speak. It would only take a phone call, and your life will change forever," Zander said, lying about the woman.

"Do you expect to leave here alive?" Tony asked. "My men are all around, and I take threats to my family and me very serious."

"Maybe, I'll just shoot you," John said.

"You'd be dead before you got to the door," Tony said smiling.

Zander thought he might have misread the situation. He decided on another tack.

"Max, if you're listening, we may need an exit plan."

Tony leaned forward but kept his hands visible.

"What kind of bullshit are you trying to run here?" Tony asked, but with concern in his voice.

Zander lifted his shirt and showed the mike taped to his chest.

"We've got a few tricks up our sleeve. One way or another, you are going to comply with our demands."

"It's never going to happen," Tony said, and started to move his right hand toward the desk drawer.

John never gave him a chance to move further. He shot him in the forehead. Tony's head snapped back and his chair went over. He was dead when his body hit the ground.

John's action stunned Zander for a moment. He never expected John to do anything so rash. He looked at him. John was still holding the gun. Zander jerked it away from his outstretched hand. John showed no resistance and turned toward Zander.

"I did it for April. The bastard needed to die."

"We need to move," Zander said, as he pushed John through the office door into the corridor.

The pair flew down the stairs and noticed April was nowhere around. That was good. She followed the directions they gave her to the letter. Zander was about to reach for the handle of the entrance door, when he heard an explosion. It sounded like it was coming right outside the door, and they both fell to the floor for protection. There were five or six other explosions that sounded farther away, and Zander took the opportunity to open the door a crack and look out.

Max's Jeep was parked in the overhang. Zander could see Mona in the backseat, but Audrey was nowhere in the vehicle. Zander threw open the door, went over to the Jeep and opened the rear door.

"Where's Audrey?"

"When April ran out after the shot, Max told Audrey to get her out of here in April's car. Don't worry, they are okay and heading to your office."

"Where's Max?"

"Target practice," Mona said.

Zander pushed John out into the parking area toward his pickup. When they got there, he told John to hide inside, and Zander grabbed the 9mm and the shotgun with every intention of helping Max.

He was too late, however. Max came around the corner of the building holding what appeared to be a grenade launcher. He had a large bag with a strap hanging from his shoulder. He reached into the bag and pulled out what looked like a flare. He lit it with a cigar that was hanging from his lip, and threw it out of Zander's field of vision. After the explosion, Zander knew it was dynamite. It was a fitting end to this used-up mine.

Max threw a few smoke bombs to mask their departure. He yelled at Zander.

"Get the hell out of here and meet up at the office."

Zander turned around and threw the guns into the bed of the pickup, and within seconds, he and John were moving toward the gate. Just as he was about to turn onto the road, he glanced into the rearview mirror. Max had tied together three or four sticks of the explosive. He opened the office door, lit the bundle, and threw it inside. Zander decided not to wait around for the report. He gunned the engine and took the corner on two wheels.

He heard the explosion 15 seconds later. He checked his mirrors to see if there was a fireball, but all he saw was the Jeep coming fast up on his tail. Zander speeded up to stay ahead of Max.

After a few miles, they both slowed to the speed limit. Zander knew they needed to avoid being picked up. It would be difficult to explain all of Max's firepower and Zander's unregistered and suppressed pistol.

Zander looked over at John. He thought he looked a little green.

"What the hell was that, John?"

"I don't know. I never shot anyone in my entire life. Something just came over me."

"You didn't just shoot him. You killed him."

John put his head into his hands.

"I know."

Zander felt bad. He was pretty hard on John, but his actions could have gotten them killed. He decided to soften his tone.

"Well, everything worked out in spite of that stupid move. You just saved the government a lot of time and effort putting this guy away."

"He'll never hurt April again, either," John said more to himself.

"How are you planning to remedy what's happened to April?"

"Everything humanly possible. Your wife has made a good case of showing me my stupidity."

"She's good at that, but she's not my wife."

"She should be."

"I know. Tell her that."

"Maybe, I will. I need straighten things out with April first."

"That's important. You need to get to know your grandson. They're living in a motel, because that's all she can afford."

John's head sunk even more. Zander could see he was struggling with what he had done.

"She and Johnny will be coming home and living with us," John said.

"I would be careful how I presented that idea."

"I don't understand."

"Think about it. You kicked April out because why?"

"It had to always be my way," John thought for a moment. "I see what you're saying. This has to be an offer and not a command. She has to make the decision, and whatever that decision is, I'll have to live with it."

"That's a great first step, John. I think this will work out just fine for everyone concerned."

"I hope you're right. There is much to rectify."

Zander and John stayed quiet the rest of the way. When they pulled up to the office, Zander saw April's car parked on the street. He pulled into a spot next to it, and a few seconds later Max's Jeep found a spot on the other side of April's car.

Audrey and April were in the conference room. The rest of the group joined them. John hung back at the entrance unsure what to do next. Zander walked over to April and put his hand on her shoulder.

"I think your father has something he wants to say to you."

John took his cue and walked over and sat next to April.

"I've been an old fool, April. I want to apologize for my behavior toward you and Johnny. There is no excuse for what I did, and I know it will be difficult for you to ever forgive me. I guess I'm not asking for that. I would like to try and make it up to you. Your mother and I would like you and Johnny to come back and live with us. I know it will need to be your decision. I wouldn't blame you if you refused because of what I've done. I think that your mother needs you, and I need to make it up to her as well. She had nothing to do with my decision, but she has suffered nevertheless. I am so very sorry, April." A tear rolled down John's cheek.

April was looking at John during his entire speech but said nothing. When he finished, she got up, sat in his lap, and put her arms around his neck.

"I forgive you. You don't know how many times I've dreamed of this very thing. Johnny and I will be coming back home to live with you and mom."

John hugged her back trying to swallow his tears.

"You won't have to worry about anything. I've got enough money, so you'll never have to work a day from now on."

April moved off his lap.

"I can't live like that. You didn't raise me to be a slacker. Besides, Audrey explained to me that I would be working here and at the real estate office below."

"I understand. What you decide for your life will be fine with your mother and me." John stood.

"I want to thank you all for what you did for April today. Things are going to be changing for the better from now on," John said.

"You'll be getting our bill," Audrey said, with a bit of a twinkle in her eyes.

"Bring it," John said, putting his arm around April.

"Let's go home to mother."

Zander listened to their footsteps going down the steps before he spoke.

"How are we going to clean up the huge mess we made today?"

"I made a phone call to one of my contacts, and men from the agency will see to everything," Max said. "You are not to be involved from here on."

"What agency would that be?" Audrey asked.

Max looked at her and said nothing.

Zander had learned to keep what questions he might have to himself. He knew it could be Homeland Security, ICE, FBI, or some other clandestine fraternal order of bullshit. Some things needed to be kept quiet. Audrey still needed to learn these things, and Zander could see that Max's response had made her reconsider her question.

Max took out his phone and left the room. There had been no audible ring, but Zander figured he had the phone on vibrate. They could hear Max talking in the outer office, and Audrey lost interest. She and Mona talked about April and her father for a few minutes. Zander listened in without saying anything. It had been mostly Audrey's case, and he could tell she was proud of how it had turned out for April.

Max came back into the conference room and took a seat.

"The agency swooped in right after my phone call and found what was left of the office and the back buildings. It sounds like there had been some nasty shit between Anthony Ritz's operation and a cartel from his drug trading. Anyway, there wasn't much left and Ritz was found dead. It appeared to be an execution. That's the story the press got, and it answers your question about cleaning up the mess."

"It's good to have connections," Zander said.

Max ignored his remark.

"If anyone in this room is having second thoughts about what happened today, you should know this. In one of the back buildings they found twenty-five girls and young women chained to the walls. It looked like they were being processed for the skin trade. That might explain why there were no guards around the office area when you got there. The girls came in on a truck overnight. We just stopped a really bad man from continuing his human trafficking trade."

"Did they find any drugs?" Zander asked.

"Could be. They were quiet on that question. I'm thinking they may be mounting some sort of sting on the cartel. It wasn't something I wanted to know or get involved in."

Zander could tell Audrey still had questions. He looked at her and shook his head. She remained quiet.

There was little need to explain what happened in the office with Ritz, because everyone had heard the dialogue through Zander's wire. Zander was about to suggest they all head down to the Branchwater for a few celebratory cocktails, when the phone rang in the outer office. Zander got up and answered the phone.

When he returned, the color had drained from his face.

"Kevin Grienne is on the move."

35

Kevin lost interest in Elaine Taggart. He had gotten what he needed and now was feeling restless. It was time to make a move, and a time to follow his protocol. He put in for vacation time and realized that he might not be returning to his position. It made no difference, one way or another, to Kevin. A job was something that filled in the time between conquests. One place was as good as another, and he could always find another position if things deviated from plan.

Kevin owned a condo garage where he stored his oversized van. It was similar to the one those American Pickers drove on their show on the History Channel. He had it tricked out with all the comforts of home. He could live in it if circumstances warranted. There was a queen bed, a small bathroom with a shower, propane stove, and a galley with a propane refrigerator. He had all the creature comforts he needed.

Kevin had the locks modified. They were keyed both inside and out. He possessed the only key. He could lock the doors from the outside, so no one could escape. He could also lock the doors from the inside, so when he was inside no one could get in or out if he fell asleep. It worked well keeping his prey in line. There was no access to the living quarters from the cab. He had an insulated wall installed between the driver's cabin and the back. The entire back end of the vehicle had been double insulated, so no one, even a few feet from the vehicle, could hear any screams.

One of his clients had given him the name of someone who asked no questions and kept no records of vehicle modifications. Miami had a number of those places it seemed. Nothing was impossible for the right amount of money. Kevin had used his van on a number of occasions. If things went sideways, the everglades would be the recipient of any protocols gone wrong. He wondered about getting rid of a body in the mountains. He was unfamiliar with the terrain. It would need to be looked into before he took any action.

Kevin backed out of the condo garage with the large vehicle. His car took its place, and he wondered if he would be returning to make the trade again. On the way back to his condo, Kevin thought about the supplies he needed to pack for the trip. He would wait until dark and then load up. He stopped at the local grocery and picked up food items he needed for the trip. He wanted no wasted time stopping at restaurants. Everything needed would be packed into the van. He would stop for gas, but time to sleep and eat would only take place in his vehicle. He would need to scout out Wal-Mart parking lots for overnight stays. There would be no record of his parking in their lots. That way, he could avoid any paper trail. When he left Florida, there would only be cash transactions. He would remain off the grid for as long as possible.

***

While Kevin was busy planning his trip to the Rockies, Elaine saw his request for vacation time. She picked up the phone and pressed the interoffice line and called Connie McGill. Connie picked up, and Elaine started to tell her about Kevin. Connie stopped her.

"Meet me in my office as quickly as you can."

Elaine got up from her desk and told the other receptionist that she was taking a break. She almost ran to Connie's office.

Connie was waiting.

"We need to stay off the phones when we're discussing this asshole."

"I think he's ready to make a move. I saw his request for vacation."

"When is he leaving?"

"The day after tomorrow."

"Good. That will give me the time I need to make arrangements."

"I hope you're not planning to leave me out of this."

Connie looked at Elaine.

"It would be better if you weren't involved."

"I am involved. I think I deserve my own revenge."

"You don't know what you are saying. This may not turn out how you think."

"I know how you feel and realize you want revenge for your sisters."

"I want more than that."

"I don't understand."

"Kevin Grienne will not be returning from this vacation of his. He will be paying the ultimate price for what he's done. That's why you need to step away from this."

Elaine sat back and considered what Connie had told her.

"It seems like you could use some help. Maybe you could use some help from someone you can trust."

"Have you ever taken part in a killing?" Connie asked.

"No. Have you?" Elaine asked her back.

It was Connie's turn to sit back and reflect.

"You might have a point," she said grinning.

"It seems to me that we need some kind of plan before we get involved in something for which there is no return."

"Let's meet after work, and we can discuss it then. I need to call this number Max Kuhn gave me. It's someone we need to warn."

"What can I do?"

"Can you leave early and go stake out Kevin's place? We need to know what he's doing. The more information we can deliver the better our chances will be to take him down."

"I'll clock out right now."

"Be sure you stay hidden. We don't want to tip him off. He doesn't know that we are on to him, and we need to keep it that way."

"I've got the perfect place. He'll never know I'm there."

"Call me on my cell when you know anything. We'll meet later."

"I'm on it," Elaine said, standing.

"Be careful. If he suspects anything, you could very well lose your life."

"He has underestimated me right from the beginning. I was just one of his conquests, because he assumed I was totally vulnerable."

"That might become his biggest mistake to date," Connie said.

"He'll never see me coming." Elaine smiled, as she left the office.

Connie hoped she was right as she reached for the phone. Someone answered on the fifth ring.

"Wood and Zander Investigations." Zander left out the 'Personal and Discreet' from the greeting. He would never use it and knew it was better if someone else answered the phone.

"My name is Connie McGill. Max Kuhn gave me this number."

"Max is here. I'll get him for you."

"That won't be necessary. He told me to relay the message to someone named Zander. I assume that would be you."

"Your assumption is correct. How can I be of service?"

"Someone named Kevin Grienne is on his way. You need to prepare yourself."

Zander knew the message was coming sometime but didn't expect it after what took place earlier in the day. He tried to reply but the line was dead. He went back to relay the information to the rest of the group.

***

Elaine Taggart found a spot a block from Kevin's condo. It was a tree-lined street, and her car would never be noticed. Kevin had never seen or been in her car so any chance at being recognized was slim at best. She turned off the engine and sat and waited. There was some country music playing on one of the FM stations, and she turned it up. She liked to listen to music and sometimes sang along. Country music was her favorite, but she liked all types. It was the only time she buried her shyness. Singing out loud had never bothered her, and she belted out some old Patsy Cline song.

She was just finishing the last of the lyrics when she noticed a large van turning the corner in front of her. It seemed out of place, so she watched it as it stopped in front of the condo complex. She wondered if someone was getting some big furniture delivery when Kevin jumped out. Elaine sat forward and grabbed her cell phone and hit Connie's number.

Connie answered before the first ring stopped.

"Do you have him?"

"Yes. What do you know about him driving a big van?"

Connie paused.

"I know nothing. I thought I had him all scoped out. He's slippery, so you can see what I mean about being careful."

"What do you want me to do?"

"Can you get the license number?"

"I think so."

"Good. Write it down along with the vehicle description. Don't get too close, and don't let him see you."

"I've got a pair of cheap binoculars in my glove box, but I think they'll do. I won't have to move."

"After you get the information text it to me. Keep the hard copy in your glove box just in case. We don't want to lose it."

"Anything else?"

"When you get that done. Stay for another hour and watch to see what he's doing. Meet me at the Bonefish Grille after that. We need to talk this thing through."

Elaine followed Connie's instructions to the letter. She watched Kevin take out bags of groceries and place them in the back of the van.

She noticed he unlocked the door with a key. It looked like he was in a hurry to get the bags into the van. It was easy to see that he wanted no one to notice what he was doing.

She waited the full hour, but nothing else happened. She decided to pull up stakes and meet Connie. She pulled into the restaurant's parking area and saw Connie getting out of her car. The timing was perfect. They entered together and got a table for two in one of the corners. They shared pleasantries and decided to wait to discuss Kevin until after receiving their drinks.

"What's the next step?" Elaine asked.

"I've texted the information you gave me to Max. He'll make sure his people know what's going on."

"So, are we giving this over to Max? I thought we were going to be involved." Elaine couldn't mask the disappointment in her voice.

"We are going to make arrangements to fly out to Denver tomorrow. I think we'll take the redeye the day after. We'll both need to take vacation days."

"What if it's not possible?" Elaine asked.

"Be prepared to take the time without pay if necessary. That is, unless you no longer want to be involved," Connie said.

"You know the answer to that."

"Good. If I haven't told you that I'm happy to have you as my partner, I'm saying it now. I don't think I could do this on my own."

"We all need a little help now and then. I'm happy you let me share in this bastard's end."

"We won't talk of it again. We need to keep quiet about what we want the final outcome to be," Connie said.

They clicked their drinks together as their food arrived. They ordered wine with the dinner and both had a slight buzz when they finished with the meal. They sat for a few minutes and then decided to take a walk together. They paid with cash and walked out into the evening air. The weather was perfect. The humidity was down, and the temps were bearable.

"So, we'll fly into the Denver airport and then what?" Elaine was anxious to know the plan.

"We'll take airport transportation into Denver. It will probably be a bus."

Elaine turned up her nose.

"I hate the bus."

"I don't like it either, but we have to stay as unnoticeable as possible."

"What will we do when we get to Denver? It's quite a distance to Frisco. I looked it up on the map."

Connie smiled. She liked the fact that Elaine was doing her homework. It meant that together they could take Kevin Grienne down.

"I have a contact in the city. He will give us access to a car, so there will be no trail. He'll take cash. That means we're both going to need to take a good deal of it along. We won't be using credit cards or checks for anything."

"Sound like a good idea."

"I'm sure we'll need the day tomorrow to think about any other details we might have missed. Write down anything you think we'll need to discuss. I'll make the flight arrangements, and we'll meet in my office just before the end of the day."

Connie and Elaine parted ways. They both were feeling good about what they were about to do. If there were other factors that needed their attention, they seemed minor. The problem was that anything connected with Kevin Grienne was never minor.

36

Zander sat down after he broke the news to his friends. Audrey got up and walked over to him.

"We knew this was something that would be happening sooner or later. Buck it up, big boy."

Her comment served to ease the tension in the room. Zander had to smile but still was concerned.

"I lost you once. I can't afford to go through that again."

"That's not going to happen. It's the reason Mona and I are here. Audrey may not like this next bit, but she will never be alone until all problems with Kevin Grienne have been neutralized," Max said.

"What will that involve?" Zander asked.

"Whatever it takes. I think what we just experienced should give you some idea of a blueprint to follow."

"Seems like death is following us around," Zander sighed.

"There are those who walk among us who don't deserve the privilege any longer." Max was firm.

Zander had nothing to say but was finding it difficult to process. His Dutch Reformed background weighed heavily on his conscience. Max could see the turmoil.

"You need to ask yourself, did I do anything that could have been avoided. Was this a necessary conclusion to a situation beyond your control? If you can answer truthfully to those questions, you should no longer have to concern yourself with questions of conscience," Max said.

Zander agreed with a nod of his head, but in his mind he was finding it difficult to put into perspective.

"What should we do while we wait for this guy to make his move?"

"Nothing. I'm expecting a call later from Miami. We should know more after that," Max said.

"I'm hungry. Let's go get something to eat," Mona said, changing the subject.

"That's a great idea, but we need to go someplace other than the Branchwater. None of us are up to facing Fats and his prosecuting dialogue," Audrey answered.

"Any suggestions?" Mona asked.

"Let's go to Breckenridge. There's lots of places to choose from there," Zander suggested.

"I'll drive," Max offered.

The four left the office together and waited for Audrey to lock up before they descended the steps. Mona had many questions about how the area had changed since she left. That took up most of the dialogue. Zander enjoyed answering many of her questions. He could see that Audrey was learning quite a bit. Mona had the advantage of having lived there before, but this was all new to Audrey who had never left the southern part of the US in the past. Zander would see that it became her new home. It had been a shaky start, however.

As they approached the Breckenridge outskirts, Zander's thoughts reverted to Sara Jane. They passed the strip mall where she had set up one of her massage businesses. It made him think of his other problem. He needed to come up with some ideas on how he was going to balance his daughter, Sandra's, life with his own. He and Audrey had some preliminary discussions on the matter, but neither had a hard and fast solution. It would take time and effort on his part. It was more complex with the inclusion of Audrey. He wanted her involved but knew it would be almost impossible with Jayne. She would never stand for another woman anywhere near her daughter.

Audrey brought him back to reality.

"Where should we have dinner?"

"Is The Bridge still operating?" Mona asked.

"Do you want to go there?" Zander asked.

Zander had not been back to his old employer since he had returned to the mountains with Audrey. It seemed like a good idea.

"Let's do it," he said, and explained to Audrey about his past ties.

The manager greeted them with open arms and sat them immediately even though there were people waiting. Sometimes knowing someone paid off.

"You've got some pull here, it seems," Audrey said.

"Did you have any doubt?"

"Shut up and order some drinks."

The night went pretty much that same way. The food was as good as Mona had remembered. When they finished, it was past 10:00.

"I think it's time to call it a night. We've had a huge day. We all could use some sleep before we tackle this Grienne problem in the morning," Max said.

Zander liked it when Max was around. He took charge and made the decisions. It meant Zander was free to follow orders rather than give them. It was a relief. There were still too many decisions that he would need to deal with on his own.

Max dropped Audrey and Zander off at the office, and he and Mona made their way back to the hotel. Zander and Audrey drove back to the cabin. Audrey surprised Zander by sitting next to him on the console. She put her arm around him, and they drove home that way. Zander loved it. Audrey had been somewhat cool throughout the Ritz affair, but he could see she was beginning to loosen up. He hoped that soon he would have his old Audrey back.

If he thought there would be some lovemaking that night, he was mistaken. The day had worn Audrey down, and before he could even rub her back in anticipation, Audrey was purring in her sleep.

Zander turned over and found that he was tired as well. It took him a long time to get the events of the day out of his head so he could fall asleep, however. Listening to Audrey in her sleep mode had a calming effect on him. It was better than music to his ears. It meant he was no longer alone.

Zander had people surrounding him his entire life but never felt that he belonged to anyone or anything. His life with Jayne had left him even more alone. When Audrey entered his life all that went away. Now he needed to make sure he could maintain that relationship. It made for some complex issues. He was thinking about all of that, when he finally fell asleep. Although still far too complex, his dreams were of the good variety that night.

Zander's phone rang at 6:00 the next morning. It scared him awake. He picked it up off the nightstand and let his eyes focus until he could read the screen. It was Max.

"Good morning. Let's meet at IHOP for breakfast."

"Damn it, Max, we're still in bed."

"Well, get up. The day's a wasting." The line went dead.

Audrey had been listening with her eyes closed.

"Does he ever sleep?"

"I don't think he needs much. I feel bad for Mona."

"Mona? I'm feeling worse for me."

"Me too." Zander put his arm around Audrey's shoulder and cupped her left breast. There would still be no romance. Audrey rolled over, raised, and pushed her feet into Zander's chest. She was sporting a wicked smile when she pushed Zander out of bed. Zander hit the floor, hard.

"Let's get going. They're probably already waiting for us," Audrey said.

"I have no doubt. You want to give me some help" Zander was wedged between the bed and the wall.

His question fell on deaf ears. Audrey was already in the bathroom running the shower. Zander decided to shave and get ready while she was showering. It was because he wanted to glance at Audrey's naked body from time to time. It seemed like it was the only time he got to see it lately.

It was 6:30, when they headed for the IHOP. Zander drove as fast as he dared because they hated keeping Max waiting. Audrey had been right. They were waiting for them. They both had coffee but were nice enough to wait to order. Zander was surprised. He supposed it was because Audrey was there. Max never seemed to show him the same courtesy.

"I got the phone call after we left you last night," Max said as they were sitting down.

"Remind me who this is again," Zander replied.

"Connie McGill and Elaine Taggart. I believe we talked about them. Audrey worked with Connie in her rehab."

Audrey nodded.

"She's a good person. What information did she give you concerning Grienne?"

"He's going to be coming here in a large van. She gave me the description and the license number. It looks like he's tricked the vehicle out for kidnapping. It sounds like he could keep someone in there indefinitely."

"Did you thank them?" Audrey asked.

"You can thank them yourself. They should be here tomorrow."

Zander choked on the coffee the server had just poured him.

"That's a problem," he said, when he finally stopped coughing. "Why didn't you tell them to stay back?"

"Have you ever tried to tell two women on a mission what to do?"

Zander sat quietly. There was no good answer to Max's question. He knew silence was his best answer.

"What's our next move?" Audrey asked.

"We let him make it. There's not much else we can do until he shows his hand."

The server came back, and they ordered breakfast. Zander waited until she left.

"What are we supposed to do until then?"

"Mona and I are going sightseeing. You can do whatever you do any other day."

Zander felt he was the only one of the four taking the thing seriously. It irritated him, but he decided to keep his mouth shut until he was alone with Audrey.

Breakfast came and went. Max told the couple they would see them at the Branchwater that evening. He would call them with the time.

"Just keep your phone handy in case we need you," Zander said, a bit stronger than he had intended.

Max smiled and saluted him. Audrey smiled, and Zander knew he had been dismissed. They walked out into the parking lot together, and soon Zander and Audrey were on their way to the office. They had agreed to open at 9:00 on Monday through Friday and by appointment all other times. It was only 8:30 but they had nothing else to do.

When they pulled up to park, Audrey saw April sitting in her car. She jumped out of the pickup and yanked open April's driver's door.

"What's wrong? Did something happen?"

"Good morning. Things are fine. They are more than fine actually. I'm here reporting for work." April smiled.

"I thought we told you to take some time before you came back."

"I did. We moved all our things back home yesterday. It's just that I need something to do, and my parents need some time to adjust to having us living with them."

"Looks like we're going to have to give April a key if she plans on coming in this early," Zander said.

Audrey pulled April from the car and gave her a hug.

"Let's get you situated," Audrey said, as she pulled her up the steps.

Zander watched them go and decided to take a walk to the Branchwater. He needed to keep Fats in the loop. Otherwise, Fats might take it upon himself to do something stupid. It might already be a lost cause, but he had to try.

Zander decided to try the back door. It was open, and he saw Fats behind the bar reading a paper.

"Hey, is that today's Denver paper?" Zander asked.

Fats almost fell off his stool.

"Please announce yourself before you burst into a room. My weakened heart cannot receive shocks of this magnitude."

Zander smiled.

"Good to see you, too."

"What brings you to my humble establishment this time of the morning? Functioning before noon never seems to fit into your modus operando."

Zander sat down and began filling Fats in on what had been happening before he had a chance to say anything else. He wanted to keep his hippie lingo at a minimum, if at all possible.

It was not at all possible.

37

Elaine made one huge mistake. She underestimated Kevin Grienne. If she thought for one moment that Kevin missed seeing something unusual down the block when he turned into his condo, she was badly mistaken. Kevin had been on high alert since he decided to find Audrey Wood. It was like clockwork. When he went after his prey, he put his senses into overdrive. It's the thing that made his work so successful. It was his ultimate calling, and he knew he was not just good at it he was perfect.

When he drove and parked the van in front of his condo, he went upstairs and found an old pair of binoculars. He turned the blinds open just a crack, stepped back, and focused in on the car down the block. The field glasses were not of the highest quality, but they would work just fine at this distance. When the driver came into focus, Kevin almost dropped the glasses.

He had a difficult time believing it was Elaine Taggart peering into some field glasses of her own. Was she stalking him? He sat down on the bed and tried to sort the entire thing out. It was pissing him off because she was tampering with his preconceived protocol.

He needed to make an adjustment if he wanted his plans to progress. There was only one thing he could do. He would need to handle Elaine Taggart before he did anything else.

Kevin got back off the bed and looked out at the street. Her car was still in place. He would have to wait her out. He knew where she lived, and he would pay her a little surprise visit later that evening.

In the meantime, he decided to put all his things together that he needed for the Colorado trip. Things were going to happen much faster than he had planned. He had always been flexible when going after his prey. He would do whatever had to be done and move on. If it meant that he had to move on before he had originally planned, then that's what he would do.

Kevin checked the street, making sure Elaine's car was still in place. It was dusk when he saw Elaine's headlights turn on. She pulled away from the curb, and he watched her go. He wondered if she was heading to her apartment. It didn't matter. He would call on her when he thought the time was right, and that time would be around 10:00.

Kevin moved all of his things out to the van and put them in place. He was meticulous in his placement of clothing and toiletries. The cupboard, refrigerator, and small pantry had enough food to last him for a week. He was satisfied that he had covered everything. It left only dealing with Elaine Taggart.

He went back into the condo. He would leave for Colorado as soon as he and Elaine came to an understanding. The protocol had changed, but he still maintained the control.

He stopped for gas at a Marathon station close to his condo. It would be the last time he would use his credit card. After tonight, it would be all cash. He went inside to pay because he wanted a few other items to take along. He found two quarts of oil and a few other items he thought would come in handy on the road. He bought the entire box of Slim Jims he found on the counter. They would have been a hell of lot cheaper at a grocery store, but he didn't care. He was on a mission, and cost was not a factor.

He paid for the gas and items he cherry picked. He stowed everything in the cab. He would keep the Slim Jims at his side. They had always been a part of his ritual. One of the main reasons was that women hated the smell on his breath. He thought it might be part of his need for control, but he enjoyed the humor in it. If you failed to get enjoyment from the things you did, you should find something else to do. His enjoyment had never come close to failure in any of his conquests. He had always told his clients they needed to find something they were good at and made them happy. Then they should pursue that happiness to the very end. It was the only thing that could keep the darkness away. Kevin had darkness before but not anymore.

He drove to Elaine's apartment and parked down the street. She would be surprised to see him because he believed she thought he didn't know where she lived. Kevin was meticulous, and he always did his homework. Elaine had been a loose end right from the start. He thought he had control over it but now realized he should have taken care of things long before things got to this point.

He looked around for her car but saw nothing. There was no light in her apartment. He put on a pair of latex gloves from a box he kept under the seat. Just to be safe, he climbed the outside stairs and banged on her patio door. No one was home. If he had to wait, then waiting on the patio in one of the recliners would be good. It was a nice night, and it was interesting hearing the sounds coming from the individual apartments.

Kevin lived in an apartment complex once and vowed it would never happen again. People lived in them who could never afford a home of their own. Sitting on Elaine's patio confirmed all of that. He was still gloating about his assessment of the have-nots, when he saw headlights turn into a parking spot adjacent to Elaine's apartment. Kevin had a good view, so he remained in the lounge chair. He assumed she would go into the main door and use the stairs inside to access her apartment. He was wrong. She came up the same way he did.

Kevin never moved from his lounge chair. Elaine went right to the door and had the key in her hand. She felt his presence before she saw him move. As she turned, Kevin jumped up and put his arm around her shoulders. She was unable to move.

"Why don't we go inside?" Kevin asked, without showing any kind of emotion.

"You scared me. What are you doing lurking around my apartment?"

"I could ask you the same thing."

Elaine put the key into the lock and opened the door. Kevin escorted her into the living room and found a light switch.

"Can I get you something to drink?" Elaine asked, trying hard to hide the fear in her voice.

"This isn't a social call."

"Then why are you here?" Elaine's fear was gone.

Kevin could feel the change in her demeanor.

"I want to know why you were stalking me at my condo earlier."

Elaine had been so sure that she had kept her presence hidden. She knew she had underestimated him.

"You've been so distant, that I wondered what was going on. I thought that maybe you had met someone else. That's why I was there tonight."

Kevin removed his arm from her shoulder. Elaine was good at thinking on her feet, but her story was far too thin.

"Let's have a beer and discuss our relationship." Elaine started to move toward the kitchen.

"Just sit down. I'll get the beers." Kevin went to the refrigerator and found two mismatched bottles. He gave Elaine the light beer, and he took the other.

They both took a sip. Elaine was first to speak.

"If I offended you, I apologize. I was just trying to see if this relationship still had legs."

"There is no relationship. You were merely a means to an end, and I'm sorry you thought you needed to insert yourself in my business."

Elaine was beginning show her anger.

"You must think pretty highly of yourself if you think that I care for one moment about your business."

Kevin smiled. He could see Elaine's temperament change. It was exactly what he wanted. Her anger would serve to let down her guard and that's what he needed. He looked around and saw two pillows on the couch. He only needed one. He wanted no blood left in the apartment. There was no time for any cleanup. He had a long knife and some firearms in the truck, but they were hidden away. There was too much risk in using a weapon. Strangulation was always preferred. Kevin finished his beer.

Kevin sat back and let Elaine stew. His dialogue with her was over. If she wanted to continue, he would listen and wait for the right moment. Elaine looked at him, and saw the latex gloves for the first time, and then she realized she was in trouble. Kevin outweighed her by at least a hundred pounds. She looked around for something to grab when Kevin sprang from his chair.

In one fluid movement, his empty beer bottle came down on the top of her head. He had calculated about how hard to hit her. He wanted to stun her without breaking the bottle and leaving any glass for someone to find. He hit her harder than he planned, but the bottle didn't break. The skin erupted on the top of her head, however.

Kevin grabbed a pillow, and before Elaine could recover from the blow, he held the pillow over her mouth and nose effectually cutting off her airway. She struggled for a few minutes, trying to break Kevin's hold. She was unsuccessful, and Kevin wondered what she had been thinking as her body went limp in his arms.

Death had always interested him. He wondered what the dying were thinking when they took their last breath. He thought about stopping at that precise moment and asking them. He knew it could never happen, however. There was just too much that could go wrong when protocols were changed. He would need to be content to wonder about these life-and-death questions. Elaine's eyes were open. He closed them with two fingers.

The pillow had a bit of blood on it from the wound on the top of her head. It was the only place he saw any blood. Kevin put the pillow under her head to catch any more of the blood. He would need to get rid of it along with her body.

Kevin needed to camouflage the body when he carried it out to his truck. A large rug would be the best bet. He looked around the apartment and found nothing suitable. Apparently, Elaine's taste did not include rugs.

The laundry room had some cupboards over the sink. He found some large garbage bags and brought the box with him into the living room. He found that if he used two bags he could cover her entire body. One went over her head and cinched at her waist. The other started at her feet and ended at the same mid-body point.

He decided to double bag her making sure nothing was visible through a possible tear in the plastic. He took one more bag and threw the pillow in it. He looked at his work, and while it was not perfect, it would have to do. He had wasted enough time and knew he needed to move.

He took the bag with the pillow out to the truck as a dry run. Looking around, he saw nothing that concerned him. Moving quickly, he brought Elaine's body out over his shoulder. Elaine was in the van and he was closing the door when a pair of headlights came around the corner. He kept his head down and moved around the front of the van without looking up. The car passed and kept going. Kevin sat behind the wheel. He knew he should go back inside and police the area. The car had made him nervous, however. He wanted to dispose of the body and make his way to Colorado. He knew a good place in the Everglades off I-75 where no one would ever find Elaine Taggart.

He went against his better judgment and started the truck. Soon, he was heading west on the interstate. Kevin realized he would not be coming back to Florida anytime soon.

38

Connie woke up early. She called Elaine in hopes they could go to the airport early and avoid traffic. Elaine's phone went to voice mail. The pair had agreed to take a cab to the airport so they could avoid the parking and fees. Connie decided to wait until the agreed-upon time and made herself some breakfast. She packed the night before, and her suitcase was waiting at the door.

She cleaned up after breakfast and put a call into the cab company. The cab would be at her door in fifteen minutes. After double checking the apartment and turning off the water, she waited at the door. The cab showed up on time, and she gave directions to Elaine's apartment. The cabbie was a nice older gentleman, and they passed the time in meaningless conversation. They pulled up in front of Elaine's apartment, and the cabbie laid on the horn per Connie's instruction. They waited a few minutes. When nothing happened, Connie got out and went to the steps leading to the deck. She saw the slider was open.

The hairs on the back of Connie's neck stood straight out. She knew something was wrong. She climbed the stairs two at a time and burst into the living room calling Elaine's name. The apartment was small, and there was no answer. She went to the bedroom expecting the worse but found nothing except Elaine's packed suitcase.

Connie was at a loss at how to proceed. It was a rare moment in her otherwise organized life. She sat on the sofa trying to collect her thoughts. As she sat down, her hand slipped into the crack of the center cushion and felt something sharp. It felt like a key ring with car keys. Connie had never been a sheller, but she recognized the funky shell on Elaine's key ring. Connie was sure that Elaine would never absently leave them anywhere but her purse.

Connie stood and removed all the cushions, looking for some kind of sign. There was a card near where she had found the keys. When she picked it up, her legs began to wobble. It was Kevin Grienne's business card. She expected the worst, and this confirmed it. Kevin Grienne somehow had got to Elaine. Connie's only hope was that she might still be alive.

Her mind raced and she made a decision. If Elaine were still alive, Grienne would be taking her along with him to Colorado. There was still a bit of hope, but it was fleeting. In her heart, Connie knew Elaine was already gone. She would not be listening to her heart today, however.

She ran down the steps and back to the cab. The cabbie could see something was wrong and kept his mouth shut all the way to the airport. After Connie checked in and went through the checkpoint, she settled into a chair at her departure gate. She and Elaine had planned to have breakfast at the airport, but she was no longer hungry.

Her cell phone was fully charged, and she made a call to Max. It rang six times and then went to voicemail. She terminated the call and fumbled through her purse until she found the card Max had given her. She had written the number of Zander's investigation business on the back. She dialed the number and waited.

***

April fit into the position immediately. Audrey had the phone rigged so she could answer for either business from whatever phone she was using. Jo loved the idea, and Audrey was concerned that she might monopolize most of April's time. She told Zander in so many words.

"We don't have that much for her to do up here. Jo and Bert's business has all kinds of clerical things that she can do. A few hours a week up here would be enough for us since she can answer the phone anywhere. That would be her biggest job for us," Zander said.

"I suppose you're right. But if that's going to be the case, then Bert and Jo will need to be paying most of her salary."

Zander smiled to himself. Audrey was indeed a businesswoman.

***

April answered the incoming call from Bert and Jo's office.

"Wood and Zander Personal and Discreet Investigations. How may I help you?"

"May I talk to Zander please? It's very important."

"Hold on, I'll see if he's in." April could tell by the tone of the woman's voice that there was a problem.

She pressed the intercom button and rang Zander's office. No one picked up. She decided to phone Audrey's office. She answered immediately.

"There's a woman on the line, and she wants to speak with Zander. She sounds upset," April said.

"He stepped out for a bit. Why don't you put me through, and I'll take it," Audrey replied.

She knew it would take some time for people to see her as an equal partner in their business venture, and she needed to be patient. It still made her angry, however.

She answered in her best business voice.

"This is Zander's partner. He isn't here at the moment. Can I help you?"

Connie was stunned and needed a few moments to regain her composure. She knew it was Audrey on the other end the moment she heard her voice. She decided not to disclose who she was.

"I have been trying to reach Max Kuhn, but he's not picking up his phone. He gave me this number for a Zander, and I'm trying to reach out." Connie was playing things close, since she had no idea how much Audrey knew about Grienne.

"Hello, Connie. Max has brought all of us up to speed. He and Mona are off sightseeing somewhere in the mountains, so I think he might be out of cell tower range."

"Back at you, Audrey. How did you know it was me?"

"I spent so much time with you, I don't think I'll ever forget the sound of your voice. It has always been a comforting thing for me."

"I'm sorry, but this will not anything close to a comforting call."

Connie went into detail about what had happened and about her fears for Elaine Taggart. She also gave Audrey all the information she had on the van Kevin Grienne was driving to Colorado.

"Please share this with Max and Zander, as soon as possible."

"We should have some time before he shows up here, don't you think?" Audrey asked.

"Grienne is unpredictable. He might decide to drive straight through. He knows who Max is and knows he has resources. I don't know how much he knows about my involvement. He may have tortured Elaine for information."

"Where are you now?"

"I'm at the airport in Miami. My flight leaves in an hour. I have an acquaintance in Denver who will provide me with a car, and I should be in Frisco late afternoon."

"Do you think it's a good idea for you to come here? This could get ugly."

"That's exactly why I'm coming. I want to end this terror. He's killed enough family and friends, and now he needs to pay for those sins."

Audrey had learned the details of Connie's sisters from Max. She knew that nothing in the world would deter her from coming to Colorado.

"I'll book you a room in the same hotel that Max is staying." Audrey gave her the information and directions to the hotel.

"Thanks for not trying to talk me down."

"I know you too well. Once you have your mind made up, there's no changing it."

"Women of Kindred spirits, don't you think?"

Audrey laughed.

"Call when you get to your hotel. We'll do dinner together and hash this out."

"Done," Connie said, and disconnected the call.

Audrey fired up her computer and put the information Connie had given her into a blank document. After she proofread the info, she printed off six copies. Everyone in the building would get one. Audrey knew that she needed to be vigilant and that meant everyone else needed to be as well. She gave it a second thought and then printed another. Fats and Fran would need to be vigilant also.

Just as she was finishing, Zander walked into the office. He had a large coffee in each hand.

"Boy, they don't give these things away. That will be the last time I buy coffee to go."

Audrey shook her head.

"Kevin Grienne is on the move."

Zander dropped both coffees on the floor.

***

Kevin dumped Elaine's body in his usual place. He had used it three times before, and there had never been a trace. He assumed the gators made fine work of the remains. He decided to put some miles between southern Florida and his first stop for the night. Six hours later he stopped at a rest area near Tallahassee. He would travel during the day when there was more traffic on the road. No attention to his vehicle was needed.

Sleep came immediately for Kevin. His nagging worry had been eliminated. Since he had no conscience, there was nothing left to keep him awake. His dreams were of Audrey Wood and how he would change her life.

He awoke at 7:00. He made himself a peanut butter sandwich and grabbed a bottle of water. It was a meager breakfast, but he wanted to get moving. As he ate, he pulled out a road atlas. He studied the best route to Colorado. He thought it looked like long a distance. He had never driven that far in a vehicle his entire life.

After doing some measuring, he decided to angle through Alabama on some of the blue highways until he got to Memphis. There he would take I-55 to St. Louis. It would be a straight shot to Denver on I-70 mostly through Kansas.

He would drive until he tired. He thought he could do the drive in two to three days, max. His plan was to only spend two nights in Wal-Mart parking lots or rest areas. He preferred the Wal-Marts because of the anonymity. Time was of the essence, however, and he would do what it took to get to Frisco as soon as he could.

It was a nice day when Kevin exited his rolling home. He went to the restrooms to take care of the day's business. It was early, and very few people were at the rest area. A few truckers had pulled in overnight, and the drivers were beginning to stir.

Kevin got back into his van and began his trip with all the excitement of someone taking a long vacation. He wondered why this woman had driven him to this point in his life. In the back of his mind, he feared it might be a huge mistake, but he buried that thought. It made him angry when it surfaced without warning. He would do his best to keep it in the darkness where it belonged.

He was nodding off somewhere south of St. Louis, so he pulled into a little town called Festus and drove to a Wal-Mart. He found a lonely corner in the lot. He thought about fixing dinner in his galley kitchen but was tired. The Wal-Mart had a Subway inside, and it appealed to him.

He picked a foot-long meatball sandwich and a root beer. He opted for that because the soft drink contained no caffeine. He paid cash and sat alone in a booth. The meatball sub was hot and tasted good. Kevin ate the entire thing and washed it down with the 20-ounce soft drink. He really wanted bourbon. He was pissed at himself for forgetting to pack a few bottles for the trip. Then he remembered that Wal-Mart had a selection of hard liquor. He wandered around the store until he found the booze near the back of the food area. He was surprised at the selection they had to offer. He chose a large bottle of Maker's Mark and another of Woodford. There was ice near the checkout, and he grabbed a small bag and paid with cash.

Soon he was in the back of his van enjoying a large pour of bourbon. He had three before he figured he should stop and get some sleep. Hangovers were brutal and not needed on this leg of his trip.

The booze helped to relax him, and he fell asleep on top of the bed without removing his clothes. He smiled as he drifted off. There would be plenty of time to remove his clothes later.

39

Connie McGill called Audrey's phone, after she checked into the hotel. The group was huddled in a corner of the Branchwater. Max had cut their tour short, when Zander finally got him to answer his phone. The only person who seemed to be worried about their situation was Zander.

Audrey started to give directions to Connie and then had a better idea. When the call to Connie was finished, Audrey stood.

"I'm going to the hotel to pick up Connie."

"Oh, can I go with you? The men are beginning to bore me," Mona said.

"You just now figured that out? We need to talk about your perception." Audrey laughed.

"Show me the way."

"With pleasure. Let's go." They both bounded out of the bar.

Max looked after them.

"Aren't they something? We are some lucky gents."

"I would very much like to keep it that way," Zander said.

"You worry too much."

"This Kevin Grienne, by all counts, is unpredictable. I'm afraid he is one step ahead of us and has been from the beginning."

"That very fact makes him more predicable than most."

"I don't know what you mean."

"We haven't been ignoring his movements. The fact that he seems unpredictable heightens our awareness. Just think of how many people are working with Audrey on this."

"I know, but one of the principals may just have been abducted and murdered. That's because he has been more dangerous than anyone had expected."

"Elaine Taggart may have let her guard down. We won't make that same mistake, will we? Besides, we don't know what happened to her for sure. Don't jump to conclusions before you have the facts."

"Do you actually believe she's still alive?"

Max thought for a moment.

"No, I don't. In situations like this it is best to expect the worst. That way if things do work out, it becomes a win and if they don't, you will have expected it."

"I'm going to stick to Audrey like glue. She's always going to be in my line of sight."

Max looked at him with a peculiar smile.

"And yet, you let her go to the hotel without your intervention."

Zander was dumfounded. He was so worried about their situation he missed doing what was the most important thing. He stood and was ready to run out of the bar when Max grabbed his arm.

"Sit."

Zander sat down immediately.

"We've got a couple of days before we need to worry about Grienne being in the vicinity. He's driving here in a large van, so he'll need to stop often for gas. He's not going to be able to drive into town and abduct Audrey. He's unfamiliar with the place, so he'll need to do some serious reconnaissance."

Zander realized he was right but was still reeling from his bonehead maneuver.

"I can't believe I let her walk out of here. What the hell was I thinking?"

"Forests and trees, my friend, forests and trees."

Zander knew what he was saying. He would never make that same mistake again. At least, that's what he told himself. He was still punishing himself mentally when the three women walked in.

Audrey introduced Connie to Zander. He did his best to give her a warm welcome. He even gave her a hug. When that was completed, he turned to Audrey.

"You can never do that again."

"What?" Audrey was confused, but she had an edge in her voice.

Zander knew he had to proceed with caution. He got up and put his arms around her.

"Until all this is over, we need to be as vigilant as humanly possible. You need to have someone with you always."

"By someone you mean you. Because if you'll remember, I had someone with me." She pointed to Mona.

"Actually, she would have been a better choice than you if something had happened. Show him Mona."

Mona lifted her jacket and pulled out a pistol from behind her back. Zander had nothing to say. He looked at Mona and then at Max.

"She's packing. I always think a woman with a 9mm is beyond sexy," Max said.

Zander could see she was enjoying the uncomfortable situation he had made for himself. He released Audrey from his bear hug and put his arms straight up into the air.

"I give up. I know when I'm beaten."

Audrey pushed him down into a chair and sat on his lap.

"Sometimes you are such a huge blockhead. You just can't help yourself. That's why I stay around. It's always such a shit show." She messed up his hair. "But your point is well taken. I will make it a point not to be alone until this Grienne mess is cleaned up."

"Thank you. That will be one less thing I need to worry about."

"Oh, come on. You'll still worry about it."

Zander knew she was right and sat back.

Connie McGill was taking the whole thing in with a bit of merriment, but she became quiet as Zander sat back.

"I'm afraid Zander is right about the danger. Elaine and I thought we were careful enough. Now she's gone." Everyone could see Connie was upset.

"Let's not jump to conclusions. I just had this same conversation with Zander before you walked in."

"There are some things you just know. I know that Elaine Taggart is dead. Kevin Grienne killed her."

"Connie you just can't…" Max never got to finish.

"Max, you need to be quiet. There are some things women just know. Connie knows this to be true. You don't have all the answers." Mona said in a raised voice.

Zander looked over at Max to see how he would react.

Max looked at Mona smiled. He knew when he was beaten, and he would tell Zander that same thing later.

After the dust settled, Connie spoke first.

"How are 'we' going to proceed?" She highlighted "we," so there would be no doubt that she would be involved.

Zander took the moment to assert his willingness to be point man in the discussion.

"We've got to get as many people we can trust up to speed. In this case, there will be strength in numbers." He called Fats and Fran over to the table.

After the introductions, Audrey passed around the information she had compiled concerning Kevin Grienne.

"This is what we know. If you need to know more about Kevin Grienne, please field your questions to Connie. She has the most knowledge concerning his character."

Fran looked at the page and asked a few questions about how to identify Grienne. Fats stayed quiet.

"From now on, we've all got to keep our senses on heightened alert. This guy won't quit until he has Audrey in his clutches or we stop him. I prefer the latter," Zander said.

Zander was astounded that Fats kept quiet. He would talk to him alone later.

It was evident that there was no plan in dealing with Kevin Grienne. It was also painfully clear, until they found him, there was little they could do. They talked over burgers and beers until well after 10:00. Everyone was tired and ready to leave. They agreed to meet for breakfast at Denny's by 8:00 the next morning.

Connie left with Max and Mona. Fats and Fran were in the process of locking up for the evening. The evening had been slow, and Zander was thankful so his friends could be brought up to speed.

"I'll drive the T-Bird home," Audrey said, and started to move to the door.

"What in the world did we all just talk about tonight?"

Audrey turned around smiling.

"It was a test. You passed."

"I'll drop the T-Bird off when we go home. You don't want to leave it on the street. Fran and I rode together this morning, so it's no imposition," Fats said from behind the bar.

"Thanks, Fats." Zander grabbed Audrey's hand and turned to leave.

"Hold on you two," Fats said.

He came from behind the bar. He put his arms around the pair and pushed them toward the door.

"I don't like any of this. This guy is an unknown, and that makes him dangerous."

"I had the same conversation with Max earlier. He says that will be one of our strengths, because it makes us more aware."

"I don't know about any of that. I'm just a dumb bartender that talks too much sometimes."

"All the time," Fran said from behind the bar.

"Just another country heard from." Fats shot Fran a glance.

"I think you should both take some extra precaution." He took out the two chrome .45 pistols he had tucked into his blue jeans.

"These things make me nervous," Zander said.

He noticed that Audrey was admiring the firearm Fats had given her.

"They are loaded and each has six shots. I'm running a bit low on ammo, so tomorrow you go to Wal-Mart and buy some extra. That one saved my life, and it might have the same good fortune for you both."

Zander tried to hand it back, but Fats pushed it back into his hand. He turned around and went back to work. The conversation had ended, and Fats was in control. Zander knew it would do no good to try and reason with him.

He and Audrey drove home in the pickup. They talked about the two pistols and how they could possibly use them.

Zander placed them on the counter when they got home. He felt some comfort having them in their possession. The feeling was foreign to him.

The next morning, both Zander and Audrey woke to the smell of coffee. Zander turned to Audrey.

"Did you set the auto-brew on the coffee pot last night?"

"No. When I smelled it, I thought that maybe you had."

Zander got up and went out into the kitchen in his jockey shorts. He saw Fats sitting at the table with a mug of coffee. He was reading a paper.

"Jees, Fats, when did you break in?"

"I've got a key. Remember?" He held up the key to the cabin.

"That was a mistake on my part."

"Maybe so, but you're not getting it back. It has come in too handy over the years. Why don't you go put on some clothes? You're making me uncomfortable."

"Damn it, Fats, this is my place. I'll walk around however I want."

"Point taken. It's a bit nippy this morning. I just thought you might be chilly. I'll make you and Audrey breakfast while you get ready." Fats got up and moved to the counter.

Zander shook his head and went back into the bedroom. Audrey was already in the shower. Zander dropped his shorts and joined her. There was no resistance. When they were finished and dressed, they both entered the kitchen together.

Fats had three plates filled with scrambled eggs and toast.

"Dig in before everything gets cold."

"What? No bacon?" Zander asked.

"Far too much cholesterol. You need to start eating with your health in mind."

"I thought we were meeting at Denny's this morning," Audrey said.

"Change of plans. I told them to have breakfast on their own. I was taking care of you this morning," Fats replied.

"So, where is Fran?"

"Home. She was less than pleased with me for this change order."

"You need to pay more attention to what she tells you. It will serve to keep you out of a good deal of trouble," Zander said, as he dug into his eggs.

He had to admit that Fats was a decent cook. The breakfast was tasty, and Audrey must have felt the same way. She was finished before Zander had time to take one bite of his toast. He was surprised that he had an appetite. His sleep had been restless, and he had spent a good deal of the night looking at Audrey. He was afraid that if he fell asleep she would be gone when he woke up.

Fats poured more coffee. When they finished, he put their dishes in the sink. He sat down.

"I wanted to have a little time to talk to you both without anyone else around," Fats said, when he sat down.

"What's on your small brain?" Zander asked.

Audrey kicked him.

"Be nice to your friend. You don't have that many."

Fats hid a smile while trying to be serious.

"I don't like this entire situation. No one seems to be taking it seriously."

"This is one time I agree with you," Zander said.

"What are we going to do about it?"

"We have little choice but to trust Max. He has the proven track record."

"What about us. We've done a masterful job in the past."

"Fats, we've been nothing but lucky, and luck has a way of running out."

"This Grienne asshole has to be stopped, and I think you know what that means."

"We've had that discussion with Max. That part will be out of our hands unless we're threatened directly."

"We've got to be ready to access the mine's air shaft again."

"Absolutely not. Don't you think we've stretched that to the limits? We can't keep taking the risk. One misstep and we would have a number of past sins to answer for."

"I see your point," Fats said.

"If you two are finished with your pity party, let's go to the office. Fran and Max will be wanting to meet us there," Audrey said.

"That's a good idea. I'll get Fran, and we'll meet you there."

"Don't you have the bar to open?" Zander asked, hoping to keep Fats out of the entire situation.

Zander's friend was having none of it, however.

"I don't open for a couple of hours. Anyway, I want to find out how this half-baked, half-assed plan is going to play out." Fats left.

Audrey did the dishes, while Zander looked through the paper Fats left. When she was finished, Audrey sat across from Zander.

"You need to go easy on Fats. He's a good friend and just wants the best for both of us."

Zander took Audrey's hands.

"I realize that. It's just that we've always had a love-hate relationship."

"I don't see any hate in Fats, only love."

The comment took Zander by surprise. It was something he knew he needed to think about. He was still thinking about it when they left for the office in his pickup.

40

Kevin Grienne drove into Frisco three days after he left Miami. True to form, he drove around the area making notes of the terrain and places of interest. He put everything into categories in a notebook. This would be a painfully slow process, but one that would necessary for his survival.

He settled on a small RV site between Frisco and Breckenridge. It had trees separating each RV pad and gave each site a great deal of privacy. Kevin chose a site near the back of the park away from most of the other campers. He hooked up the electricity, the water, and sewer.

When he made the trip from Florida, he had time to think. One of the things that bothered him was that he would be driving the large van around the community. It would draw too much attention. While driving through Denver, he made up his mind to find a supplementary mode of transportation.

He stopped at a Yamaha cycle dealer and found a pretty good used Yamaha 150cc motorcycle. It was small enough to fit into the back of the van. He had it equipped with two saddlebags, so he could fit in the supplies needed for an extended stay at the park. It looked like it had been modified as a dirt bike. It was loud, and that was the last thing he needed. The dealer agreed to put new guts in the muffler at no extra charge.

Kevin knew he looked like a dufus riding the small cycle, but he would be in disguise. After he settled in and had a good night's sleep, Kevin decided to begin his reconnaissance mission. He took out a small gym bag and began placing items on the counter next to his mirror.

There was a good deal of make-up, a number of different-colored wigs, and a few eyeglasses with clear lenses. Kevin began his makeover process and within forty minutes had completed his transformation. He looked at himself in the mirror and was satisfied with the artwork. He transformed into an old man with longer white hair, beard, and eyebrows. He dressed in baggy clothes and wrapped a sweatshirt around his middle to simulate a paunch. It was a disguise he had used previously with effective outcomes. No one would suspect that it was Kevin Grienne behind the mask.

His day consisted of riding every street in both Frisco and Breckenridge. He stopped at a park or two and made notes. Being well prepared took away any anxiety he might experience when he worked a place that was formerly unknown. Being forewarned was being forearmed. Once a system worked, there was no need to change. At noon he stopped at a fast food joint. He sat outside not wishing to draw attention from the inside diners. He studied his notes and liked what he saw. Neither Breckenridge nor Frisco was all that big. It would be easy enough to get his bearings in a few short days.

Late in the afternoon, Kevin parked his bike in front of a hotel across the street from the Branchwater. He found a seat in the bar on the second level. It was outdoors and faced the Branchwater. He could watch the comings and goings of the patrons without being seen.

He ordered bourbon and water. He wanted it on the rocks, but he knew he had to keep his wits about him. After the third drink, he realized he should eat something. The menu showed finger food. He ordered fried pickles and a basket of fries. He needed something to help absorb the alcohol. The last thing he needed was to be picked up.

Kevin's stakeout paid off. He watched a pickup pull up, and Audrey Wood jumped out of the passenger seat. Kevin almost choked on a French fry. The man he had met at the motel in Cedar Key followed Audrey into the bar. Kevin was on high alert. Moments later, he saw a light-colored car park next to the pickup. Three people got out of the vehicle. He recognized Max from the office. His eyes bugged out, when he saw Connie McGill following another woman into the bar.

"What the hell is she doing here?" Kevin asked himself.

Something told him he was in dangerous waters. For the first time in his life, Kevin was unsure how to proceed. He sat stunned and lost his appetite. He knew he had to regroup. He called for his check and paid with cash. He needed to get to his van and sort through the Connie McGill problem.

When he got to the van, Kevin poured himself a tumbler of bourbon. He drank half of it while removing his makeup. He had no ice but felt no need to dilute his drink. He needed a buzz before he lost his edge. After his disguise was removed, he filled the glass again. He sat outside under a canvas sunscreen that was attached to the van. He had to think and did better at it when surrounded by nature.

It was dark, and after three large glasses of bourbon, Kevin went back into the van. He was quite drunk but had made a decision. He would take the offensive. The next day, he would continue plotting the area. He needed to end up at the Branchwater. He knew his makeup needed to be stellar in order to keep his identity a secret. It made him smile as the room spun around. He found his way to the bed and was sleeping in his clothes before his head hit the pillow. He dreamed of Audrey Wood and what he would do to her.

He woke the next day with his head pounding. Drinking that much was something he seldom did. He understood the reason after choking down the fourth aspirin. He felt nauseated and dreaded the idea of puking. He swallowed the water from the glass he had used the night before. There was still a hint of the bourbon, and it made him gag. He walked into the mountain air and strode around the campground until he started to feel better.

He went back to the van and made an effort to work on his makeup. His hands shook as he tried to put on some foundation, but he gave up. They were out of control. He needed more mountain air, so he grabbed a map and looked at it. Today would be a sightseeing adventure, and there would be no drinking. He decided on a trip to Steamboat Springs. It looked like it was about a hundred and twenty-five miles one-way. He could access the road in Dillon. There was a town called Kremmling about halfway. There he could get something to eat. The food would need to be greasy and salty to help with his hangover. The trip would take most of the day, and he needed to time it right so he would be back before dark. He grabbed a Coke and downed most of it. Someone told him once that Coke was the best thing for a hangover. He would try anything to feel better. He stowed the rest of the bottle in his saddlebag and left town following all speed limits.

He started to feel better an hour into the trip. The mountain air did wonders. He had heard of many people who experienced altitude sickness. Kevin had never been bothered by it in the past and thought it might be a myth. He wondered, however, if it had added to his hangover. Maybe there was more to it than he realized. He tried to put it out of his mind.

He stopped at a burger joint in Kremmling and ordered a double cheeseburger, fries, and another Coke. This time it was in a thirty-ounce cup. He drank a third of it while he ate. He forced down the last of the fries and went back to the bike. He took off the lid of the Coke and poured the rest of the bottle from the saddlebag into the cup. He would drink the rest of it through the straw provided. He knew it would mean countless stops to relieve his bladder. It would be a small price to pay if it made him feel like himself once again.

When he came over the mountain crest that led to Steamboat Springs, he pulled over on a turnout. He couldn't believe his eyes. There were hot air balloons all over the sky. Kevin watched from his perch. He decided this was worth the trip, and as a bonus, he forgot about his hangover.

Kevin rode through town and found the meadow where the balloons were launched. It was a festive atmosphere, and he enjoyed some of the food they offered. He stayed away from the alcohol.

When he looked at his watch, he knew he would need to go back to Frisco. He needed to get there before dark. He made a pass through town and saw people tubing down the Yampa River. It looked like fun. Maybe he and Audrey would come back and try it. He knew it was a pipedream. He was incapable of that type of relationship. He had his chances, but something always got in the way. It wasn't anything he tried to dwell on. He just knew he was different from most. It had served him well in the past, and there was no reason to change.

The trip back to Frisco was much more pleasant. His hangover was gone, and he felt great. The vistas were breathtaking, and it was hard to take it all in. His wits would be sharper the next day without the alcohol to screw things up. He stopped in Silverthorne at Pizza Hut and ordered a small combination with everything. This was the kind of food he seldom ate, but today it was the only thing he could stomach.

It was dusk when he pulled the bike next to his van. He was tired, and his back ached from riding that far on a motorcycle. He knew it would have been different had he been used to it, but he hadn't ridden a bike in years.

The thought reminded him of his youth. It was something that he had no desire to revisit. He tried to put everything out of his mind from before his college days. Being abused sexually by a close family member had taken its toll.

Had he been able to get help for what happened to him, Kevin's life might have turned out differently. He might have been able to have a lasting relationship. He might have been able to look at a woman without all the darkness.

He would never know, however, because he never got the help he deserved and needed.

41

The day was brighter for Kevin when he woke the next morning. He was in a good mood because he knew today would be the day he would take control. He whistled while he made breakfast. When the coffee was ready, he went out to the picnic table next to the van and enjoyed breakfast in all of the majesty of the mountains. He was in no hurry. Finding Audrey would not take much effort. Finding her alone and vulnerable would take much more patience. Kevin knew it would be the hardest part for him.

He decided to take a walk on the path that led to Breckenridge. He felt comfortable enough not to have to put on makeup. He needed the exercise and makeup would only get in the way of a good sweat. Besides, most of the path was away from the road, so recognition by anyone would be difficult. The morning was cool, but the air was thin. Soon, Kevin was working up the sweat he believed he needed.

He was focused on his power walking. He failed to see a car slowing down as the path curved toward the road. It was a nondescript white vehicle with Colorado plates just like countless others. When Kevin passed the vehicle, it sped up again. No bells or whistles went off in his head, and he continued for another mile before turning back to the RV Park.

***

What Kevin failed to notice was that the car contained Max Kuhn. He was on one of his fact-finding excursions and just happened to find what he had been seeking. He knew it was more luck than sense finding Kevin Grienne in such a random fashion.

What the chance meeting told him was that Grienne was stowed away somewhere close. Max turned into the RV site, because it was the only place between Breckenridge and Frisco that could hide a big van like the one Grienne was driving.

Max drove through the park and headed to the far edge where he thought someone could easily hide out. He was not disappointed. The glaring Florida state license plate caught his eye immediately. Max smiled at the mistake. Grienne should have changed plates when he got to Colorado. Overconfidence generally leads to mistakes. This one was huge. What interested Max more was the small motorcycle leaning against the front bumper. It made sense that Grienne would need other transportation when scouting the area. Max wondered how long he had been around. He would need more information.

The rear door of the van was locked. The driver's door and passenger door also were locked. Max went back to his car and pulled out a small bag. He fished out a few tools, and within seconds, he had the rear door open.

He realized he needed to work fast and did a quick once-over of Kevin's living space. Nothing seemed out of the ordinary until he reached the bedroom space. On the shelf by the mirror were a makeup bag and a white wig.

Max fingered the wig and realized that Grienne was smarter than he had first given him credit. The disguise idea was a good one. Max knew this whole chance encounter had been a stroke of luck for his team.

Max put the wig back in place. He needed to get back to Zander's office and share what he had learned. When Max turned out of the park and onto the road toward Frisco, Kevin was walking back to his van. He was still a long distance from being able to recognize Max. He left no trail for Kevin to follow.

Max went to Zander and Audrey's office. He meant to pick up Mona at the hotel first, but this news needed to be shared immediately. When he climbed the stairs, he was disappointed at not seeing his friends. April was at the receptionist desk and smiling broadly at him.

"Good morning. Zander and Audrey have not yet arrived for the day. Is there something I might help you with?"

Max liked her style. It was very professional.

"What time do they usually get here?"

"Well, the office hours begin at 9:00. They usually show up around that time."

Max looked at his watch. It showed 7:45.

"Why are you here so early?"

"I love coming here and looking out the window and seeing the community waking up. I've got such a good vantage point from up here."

Max went over to the window and looked out. People were driving down the street, and a few of the locals were coming out of some of the coffee shops after their morning breakfast.

"I see what you mean," Max said.

"I love it here. I just wish I could work up here full time," April said, and then had a stricken look in her eye. "I mean Jo and Bert are wonderful, and I realize that there just isn't enough for me to do up here for a full-time job. It's just that I like being around Zander and Audrey. You all saved my life."

Max smiled. He had no comment that he felt would be appropriate.

"I've got to make a call. Please excuse me."

Max went back down the stairs and found a seat on a bench in front of the building. He made his call to Mona, and after explaining what had happened, he told her to hook a ride with Connie and come to the office a soon as possible.

Max decided to take a stroll over to the Branchwater while he waited. He thought he might be able to catch Fats coming to work. Everyone needed to be brought up to speed concerning Grienne.

The front door was locked, but Max could see Fats moving around. He decided not to bother him by pounding on the door and went around to the back instead. When he walked in, Fats was leaning over a dustpan picking up yesterday's dirt from the floor.

"Good morning, Fats," Max said firmly.

Fats jumped up almost hitting his head on the edge of the bar.

"Jesus, Mary and Joseph. You need to warn someone before you send them off into repose."

"I didn't know you were Catholic, Fats."

"I'm not. But maybe I should turn to it after that near-death experience."

Max liked Fats' sense of humor. He could see why Zander was his friend.

"Do you have some time to come over to Zander's office around 9:00?"

"What's shakin'?"

"A bit of a new wrinkle concerning Grienne. He's here and been sporting a disguise. Can you make it at 9:00?"

"We open for the coffee guys then, but I'll call Fran and she can come in a little early today."

"Won't she want to be involved?"

"Nupe. She's had her fill of bad folks. I try to keep her out of things like this."

"Okay, see you at 9:00." Max left the same way he entered.

Max caught Jo before she opened for the day and asked if they could keep April on duty. After an amended version of the Grienne saga, Jo agreed.

"Can we be of any help?" Jo asked.

"We need to just go about our usual business. We don't want to draw attention to anything."

At 9:00, all the involved parties were sitting around the conference table in the office. Max detailed what he had found earlier that morning. No one spoke when he finished.

"Here's what we're going to do. We will all split up and take a position around town. We'll be looking for an old man riding a Yamaha motorcycle. There is no tag, but a cardboard sign states that the owner's license has been applied for. April will keep her eyes open from her perch above the street. If anyone sees anything I'm your first call." Max held up his phone. "I will then call April, and she will relay the information I give her to each one of you. So, make sure she has your phone numbers."

"What's the plan after that? I don't want anyone with just their phone in their hand when this guy is confronted," Zander asked.

"Grienne is not to be confronted. Is that clear?"

Everyone nodded.

"Give us something we can understand," Zander said.

"I believe he will stake out this place. If someone sees him, make the call, and then stay where you are. Audrey will be here in the office with April. When he's spotted, I'll let Audrey know she is to move quickly to the Branchwater."

"I won't let her on the street alone with this killer on the loose. I'll walk her over." Zander was hot.

"You think I can't take care of myself?" Audrey asked.

Zander knew it was a bad sign and realized he had overstepped his boundaries.

"Of course not. It's just that this asshole is unpredictable."

"We need you out on the street, Zander. She won't be going to the bar alone. I'll be shadowing her." Max pulled up his shirt to reveal a .45 automatic pistol. "It's loaded with fifteen hollow points. If he's dumb enough to try anything, they'll be mopping the street with his brains."

Mona rolled her eyes.

"I think we can quit with the hysterics."

"Drama for effect," Max said and smiled.

Fats had been quietly listening which was unusual.

"It appears that my watering hole will be the epicenter of whatever will happen. I surmise that I will be point man on this excursion."

"That would be correct. If anything happens we want it to be at the Branchwater," Max said.

"I don't want Fran involved in this. She's already had to shoot someone in the bar, and I don't think she could go through that again."

"There won't be shooting in the bar. We will argue with Grienne. I believe when he sees the numbers he will figure out his best exit strategy." Max looked at everyone. "The first plan of attack is to talk him down."

"Ah, it's a come-to-Jesus meeting. I like it. See you all later at the Branchwater. When we put this baby to bed, the drinks will be on me." Fats left the room and bounded down the stairs two at a time.

Zander looked across the table at Connie McGill. She was not happy. Her face gave her away. Zander watched thinking she might object to the plan, but she said nothing. She remained quiet as Max assigned everyone to his or her individual places on Main Street.

"We need to move. He's ready to try something, and I believe it will be today." Max said.

Everyone filed out of the room and down the steps without talking. They were trying to digest everything Max had just told them. Zander hung back.

"Do you think you can talk a psychopath down?"

"One way or another." Max pointed to his pistol and made his exit.

Audrey was sitting next to April and looking out the window. Zander went over and gave Audrey a kiss on the top of her head.

"Just promise me you'll be careful."

"You know the answer to that," Audrey replied. "Now go to your assigned spot, and let's get this over with.

Zander left feeling like he had no control over any part of his life. Someday all this would have to end. He hoped it would be the two of them together. He would be happy to be with Audrey anywhere.

Then, that other thought hit him. He had pretty successfully buried it when all this nonsense came about. He had a daughter. That whole thing was still out there without any resolution whatsoever.

The black cloud just never went away.

42

Kevin took a long shower and got dressed in his old-man uniform. He painstakingly put on his makeup and fitted the wig with some double stick tape. His last look in the mirror was a good one, and he was satisfied.

He unhooked the van from the services and made sure he left nothing that would identify him. He took the cycle and put it into the rear of the van. He needed the van today for the final run. He would leave the bike somewhere after Audrey was secured. It would no longer be necessary. He had a bit of anxiety about where he could park the van. He needed it to be accessible but not some place where it would be noticed.

As he drove into Frisco, he tried to remember some of places he had scouted previously. He recalled a storefront on a side street between Audrey's office and the Branchwater. The store was empty and paper was taped to the windows on the inside. There was an old covered carport around the back that the van could fit under. There was a padlock on the back door but a crowbar would make easy work of that. He could use the place as a staging area and take Audrey there if things got too messy.

He avoided Main Street. He turned and drove through a series of apartment complexes. It appeared that many of the local workers could find affordable housing in Frisco rather than Breckenridge.

The storefront was just as he remembered it, and he turned into the alley behind it and slid under the carport. He sat in the vehicle for fifteen minutes before he decided the dust had settled enough for him to get out the cycle.

No one had seen what he had done, and it was time to make some movement.

He had been wrong about no one seeing him. From her assigned spot Connie McGill had seen exactly what he had done. She decided to wait until he made a move before she would make the call to Max.

When he got out of the van and pulled out the cycle, Connie took out her phone. She waited until he started up.

She dialed Max's number.

"He's on the move. Driving the cycle east on Main." She hung up.

Max made the calls, and the plan began to take shape. Zander was stationed in the bar at the hotel. He saw Grienne climb the stairs and take a seat streetside.

Zander slipped down a set of back stairs that were used by the wait staff. He called Max and told him that Grienne was in position overlooking the Branchwater.

"What do you want me to do now?" Zander asked Max.

"Make your way down the back street toward the Branchwater. Don't let him see you. I'm going to wait until we have everyone in position. Then I'll cue Audrey to move to the Branchwater. We want this thing to go seamlessly."

Zander understood and did what he was told. Grienne wouldn't be playing by the same set of rules this day, however.

Zander stopped when he saw Grienne coming back down the stairs. He ducked back behind and climbed back up as Grienne went down. He called Max.

"What's wrong?" Max asked.

"Grienne's on the move," Zander replied.

"Stay on the line and watch him. Tell me where he goes." Max sounded excited.

Zander climbed the steps and watched as Grienne parked his Yamaha in front of the Branchwater.

"What the hell?" Zander blurted out into the phone.

"What's wrong?" Max asked.

"He's in front of the Branchwater. Wait. He just went in through the front door."

"That's interesting. He's pushing."

"Now what?"

"This is a good thing. We don't need to involve Audrey directly. Make your way to the bar. I'll meet you at the back entrance, and we'll go in together. I'll call the rest and have them go in the front."

"We need to move fast. Fats will be in there with him alone. Who knows what he might do."

"Agreed. Let's move." Max was almost in position and made his calls, as he walked to the rear entrance of the Branchwater.

Zander arrived moments later. He was out of breath.

"Let's go," he said to Max.

"You need to take a moment. We want to appear relaxed. You're far from that right now. It will give the rest of the group time to catch up."

Zander leaned against the wall and tried to catch his breath. He wondered if he was out of shape, or he was just excited to finally confront Grienne.

***

One of the locals was shooting pool with Fats when Grienne walked in. He took a seat at one of the tables and ordered coffee. Fats noticed he used an old man's voice, when he asked for the coffee. His disguise would not have caught anyone's eye had they not known about it prior. Grienne impressed Fats, and he might have liked to quiz him under different circumstances.

Fran brought the coffee and Grienne gave her a few bills he pulled from his pocket. Fats noted that he had no wallet and figured he had no identification with him. That was a smart move. Fats had an appreciation for anyone who planned ahead.

Fats had been toying with his pool-shooting friend, letting him sink a few balls. Things had changed, however, and Fats needed to give this his undivided attention. He ran the table until the eight ball was the only thing left. Fats thought about what he would do and then scratched on the final shot. That gave the game to his rival. They were playing for a buck, and Fats shoved the money across the table. He was still holding his favorite pool cue.

"Thanks for the game. I'll get you next time."

The man took the money but looked at Fats like he had just witnessed the end of the world. Fats put his finger to his lips before the man could say anything. He shrugged and took a seat with the rest of his group.

Fats walked over to where Grienne was sitting.

"Hello and welcome to the Branchwater."

Grienne nodded.

"I haven't seen you in here before. I know most of the locals, so you must be a vacationer."

"Just passing through." Grienne used his old man's voice.

Fats looked at him still impressed but not as much as when he was at a greater distance.

"You look like someone who hails from Florida."

Grienne tensed up. He eyeballed Fats and decided he needed to leave. Before he could make a move, Fats took his pool cue and pushed it into the wig Grienne was wearing. He flipped the wig into the air, and it floated gently to the floor.

"Are you with a traveling theatre group? Your disguise is quite impressive."

Grienne reached for his waistband where he had placed his pistol. Fats' experience with his pool cue caught Grienne before he could raise the weapon. Fats knocked the gun out of his hand breaking his thumb and forefinger in the process. Grienne howled in pain.

Fats leaned over and picked up the .38 special and was placing it on the bar when Zander and Max walked in. They saw Grienne holding his right hand. Fats was holding the pistol. Zander rubbed his forehead. He could feel a headache coming on.

"See what I mean."

Max said nothing. He walked over to Grienne and pushed him back into his chair. Mona, April, Jo, Bert, and Audrey walked in and surrounded the table. Zander was upset when he saw Audrey. He had hoped to keep her away from the confrontation. He was surprised when he noticed that Connie McGill was not present.

Max placed a chair next to Grienne and sat.

"Kevin Grienne, I presume. You must realize that you are not nearly as clever as you thought you were. These people have been monitoring your movements since you left Florida. Do you care to tell us what happened to Elaine Taggart?"

Grienne was silent.

"I thought as much. That's a problem for law enforcement in Florida. We are here to deal with the here-and-now. Please listen to me carefully, so there will be no question about how this will end."

Grienne was in pain but was damned if was going to show it. He nodded at Max, indicating he understood.

"Good. You will leave Colorado immediately. I don't care where you go or what you do. You will never return here, and you will never again stalk or have any contact with Audrey Wood. If you do not follow these instructions you will be killed."

Grienne blinked hard. It was apparent no one had talked to him this frankly before. He could only stare at Max.

"I don't believe you are a stupid man, and I think you know my status. It would not be prudent for you to ignore what I'm saying.

There is no expiration date on any of this." As a way of punctuating what he said, Max grabbed the fingers of his right hand. Grienne howled again.

Audrey stepped forward.

"He's giving you a chance here. You've done some horrible things and should be punished for them. That will be someone else's responsibility because we don't want to stoop to your level. Just be certain that if you don't follow Max's instructions, I'll kill you myself."

Grienne looked at her with nothing but hatred in his eyes. It did not scare Audrey, but she knew he would never let this go. He was a psychopath, and they needed to have the upper hand.

No one was fooled into believing that Grienne was through, but they had to give him time to follow the directive.

"It's time for you to leave. Do you have anything to say?"

Grienne shook his head. He stood and found the door. He turned and was about to say something. He thought better of it and left.

"This isn't over," Zander said.

"You are probably right, but we need to let it play out. One thing is for certain: he'll need to lay low for quite some time. I've already made some calls to Florida, and there will be an investigation concerning his actions over the years," Max said.

"Do you think he'll go back to Florida?" Audrey asked.

"It's all he knows. He's comfortable there and in his element. You saw how badly he screwed up in unfamiliar territory."

"I hope you're right," Zander said.

"You should have let me take him out," Fats said.

"You've done quite enough the way it is," Zander replied.

"Perhaps, but I also promised that drinks would be on me. So, order what you want. That goes for the rest of the bar as well."

A cheer went up from the locals' table.

"It's pretty early for drinking," Mona said.

"Everyone can make an exception this once," Max said. "This does call for a celebration."

***

Grienne stumbled out of the bar and started his Yamaha. He planned to drive to his van and leave. He would return when they least expected. No one treated Kevin Grienne the way he had been treated this day. Things like this could not go unpunished. He was already plotting what he would do when he returned. He turned the corner and drove into the carport behind the storefront.

His van was gone. He tried to remember what he had done with the keys. In his haste, he must have left them in the ignition. He thought he had locked the door, but he was unsure of anything at the moment.

Kevin paused for a few moments to try and decide how to proceed. He needed to find his van. He would go back to the RV Park. Maybe someone had moved it back there. It made no sense, but he had no other explanation. His fingers hurt so badly that he realized he wasn't thinking straight. He was running out of options. When he decided to move, he saw his van move down Main Street toward the west.

He put the cycle in gear and tried to follow. The van had a huge head start and was speeding away. The best he could do was to follow along. He lost sight of the vehicle but continued on hoping to catch a glimpse of it through the trees.

Just as he was running out of road, he caught something in the corner of his left eye. It was the last thing he would ever see.

Connie McGill came from behind a stand of trees moving fast. She broadsided the bike, and Grienne went flying. There was a large pine tree on the other side of the road that was in Kevin's way. As he hit the gnarled trunk, Kevin thought about Christmas trees. He hadn't thought about the smell of pine since he had been a little boy. The pine tar was sticky on his hands as he pushed himself away from the trunk. The pain was excruciating. He knew he had broken a few ribs and he had no idea how much damage had been done to his back. As he struggled to stand, Connie hit the gas and rammed the van into the tree. Kevin looked up in disbelief. This should not have been happening to him. It wasn't part of his protocol, and he had been so careful in following it.

As the light began to fade from Kevin's eyes, Connie grinned and saluted. She smiled as Kevin Grienne took his last breath.

Connie tried to open the driver's door but it was sprung. She put her shoulder to it and as it creaked open, a notebook fell into her lap from under the dash. It was Kevin's protocol notebook. She paged through it quickly and thought about taking it with her. She knew it would be better to leave it for the authorities. All of Kevin Grienne's sins would be made public. That would be the best revenge of all.

She got out of the van and felt his neck for a pulse. She felt nothing. Connie walked away through some trees and wound her way on the back streets toward her car. She moved, drawing little attention to herself. When she reached her car, she took off the vinyl gloves she was wearing and stuffed them in her pocket. She would remember to dispose of them later.

Connie drove back to Denver, returned her friend's car, and took a cab to the airport. She was home before midnight and back in her office in Miami the next day. All was right with the world.

Epilogue

Ieder Kaasje Heeft Zijn Gaatje
Every cheese has its hole.
–Dutch Proverb

The party at the bar was interrupted by a series of sirens outside. After the first police vehicle went by, the group looked out the window to see what was going on. There was a fire truck, rescue vehicle, and first responders in addition to a number of cop cars.

"That doesn't sound good," Mona said.

Bert and Jo ran out of the bar to find out what was going on. The rest of the group went back to their drinks after Zander warned them not to get in the way. They would find out from Bert and Jo what happened.

Fats was doing his usual hippie-speak explaining how he would have handled Grienne differently. No one was really listening to him.

Things were winding down when Jo rushed back in with news of an accident.

"There was a motorcycle crash. Someone driving a large van hit Grienne. They hit him and then pinned him to a tree. He's dead."

"Who was driving the van?" Zander asked.

"That's the weird part. There was no one at the scene. Looks like a hit-and-run. The van had Florida plates."

No one said a word. Everyone knew who had been driving. Connie McGill was smart and pulled off the killing of Kevin Grienne. She had more reasons than anyone at the bar. No one said another word about it.

Law enforcement never found out who was driving the van registered to Kevin Grienne. No one ever claimed the vehicle or the Yamaha. The van was claimed by the police department after a year of sitting in the impound lot.

No one in the world shed a tear for the late Kevin Grienne. No one in the world was ever apprehended for his killing.

***

A week went by, and there was no more said about Kevin Grienne. It was as if he never existed, and that was fine with Zander. Max and Mona returned home to Key West. Zander could never thank them enough. He knew he could never repay his friend for what he had done for them.

Max advised everyone not to involve Connie McGill in any type of correspondence. It would be better if no one knew she had been in Colorado at all. The world was better without Kevin Grienne in it. If anyone had been justified in the killing, it was Connie McGill.

Audrey and Zander's investigation business was seeing a bit of success. Mostly, it concerned spying on cheating spouses or catching an employee stealing from a company. There had been nothing close to their rescue of April, and that was fine with Zander. He tried to keep Audrey out of harm's way without tipping his hand. She was always watching and reminding Zander that they were equal partners.

Note from the Author

Word-of-mouth is crucial for any author to succeed. If you enjoyed *Protocol*, please leave a review online—anywhere you are able. Even if it's just a sentence or two. It would make all the difference and would be very much appreciated.

Thanks!
Jeff Zwagerman

We hope you enjoyed reading this title from:

BLACK ROSE writing™

www.blackrosewriting.com

Subscribe to our mailing list – *The Rosevine* – and receive **FREE** books, daily deals, and stay current with news about upcoming releases and our hottest authors.
Scan the QR code below to sign up.

Already a subscriber? Please accept a sincere thank you for being a fan of Black Rose Writing authors.

View other Black Rose Writing titles at www.blackrosewriting.com/books and use promo code **PRINT** to receive a **20% discount** when purchasing.

www.ingramcontent.com/pod-product-compliance
Lightning Source LLC
Chambersburg PA
CBHW010728100726
47899CB00009B/2965